John Buchan was born in Perth in 1875, the son of a Free Kirk minister. After completing his studies at Oxford, he spent two years as Lord Milner's secretary in South Africa after the Boer War. During his life he was a barrister, a publisher, a wartime Director of Intelligence, a director of Reuters, a Member of Parliament and became Governor-General of Canada as Lord Tweedsmuir. He wrote over a hundred books, among them nearly thirty novels, many of which are widely read and enjoyed today. John Buchan died in 1940.

David Daniell, like Buchan son of a North-country manse, was educated at Oxford and Tübingen. He is a lecturer in English Language and Literature at University College, London. He has written extensively on Shakespeare, most recently on the RSC's European tour of *Coriolanus*. David Daniell wrote the definitive account of Buchan's writings, *The Interpreter's House*.

Also by John Buchan

Grey Weather
The Watcher by the Threshold
Prester John
The Moon Endureth
Montrose
The Thirty-Nine Steps
Greenmantle
The Power-House
Mr Standfast
The Path of the King
Huntingtower
Midwinter
The Three Hostages
The Dancing Floor
The Runagates Club
The Blanket of the Dark
Gap in the Curtain
Sir Walter Scott
Julius Caesar
Oliver Cromwell
The King's Grace: 1910–1935
Memory Hold-the-Door

Also by David Daniell

The Interpreter's House
Coriolanus in Europe
The Best Short Stories of John Buchan, Vol 1 (Ed)

JOHN BUCHAN

The Best Short Stories
of John Buchan

VOLUME 2

Edited by David Daniell

PANTHER
Granada Publishing

Panther Books
Granada Publishing Ltd
8 Grafton Street, London W1X 3LA

Published by Panther Books 1984

First published in this edition in Great Britain by
Michael Joseph Limited 1982

Copyright in the stories of John Buchan, Lord Tweedsmuir
of Elsfield
Introduction and selection © David Daniell 1982

ISBN 0-586-05939-4

Printed and bound in Great Britain by
Collins, Glasgow

Set in Times

To
my mother
and in memory of my father,
with love.

Contents

I acknowledge once again with gratitude the permission of Lord Tweedsmuir to reprint these stories, and again take the opportunity to thank the members of John Buchan's family for their most generous interest, help and encouragement. It gives me pleasure too to thank Dr David French and John Spiers, both of University College, London.

Introduction

When I introduced the first volume of *The Best Short Stories of John Buchan* I gave a brief account of Buchan's life, and described the significance of his contribution to the short history of the short story in Great Britain. In this present volume, as before, I have again tried to show his special narrative qualities as a writer, and demonstrate his extraordinary range. I have therefore included a *locus amoenus* story, about a special and powerful place; but this one, 'Fullcircle', is delicately oblique. In 'The Wind in the Portico', like 'The Grove of Ashtaroth' in the previous collection, there is another example of a place distorted. Buchan contributed to forty-six issues of *Blackwood's Magazine*, and stories from there must, I feel, be represented: so in this collection there are two from 'Maga'. The wise and imaginative classical scholar in Buchan is seen in 'The Lemnian'. Three stories are reprinted for the first time from his early collection, *Grey Weather* of 1899. Scottish moorland romance, and the power of the irrational, occupy more than one story in this new volume, and the collection ends with a classic, and early, 'flight north' story, 'Fountainblue'.

Once again Buchan's artistry in the new form can be seen in his interest in the small moment at the point of balance of large events. The small frame allows for finely tuned effects. Thus, for example, in the first story here, 'On Cademuir Hill' – one of his earliest published – large matters relating to the power of the imagination, of nature and of theology are focused on the pain in part of a man's hand. It is a topsy-turvy world, too, where it is the gamekeeper who is trapped, the stolid man's imagination which is unexpectedly released. In 'Fullcircle' the organization of the tale allows each of Leithen's visits to the house to be made through a special but quite unobtrusive ceremonial experience, the last and most 'sacred' being through something not unlike the waters of baptism. In 'The Earlier Affection', a story in which Buchan comes closest to his acknowledged master Robert Louis Stevenson, the inadequacy of the strange religion of the Whig merchants is shown obliquely by their response to a more ancient and altogether larger call. The narrator of 'A Lucid Interval' is fastidious and a little conceited, given to spattering his remarks with random fragments of his education: this makes the simplicity of the truth he is reporting all the more devastating. In spite of Nightingale's 'quick imagination and flawless courage' with Bedouin tribesmen, his textual pedantry as narrator of 'The Wind in the Portico' seems to cut him off from the fullest meaning of the strong events in Shropshire he has to report. In fact, the relation between a page of written text and powerful events is often Buchan's prime interest. The secret deciphering team in 'The Loathly Opposite' are astounded when the Armistice ends their work.

The use of imagination is one of Buchan's strongest interests: in all his writing, and in these stories especially, it is important to note who has it and who has not. The young gamekeeper in 'On Cademuir Hill' owns, it turns out, a powerful imagination fed by nature and the Bible: he will never be the same plodding man again, we may feel. Hannay in the opening lines of 'The Wind in the Portico' shows he has no historical response to his environment, and is corrected. The prime connection between imagination and the creative process, in controlling metaphors of wind or water, is never far away, and makes, for example, the sense of release in 'Streams of Water in the South' stronger still.

Buchan began to appear in print in the early 1890s when he was an undergraduate at Glasgow University. His earliest novels, essays and stories reflect his first great interests: the landscape and people of Upper Tweeddale, where his mother came from and where he spent much of his boyhood; his classical studies, especially under Gilbert Murray at Glasgow, and then reading Greats at Oxford; and, as a son of a Presbyterian manse, the history and theology of Scottish Christianity. These matters helped largely to form his mind, and were never lost to him. The volume and breadth of his reading throughout his life is extraordinary. He was a classical scholar and Platonist, for forty years a leader-writer who was completely at home in world events, a novelist well abreast of modern fictional trends, from his Oxford days a publisher's reader and then publisher, a writer with a special interest in English seventeenth-century prose writers like Sir Thomas Browne or Izaac Walton or John Bunyan, and in hugely prolific eighteenth-century figures like Edmund Burke. There seems to have been enough reading – let alone anything else – for several lifetimes. His writing does in fact benefit from scholarly annotation, a matter not commonplace among best-selling writers of fiction.

Bunyan was for Buchan a particular interest: and behind both writers stands the Apostle Paul. Buchan was influenced by Paul profoundly. Indeed, I was told by his family that his death in 1940 came unexpectedly to him. He was confidently planning to leave Canada after the war and return to the Cotswolds and devote himself to writing a life of Paul. It was Bunyan who helped Buchan to develop a cool English prose, and gave him a model for a country of the spirit, a territory beset with dangers. Buchan always communicates the whole topography of a country, real or imaginary, and in more than its purely physical dimensions.

The Pauline Platonist steeped in Bunyan made a very unusual war correspondent. Buchan was *The Times* Special Correspondent in France from May 1915, after spending the second half of 1914 as an invalid. From the start of the war he wrote the million-and-a-quarter words of *Nelson's History of the War*, in twenty-four volumes, partly undertaken as a public service and partly to try to keep the Nelson plant in Edinburgh at work. He gives a world-sized picture. The tone is restrained, spare, even astringent. And this was at a time when the fashion was for the most lurid colouring and jingoistic huckstering. Here, more or less at random, is a passage from Buchan's *History*, from Volume VIII. Those qualities which make him a good short-story writer are vividly seen.

The last stages of the Artois battle were as bloody and desperate as any action of the campaign. In the famous Labyrinth, which by the middle of the month was practically in French hands, a murderous subterranean warfare endured for weeks. Tunnels ran thirty and forty feet below the ground, and that triangle between the Bethune and Lille roads was the scene of a struggle which for nightmarish horror can be paralleled only from the sack of some medieval city. The French, no longer moving freely in the open with flowers in their caps, as on the first day of the advance, fought from cellar to cellar, from sap-head to sap-head, hacking their way through partition walls. The only light came from the officers' electric torches. The enemy resisted stubbornly, and there, far below the earth, men fought at the closest quarters with picks and knives and bayonets – often like wild beasts with teeth and hands.

But the great movement had failed. It was now a matter of reducing separately the many forts, and the slowness of the task enabled reserve lines to spring up, so that the Allies were as far from Vimy heights and Lens as before their effort began.

The movement from above to below ground, then to picks and knives and bayonets, and then to teeth and hands, is extraordinary in itself. Yet it leads not to sentences of a misty patriotism but instead to the truth of the harsh conclusion, 'the great movement had failed'. Again, the following passage from Volume XVII describes events of 2 September 1916, the first encounter between an aeroplane and an airship by night. The scene is set easily, and then develops dimensions of height and space culminating in a sudden expansion.

Saturday, 2nd September, was a heavy day, with an overcast sky, which cleared up at twilight. The situation on the Somme was getting desperate, and Germany resolved to send against Britain the largest airship flotilla she had yet dispatched. There were ten Zeppelins, several of the newest and largest type, and three Schütte-Lanz military airships,* and their objective was London and the great manufacturing cities of the Midlands. The Zeppelins completely lost their way. They wandered over East Anglia, dropping irrelevant bombs, and received a warm reception from the British guns. At least two seem to have been hit. One lost her observation car, which was picked up in East Anglia, and this may have been the airship which was seen next morning by Dutch fishermen, travelling slowly and in difficulties, jettisoning stuff as she moved.

The military airships made for London. Ample warning of their coming had been given, and the city was in deep darkness, save for the groping searchlights. The streets were full of people, whose curiosity mastered their prudence, and they were rewarded by one of the most marvellous spectacles which the war had yet seen. Two of the marauders were driven off by our gun-fire, but one attempted to reach the city from the east. After midnight the sky was clear and star-strewn. The sound of the guns was

---

* The largest type of Zeppelin was close on 700 feet long, and its framework was made of aluminium. The Schütte-Lanz was some 500 feet long, with a framework of wood bound with wire.

heard and patches of bright light appeared in the heavens where our shells were bursting. Shortly after two o'clock on the morning of the 3rd, about 10,000 feet up in the air, an airship was seen moving south-westward. She dived and then climbed, as if to escape the shells, and for a moment seemed to be stationary. There came a burst of smoke which formed a screen around her and hid her from view, and then far above appeared little points of light. Suddenly the searchlights were shut off and the guns stopped. The next second the airship was visible like a glowing cigar, turning rapidly to a red and angry flame. She began to fall in a blazing wisp, lighting up the whole sky, so that countryfolk fifty miles off saw the portent. The spectators broke into wild cheering, for from some cause or other the raider had met its doom.

The cause was soon known. Several airmen had gone up to meet the enemy, and one of them, Lieutenant William Leefe Robinson, formerly of the Worcester Regiment, a young man of twenty-one, had come to grips with her. When he found her, he was 2,000 feet below her, but he climbed rapidly and soon won the top position. He closed, and though the machine gun on the top of the airship opened fire on him, he got in his blow in time. No such duel had ever been fought before, 10,000 feet up in the sky, in the view of hundreds of thousands of spectators over an area of a thousand square miles.

The victory was a matter of pride: but Buchan seems as much interested in communicating the display in the heavens, the Miltonic duel and flaming fall witnessed by hundreds of thousands of people over a thousand square miles.

Here he is recording history, but doing so with the novelist's grasp of the importance of narrative stance. It is no surprise to find him a born biographer, and if all else were lost, he would still be hailed for the biography of Sir Walter Scott of 1923. He wrote full biography, or biographical sketches of good length, all his life – the first in 1894, on Bacon. He wrote two books on Montrose and two on Raleigh; on Walton, Emerson, Burke, Murray, a host of Oxford men, Lord Ardwall (book), Lord Minto (book), Lord Rosebery, Julius Caesar (book), Gordon of Khartoum, Cromwell (a big book), Augustus Caesar (book). We should lament the loss of the planned life of the Apostle Paul.

Buchan was a historian of the war, as we have seen. He wrote history of a whole nation, South Africa; of regiments, Scottish and South African; of individual feats and sporting events; of a Scottish county, Peebles-shire; of a sect, Presbyterianism. He gives the steady clear-eyed view of his principal subject. Here is a taste of the flavour of his handling of a dreadful moment in the Gordon Riots in a biographical essay on Lord Mansfield:

On Tuesday, the 6th of June 1780, the mob attacked his house in Bloomsbury Square. He had received warning, but in a spirit of commendable tolerance he refused to have soldiers keeping guard round his door, lest the passions of the crowd should be more seriously inflamed. He trusted to the reverence traditionally shown to the English justices; but he had underrated Protestant zeal. When the rioters battered at his door, he escaped with his wife by a back passage. Then, for a little, anarchy was triumphant. Books, pictures, and furniture were burned in a bonfire on the pavement; the cellars were pillaged, and the miscreants grew drunk on the Chief-Justice's claret; soon the flames reached the house, and in the morning nothing remained but a blackened shell. It is impossible to overestimate the gravity of the misfortune to a man of Mansfield's nature. He had taken much pride in his career, and he had filled his house with remembrances. But now his own diaries, the books in which Pope and Bolingbroke had written their names, his pictures, busts, and prints, his rare and curious furniture, all had perished utterly. He had founded a family, but the heirlooms were gone which he had hoped to hand down to posterity. To one so tenderly attached to his past, it must have seemed as if he stood again bare and isolated in the world, beggared of the fruits of his life's work. The town sympathized with his misfortune, and for once there is no word spoken on his conduct but the highest praise. When he took his seat on the bench, he was received, we are told, 'with a reverential silence more affecting than the most eloquent address'. He rejected with dignity all proposals of compensation, and when he presided at the trial of Lord George Gordon he showed not a trace of prejudice or resentment. Once only he referred indirectly to his loss. He defended the strong measures taken by the Government in quelling the riots. 'I will give you my reasons within as short a compass as possible. I have not consulted books; indeed, I have no books to consult.'

Such directness and dignity are the marks of Buchan as historian – and his historical interests are widespread, and not only in the historical short stories and novels. Three historical novels, all set in Tweeddale, came very early. Most are from his high maturity. *Salute to Adventurers* tells of people in elemental, almost biblical, situations of promise and threat in seventeenth-century Virginia. (He was congratulated on his sharp observation of the Virginian landscape: he had not yet been there.) *The Path of the King* tells of the transmission of royal blood from a Viking boy to Abraham Lincoln. *Witch Wood* is about Calvinism among the herdsmen and cottagers of seventeenth-century Tweeddale. *Midwinter* tells of Dr Johnson and high aspirations around the events of 1745, seen from England, and from outcasts, from the Naked Men and the Spoonbills:

Lords and Parliament-men bustle about, but the dust of their coaches stops at the roadside hedges, and they do not see the quiet eyes watching them at the fords.

Buchan's Tudor novel, *The Blanket of the Dark*, is about plots against Henry the Eighth seen from the lowest of all social scales, and *The Free Fishers* is a Regency tale showing marvellous expertise of *manège* in the high coaching days just before the railways came.

This richness can be illustrated in another way. In the dozen years from 1923 to Buchan's departure for Canada to become Governor-General, he wrote about forty books as well as producing a remarkable amount of journalism, for *The Times*, *The Sunday Times* (as Atticus for a long spell) and his old weekly, the *Spectator* (which at the turn of the century he had virtually edited). Reading those books is to assemble an anthology of experiences, possibly without noticing in how many different areas Buchan is at home; with witch-pricking incidents in seventeenth-century *Witch Wood*; Jacobite Dr Johnson; the modern Gorbals Die-Hards; the Norse powers of *The Island of Sheep*; Trades Unions in a Midland city; guerrilla tactics in a South American state; Easter ceremonies on a Greek Island; the politics of imaginary European states; the campaigns of Montrose; the genius of Scott and Augustus Caesar. Who else could encompass this range and do it with such power? And that list excludes poetry, both his own and editions of other people's. The stories that follow here give a good idea of his strengths.

In the last story in this collection Maitland, the hero, has attained the highest worldly success. He has been lonely all his life. Worse, he has lost touch with the country boy he once was. Buchan was not lonely and did not ruthlessly pursue office. But most of all, he never lost the simplicities of his Tweeddale boyhood. All his life he felt the moorland turf under his feet.

David Daniell
University College, London

On Cademuir Hill

This story was probably written when Buchan was in his teens, beginning his final year as an undergraduate at Glasgow University. It first appeared in Glasgow University Magazine *in December 1894, and was reprinted in the collection of essays which Buchan called* Scholar Gipsies, *published in London and New York in 1896, with three later editions.*

The combination of strong physical sensations and imaginative experience, is not just set in, but grows out of the pastoral landscape in Upper Tweeddale.

On Cademuir Hill

I

The gamekeeper of Cademuir strode in leisurely fashion over the green side of the hill. The bright chilly morning was past, and the heat had all but begun; but he had lain long a-bed, deeming that life was too short at the best, and there was little need to hurry it over. He was a man of a bold carriage, with the indescribable air of one whose life is connected with sport and rough moors. A steady grey eye and a clean chin were his best features; otherwise, he was of the ordinary make of a man, looking like one born for neither good nor evil in any high degree. The sunlight danced around him, and flickered among the brackens; and though it was an everyday sight with him, he was pleased, and felt cheerful, just like any wild animal on a bright day. If he had had his dog with him, he would have sworn at it to show his pleasure; as it was, he contented himself with whistling 'The Linton Ploughman',* and setting his heels deep into the soft green moss.

The day was early and his way was long, for he purposed to go up Manor Water to the shepherd's house about a matter of some foxes. It might be ten miles, it might be more; and the keeper was in no great haste, for there was abundant time to get his dinner and a smoke with the herd, and then come back in the cool of the

* An asterisk in the text denotes an entry in the appendix at the back of the book.

evening; for it was summer-time, when men of his class have their holiday. Two miles more, and he would strike the highway; he could see it even now coiling beneath the straight sides of the glen. There it was easy walking, and he would get on quickly; but now he might take his time. So he lit his pipe, and looked complacently around him.

At the turn of the hill, where a strip of wood runs up the slope, he stopped, and a dark shadow came over his face. This was the place where, not two weeks ago, he had chased a poacher, and but for the fellow's skill in doubling, would have caught him. He cursed the whole tribe in his heart. They were the bane of his easy life. They came at night, and took him out on the bleak hillside when he should have been in his bed. They might have a trap there even now. He would go and see, for it was not two hundred yards from his path.

So he climbed up the little howe* in the hill beside the firwood, where the long thickets of rushes and the rabbit-warrens made a happy hunting-ground for the enemies of the law. A snipe or two flew up as he approached, and a legion of rabbits scurried into their holes. He had all but given up the quest, when the gleam of something among the long grass caught his attention, and in a trice he had pulled back the herbage, and disclosed a neatly set and well-constructed trap.

It was a very admirable trap. He had never seen one like it; so in a sort of angry exultation, as he thought of how he would spoil this fine game, he knelt down to examine it. It was no mere running noose, but of strong steel, and firmly fixed to the trunk of an old tree. No unhappy pheasant would ever move it, were its feet once caught in its strong teeth. He felt the iron with his hand, feeling down the sides for the spring, when suddenly with a horrid snap the thing closed on him, pinning his hand below the mid-finger, and he was powerless.

The pain was terrible, agonizing. His hand burned like white fire, and every nerve of his body tingled. With his left hand he attempted to loosen it, but the spring was so well concealed, that he could not find it. Perhaps, too, he may have lost his wits, for in any great suffering the brain is seldom clear. After a few minutes of feeble searching and tugging, every motion of which gave agony to his imprisoned hand, he gave it up, and, in something very like panic, sought for his knife to try to cut the trap loose from the trunk. And now a fresh terror awaited him, for he found that he had no knife; he had left it in another coat, which was in his room at home. With a sigh of infinite pain, he stopped the search, and stared drearily before him.

He confusedly considered his position. He was fixed with no possibility of escape, some two miles from the track of any chance passer-by. They would not look for him at home until the evening, and the shepherd at Manor did not know of his coming. Someone might be on the hill, but then this howe was on a remote side where few ever came, unless their duty brought them. Below him in the valley was the road with some white cottages beside it. There were women in those houses, living and moving not far from him; they might see him if he were to wave something as a signal. But then, he reflected with a groan, that though he could see their dwellings, they could not see him, for he was hidden by the shoulder of the hill.

Once more he made one frantic effort to escape, but it was unsuccessful. Then he leant back upon the heather, gnawing his lips to help him to endure the agony of the wound. He was a strong man, broad and sinewy, and where a weaker might have swooned, he was left to endure the burden of a painful consciousness. Again he thought of escape. The man who had set the trap must come to see it, but it might not be that day, nor the next. He pictured his friends hunting up and down Manor Water, every pool and wood, passing and re-passing not two hundred yards from where he was lying dead, or worse than dead. His mind grew sick at the thought, and he had almost fainted in spite of his strength.

Then he fell into a panic, the terror of rough 'hard-handed men, which never laboured in their mind'*. His brain whirled, his eyes were stelled*, and a shiver shook him like a reed. He puzzled over his past life, feeling, in a dim way, that it had not been as it should be. He had been drunk often, he had not been over-careful of the name of the Almighty; was not this some sort of retribution? He strove to pray, but he could think of no words. He had been at church last Sunday, and he tried to think of what he had heard; but try as he would, nothing came to his mind, but the chorus of a drinking-song he had often heard sung in the public-house at Peebles:

> When the hoose is innin' round about,
>   It's time eneuch to flit;
> For we've lippened* aye to Providence,
>   And sae will we yet.

The irony of the words did not strike him; but fervently, feverishly, he repeated them, as if for the price of his soul.

The fit passed, and a wild frenzy of rage took him. He cursed like a fiend, and yelled horrible menaces upon the still air. If he had the man who set this trap, he would strangle the life out of him here on this spot. No, that was too merciful. He would force his arm into the trap, and take him to some lonely place where never a human being came from one year's end to the other. Then he would let him die, and come to gloat over his suffering. With every turn of his body he wrenched his hand, and with every wrench he yelled more madly, till he lay back exhausted, and the green hills were left again in peace.

Then he slept a sleep which was half a swoon, for maybe an hour, though to him it seemed like ages. He seemed to be dead, and in torment; and the place of his torment was this same hillside. On the brae* face, a thousand evil spirits were mocking his anguish, and not only his hand, but his whole body was imprisoned in a remorseless trap. He felt the keen steel crush through his bones, like a spade through a frosted turnip. He woke screaming with nameless dread, looking on every side for the infernal faces of his dreams, but seeing nothing but a little chaffinch hopping across the turf.

Then came for him a long period of slow, despairing agony. The hot air glowed, and the fierce sun beat upon his face. A thousand insects hummed about him, bees and butterflies and little hill-moths. The wholesome smell of thyme and bent was all about him, and every now and then a little breeze broke the stillness, and sent a ripple over the grass. The genial warmth seemed stifling; his head ached, and his breath came in sudden gasps. An overpowering thirst came upon him, and his tongue was like a burnt stick in his mouth. Not ten feet off, a little burn danced over a minute cascade. He could see the dust of spray, which wet the cool green rushes. The pleasant tinkle sang in his ears, and mocked his fever. He tried to think of snow and ice and cold water, but his brain refused to do its part, and he could get nothing but an intolerable void.

Far across the valley, the great forehead of Dollar Law raised itself, austere and lofty. To his unquiet sight, it seemed as if it rolled over on Scrape, and the two played pranks among the lower hills beyond. The idea came to him, how singularly unpleasant it would be for the people there – among them a shepherd to whom he owed two pounds. He would be crushed to powder, and there would be no more of the debt at any rate. Then a text from the Scriptures came to haunt him, something, he could scarce tell exactly, about the hills and mountains leaping like rams*. Here it was realized before his very eyes. Below him, in the peaceful valley, Manor Water seemed to be wrinkled across it, like a scrawl from the pen of a bad writer. When a bird flew past, or a hare started from its form, he screamed with terror, and all the wholesome sights of a summer day were wrought by his frenzied brain into terrible phantoms. So true is it that Natura Benigna and Natura Maligna may walk hand in hand upon the same hillside.

Then came the time when the strings of the reason are all but snapped, and a man becomes maudlin. He thought of his young wife, not six weeks married, and grieved over her approaching sorrow. He wept unnatural tears, which, if anyone had been there to see him, would have been far more terrible than his frantic ravings. He pictured to himself in gruesome detail, the finding of his body, how his wife would sob, and his friends would shake their heads, and swear that he had been an honest fellow, and that it was a pity that he was away. The place would soon forget him; his wife would marry again; his dogs would get a new master, and he – ay, that was the question, where would he be? and a new dread took him, as he thought of the fate which might await him. The unlettered man, in his time of dire necessity, has nothing to go back upon but a mind full of vivid traditions, which are the most merciless of things.

It might be about three or four o'clock, but by the clock

in his brain it was weeks later, that he suffered that supremacy of pain, which anyone who has met it once, would walk to the end of the earth to avoid. The world shrank away from him; his wits forsook him; and he cried out, till the lonely rocks rang, and the whaups* mingled their startled cries with his. With a last effort, he crushed down his head with his unwounded hand upon the tree-trunk, till blessed unconsciousness took him into her merciful embrace.

II

At nine o'clock that evening, a ragged, unshorn man, with the look of one not well at ease with the world, crept up the little plantation. He had a sack on his back for his ill-gotten plunder, and a mighty stick in case of a chance encounter. He visited his traps, hidden away in little nooks, where no man might find them, and it would have seemed as if trade were brisk, for his sack was heavy, and his air was cheerful. He looked out from behind the dyke at his last snare carefully, as behoved one in danger; and then with a start he crouched, for he saw the figure of a man.

There was no doubt about it; it was his bitterest enemy, the keeper of Cademuir. He made as if to crawl away, when by chance he looked again. The man lay very still. A minute later he had rushed forward with a white face, and was working as if for his life.

In half an hour two men might have been seen in that little glen. One, with a grey, sickened face, was gazing vacantly around him, with the look of someone awakened from a long sleep. By dint of much toil, and half a bottle of brandy, he had been brought back from what was like to have been the longest sleep he had ever taken. Beside him on the grass, with wild eyes, sat the poacher, shedding hysterical tears. 'Dae onything ye like wi' me,' he was saying, 'kick me or kill me, an' I'm ready. I'll gang to jail wi' ye, to Peebles or the Calton, an' no say a word. But oh – ! ma God, I thocht ye were bye wi't.'

A Lucid Interval

This story first appeared in Blackwood's Magazine *for February 1910, and simultaneously under the title 'God's Providence' in the* Atlantic Monthly; *two years later it was one of those collected under the title* The Moon Endureth *published by Blackwood in 1912. It is a product of that happy time of Buchan's early thirties when, living in London, married and with a growing family, he was barrister and publisher, already with a score of books of many kinds behind him. By this time he also had a wide reputation for distinguished journalism, and the entrée in his own right to the inner circles of public affairs.*

The pleasant irony of the application of the phrase 'a lucid interval', making politics a settled insanity, and the hyperbole of 'the terrible fortnight', are helped by the nervous pomposity of Buchan's narrator. His tone, as he views himself, is caught by the phrase, 'When I have not to wait upon the adornment of the female person I am a man of punctual habits' or, 'I was tactless enough to say'. In his observation of others he is admirable, from the unctuous Home Secretary to the general relation of politics to acting, and in particular the noting of people shifting their feet 'to positions loved by sculptors'. The unobtrusive breadth of reference shown in incidental detail is typical of Buchan's characteristically wide canvas. The confidence of the narrator flatters the reader into a sense of sharing the understanding of hidden matters, by means of clarity of fine detail about local Indian politics, House of Commons procedure and much else.

Students of the domestic politics of 1909–10 observe that the characters in the story have points of resemblances to well-known political figures, though Buchan has felt free to change their offices, and even their parties, for the sake of his story. Thus Lord Caerlaverock's time as Indian Viceroy – but not, of course, his party – matches Lord Curzon. The physical description of Alexander Cargill might fit R. B. Haldane, who was a bachelor all his life. Aspects of Abinger Vennard resemble Lloyd George. There are also references to the issues of the time: both suffrage and the question of reforming the government of India were very much alive in 1909. The Liberal party contained many temperance reformers; the scandal of Cargill's 'inebriation' would have been appalling. Most of all, of course, the issue of free trade was the great political divide in Edwardian politics.

A Lucid Interval

I

To adopt the opening words of a more famous tale, 'The truth of this strange matter is what the world has long been looking for.'* The events which I propose to chronicle were known to perhaps a hundred people in London whose fate brings them into contact with politics. The consequences were apparent to all the world, and for one hectic fortnight tinged the soberest newspapers with saffron, drove more than one worthy election agent to an asylum, and sent whole batches of legislators to Continental 'cures'. But no reasonable explanation of the mystery has been forthcoming until now, when a series of chances gave the key into my hands.

Lady Caerlaverock is my aunt, and I was present at the two remarkable dinner-parties which form the main events in this tale. I was also taken into her confidence during the terrible fortnight which intervened between them. Like everybody else, I was hopelessly in the dark, and could only accept what happened as a divine interposition. My first clue came when James, the Caerlaverocks' second footman, entered my service as valet, and, being a cheerful youth, chose to gossip while he shaved me. I checked him, but he babbled on, and I could not choose but learn something about the disposition of the Caerlaverock household below-stairs. I learned – what I knew before – that his lordship had an inordinate love for curries, a taste acquired during some troubled years as

Indian Viceroy. I had often eaten that admirable dish at his table, and had heard him boast of the skill of the Indian cook who prepared it. James, it appeared, did not hold with the Orient in the kitchen. He described the said Indian gentleman as a 'nigger', and expressed profound distrust of his ways. He referred darkly to the events of the year before, which in some distorted way had reached the servants' ears. 'We always thought as 'ow it was them niggers as done it,' he declared; and when I questioned him on his use of the plural, admitted that at the time in question 'there 'ad been more nor one nigger 'anging about the kitchen.'

Pondering on these sayings, I asked myself if it were not possible that the behaviour of certain eminent statesmen was due to some strange devilry of the East, and I made a vow to abstain in future from the Caerlaverock curries. But last month my brother returned from India, and I got the whole truth. He was staying with me in Scotland, and in the smoking-room the talk turned on occultism in the East. I declared myself a sceptic, and George was stirred. He asked me rudely what I knew about it, and proceeded to make a startling confession of faith. He was cross-examined by the others, and retorted with some of his experiences. Finding an incredulous audience, his tales became more defiant, until he capped them all with one monstrous yarn. He maintained that in a Hindu family of his acquaintance there had been transmitted the secret of a drug, capable of altering a man's whole temperament until the antidote was administered. It would turn a coward into a bravo, a miser into a spendthrift, a rake into a fakir*. Then, having delivered his manifesto, he got up abruptly and went to bed.

I followed him to his room, for something in the story had revived a memory. By dint of much persuasion I dragged from the somnolent George various details. The family in question were Beharis, large landholders dwelling near the Nepal border. He had known old Ram Singh for years, and had seen him twice since his return from England. He got the story from him, under no promise of secrecy, for the family drug was as well known in the neighbourhood as the nine incarnations of Krishna. He had no doubt about the truth of it, for he had positive proof. 'And others besides me,' said George. 'Do you remember when Vennard had a lucid interval a couple of years ago and talked sense for once? That was old Ram Singh's doing, for he told me about it.'

Three years ago, it seems, the Government of India saw fit to appoint a commission to inquire into land tenure on the Nepal border. Some of the feudal Rajahs had been 'birsing yont'*, like the Breadalbanes*, and the smaller zemindars* were gravely disquieted. The result of the commission was that Ram Singh had his boundaries rectified, and lost a mile or two of country which his hard-fisted fathers had won. I know nothing of the rights of the matter, but there can be no doubt about Ram Singh's dissatisfaction. He appealed to the law courts, but failed to upset the commission's finding, and the Privy Council upheld the Indian judgement. Thereupon in a flowery and eloquent document he laid his case before the Viceroy, and was told that the matter was closed. Now Ram Singh came of fighting stock, so he straightway took ship to England to petition the Crown. He petitioned Parliament, but his petition went into the bag behind the Speaker's chair, from which there is no return. He petitioned the King, but was courteously informed that he must approach the Department concerned. He tried the Secretary of State for India, and had an interview with Abinger Vennard, who was very rude to him, and succeeded in mortally insulting the feudal aristocrat. He appealed to the Prime Minister, and was warned off by a harassed private secretary. The handful of members of Parliament who make Indian grievances their stock-in-trade fought shy of him, for indeed Ram Singh's case had no sort of platform appeal in it, and his arguments were flagrantly undemocratic. But they sent him to Lord Caerlaverock, for the ex-viceroy loved to be treated as a kind of consul-general for India. But this Protector of the Poor proved a broken reed. He told Ram Singh flatly that he was a belated feudalist, which was true; and implied that he was a land-grabber, which was not true, Ram Singh having only enjoyed the fruits of his forebears' enterprise. Deeply incensed, the appellant shook the dust of Caerlaverock House from his feet, and sat down to plan a revenge upon the Government which had wronged him. And in his wrath he thought of the heirloom of his race, the drug which could change men's souls.

It happened that Lord Caerlaverock's cook came from the same neighbourhood as Ram Singh. This cook, Lal Muhammad by name, was one of a large poor family, hangers-on of Ram Singh's house. The aggrieved landowner summoned him, and demanded as of right his humble services. Lal Muhammad, who found his berth to his liking, hesitated, quibbled, but was finally overborne. He suggested a fee for his services, but hastily withdrew when Ram Singh sketched a few of the steps he proposed to take on his return by way of punishing Lal Muhammad's insolence on Lal Muhammad's household. Then he got to business. There was a great dinner next week – so he had learned from Jephson, the butler – and more than one member of the Government would honour Caerlaverock House by his presence. With deference he suggested this as a fitting occasion for the experiment, and Ram Singh was pleased to assent.

I can picture these two holding their meetings in the South Kensington lodgings where Ram Singh dwelt. We know from James, the second footman, that they met also at Caerlaverock House, no doubt that Ram Singh might make certain that his orders were duly obeyed. I can see the little packet of clear grains – I picture them like small granulated sugar – added to the condiments, and soon dissolved out of sight. The deed was done; the cook returned to Bloomsbury and Ram Singh to Gloucester Road, to await with the patient certainty of the East the consummation of a great vengeance.

II

My wife was at Kissingen*, and I was dining with the Caerlaverocks *en garçon**. When I have not to wait upon the adornment of the female person I am a man of punctual habits, and I reached the house as the hall clock chimed the quarter-past. My poor friend, Tommy Deloraine, arrived along with me, and we ascended the staircase together. I call him 'my poor friend', for at the moment Tommy was under the weather. He had the misfortune to be a marquis, and a very rich one, and at the same time to be in love with Claudia Barriton. Neither circumstance was in itself an evil, but the combination made for tragedy. For Tommy's twenty-five years of healthy manhood, his cleanly made up-standing figure, his fresh countenance and cheerful laugh, were of no avail in the lady's eyes when set against the fact that he was an idle peer. Miss Claudia was a charming girl, with a notable bee in her bonnet. She was burdened with the cares of the State, and had no patience with anyone who took them lightly. To her mind the social fabric was rotten beyond repair, and her purpose was frankly destructive. I remember some of her phrases: 'A bold and generous policy of social amelioration'; 'The development of a civic conscience'; 'A strong hand to lop off decaying branches from the trunk of the State'. I have no fault to find with her creed, but I objected to its practical working when it took the shape of an inhuman hostility to that devout lover, Tommy Deloraine. She had refused him, I believe, three times, with every circumstance of scorn. The first time she had analysed his character, and described him as a bundle of attractive weaknesses. 'The only forces I recognize are those of intellect and conscience,' she had said, 'and you have neither.' The second time – it was after he had been to Canada on the staff – she spoke of the irreconcilability of their political ideals. 'You are an Imperialist,' she said, 'and believe in an empire of conquest for the benefit of the few. I want a little island with a rich life for all.' Tommy declared that he would become a Doukhobor* to please her, but she said something about the inability of Ethiopians* to change their skin. The third time she hinted vaguely that there was 'another'. The star of Abinger Vennard was now blazing in the firmament, and she had conceived a platonic admiration for him. The truth is that Miss Claudia, with all her cleverness, was very young and – dare I say it? – rather silly.

Caerlaverock was stroking his beard, his legs astraddle on the hearthrug, with something appallingly viceregal in his air, when Mr and Mrs Alexander Cargill were announced. The Home Secretary was a joy to behold. He had the face of an elderly and pious bookmaker, and a voice in which lurked the indescribable Scotch quality of 'unction'.

When he was talking you had only to shut your eyes to imagine yourself in some lowland kirk on a hot Sabbath morning. He had been a distinguished advocate before he left the law for politics, and had swayed juries of his countrymen at his will. The man was extraordinarily efficient on a platform. There were unplumbed depths of emotion in his eye, a juicy sentiment in his voice, an overpowering tenderness in his manner, which gave to politics the glamour of a revival meeting. He wallowed in obvious pathos, and his hearers, often unwillingly, wallowed with him. I have never listened to any orator at once so offensive and so horribly effective. There was no appeal too base for him, and none too august: by some subtle alchemy he blended the arts of the prophet and the fishwife. He had discovered a new kind of language. Instead of 'the hungry millions', or 'the toilers', or any of the numerous synonyms for our masters, he invented the phrase, 'Goad's people'. 'I shall never rest,' so ran his great declaration, 'till Goad's green fields and Goad's clear waters are free to Goad's people.' I remember how on this occasion he pressed my hand with his famous cordiality, looked gravely and earnestly into my face, and then gazed sternly into vacancy. It was a fine picture of genius descending for a moment from its hill-top to show how close it was to poor humanity.

Then came Lord Mulross, a respectable troglodytic* peer, who represented the one sluggish element in a swiftly progressing Government. He was an oldish man with bushy whiskers and a reputed mastery of the French tongue. A Whig, who had never changed his creed one iota, he was highly valued by the country as a sober element in the nation's councils, and endured by the Cabinet as necessary ballast. He did not conceal his dislike for certain of his colleagues, notably Mr Vennard and Mr Cargill.

When Miss Barriton arrived with her stepmother the party was almost complete. She entered with an air of apologizing for her prettiness. Her manner with old men was delightful, and I watched with interest the unbending of Caerlaverock and the simplifying of Mr Cargill in her presence. Deloraine, who was talking feverishly to Mrs Cargill, started as if to go and greet her, thought better of it, and continued his conversation. The lady swept the room with her eye, but did not acknowledge his presence. She floated off with Mr Cargill to a window-corner, and metaphorically sat at his feet. I saw Deloraine saying things behind his moustache, while he listened to Mrs Cargill's new cure for dyspepsia.

Last of all, twenty minutes late, came Abinger Vennard. He made a fine stage entrance, walking swiftly with a lowering bow to his hostess, and then glaring fiercely round the room as if to challenge criticism. I have heard Deloraine, in a moment of irritation, describe him as a 'Pre-Raphaelite attorney', but there could be no denying his good looks. He had a bad, loose figure, and a quantity of studiously neglected hair, but his face was the face of a young Greek. A certain kind of political success gives a man the manners of an actor, and both Vennard and Cargill bristled with self-consciousness. You could see it in the way they patted their hair, squared their shoulders, and shifted their feet to positions loved by sculptors.

'Well, Vennard, what's the news from the House?' Caerlaverock asked.

'Simpson is talking,' said Vennard wearily. 'He attacks me, of course. He says he has lived forty years in India – as if that mattered! When will people recognize that the truths of democratic policy are independent of time and space? Liberalism is a category, an eternal mode of thought, which cannot be overthrown by any trivial happenings. I am sick of the word "facts". I long for truths.'

Miss Barriton's eyes brightened, and Cargill said, 'Excellent.' Lord Mulross, who was a little deaf, and in any case did not understand the language, said loudly to my aunt that he wished there was a close time for legislation. 'The open season for grouse should be the close season for politicians.'

And then we went down to dinner.

Miss Barriton sat on my left hand, between Deloraine and me, and it was clear she was discontented with her position. Her eyes wandered down the table to Vennard, who had taken in an American duchess, and seemed to be amused at her prattle. She looked with complete disfavour at Deloraine, and turned to me as the lesser of two evils.

I was tactless enough to say that I thought there was a good deal in Lord Mulross's view.

'Oh, how can you?' she cried. 'Is there a close season for the wants of the people? It sounds to me perfectly horrible the way you talk of government, as if it were a game for idle men of the upper classes. I want professional politicians, men who give their whole heart and soul to the service of the State. I know the kind of member you and Lord Deloraine like – a rich young man who eats and drinks too much, and thinks the real business of life is killing little birds. He travels abroad and shoots some big game, and then comes home and rants about the Empire. He knows nothing about realities, and will go down before the men who take the world seriously.'

I am afraid I laughed, but Deloraine, who had been listening, was in no mood to be amused.

'I don't think you are quite fair to us, Miss Claudia,' he said slowly. 'We take things seriously enough, the things we know about. We can't be expected to know about

everything, and the misfortune is that the things I care
about don't interest you. But they are important enough
for all that.'

'Hush,' said the lady rudely. 'I want to hear what Mr
Vennard is saying.'

Mr Vennard was addressing the dinner table as if it
were a large public meeting. It was a habit he had, for he
had no mind to confine the pearls of his wisdom to his
immediate neighbours. His words were directed to Caerlaverock at the far end.

'In my opinion this craze for the scientific standpoint is
not merely overdone – it is radically vicious. Human
destinies cannot be treated as if they were inert objects
under the microscope. The cold-blooded logical way of
treating a problem is in almost every case the wrong way.
Heart and imagination to me are more vital than intellect.
I have the courage to be illogical, to defy facts for the sake
of an ideal, in the certainty that in time facts will fall into
conformity. My creed may be put in the words of Newman's favourite quotation*: *Non in dialectica complacuit
Deo salvum facere populum suum* – Not in cold logic is it
God's will that His people should find salvation.'

'It is profoundly true,' sighed Mr Cargill, and Miss
Claudia's beaming eyes proved her assent.

The moment of destiny, though I did not know it, had
arrived. The entrée course had begun, and of the two
entrées one was the famous Caerlaverock curry. Now on a
hot July evening in London there are more attractive
foods than curry seven times heated, *more Indico*. I
doubt if any guest would have touched it, had not our host
in his viceregal voice called the attention of the three
Ministers to its merits, while explaining that under doctor's orders he was compelled to refrain for a season. The
result was that Mulross, Cargill, and Vennard alone of the

men partook of it. Miss Claudia, alone of the women, followed suit in the fervour of her hero-worship. She ate a mouthful, and then drank rapidly two glasses of water.

My narrative of the events which followed is based rather on what I should have seen than on what I saw. I had not the key, and missed much which otherwise would have been plain to me. For example, if I had known the secret, I must have seen Miss Claudia's gaze ceased to rest upon Vennard and the adoration die out of her eyes. I must have noticed her face soften to the unhappy Deloraine. As it was, I did not remark her behaviour, till I heard her say to her neighbour, – 'Can't you get hold of Mr Vennard and forcibly cut his hair?'

Deloraine looked round with a start. Miss Barriton's tone was intimate and her face friendly.

'Some people think it picturesque,' he said in serious bewilderment.

'Oh yes, picturesque – like a hairdresser's young man!' She shrugged her shoulders. 'He looks as if he had never been out of doors in his life.'

Now, whatever the faults of Tommy's appearance, he had a wholesome sunburnt face, and he knew it. This speech of Miss Barriton's cheered him enormously, for he argued that if she had fallen out of love with Vennard's looks she might fall in love with his own. Being a philosopher in his way, he was content to take what the gods gave, and ask for no explanations.

I do not know how their conversation prospered, for my attention was distracted by the extraordinary behaviour of the Home Secretary. Mr Cargill had made himself notorious by his treatment of 'political' prisoners. It was sufficient in his eyes for a criminal to confess to political convictions to secure the most lenient treatment and a speedy release. The Irish patriot who cracked skulls in the

Scotland Division of Liverpool, the Suffragist who broke windows and the noses of the police, the Social Democrat whose antipathy to the Tsar revealed itself in assaults upon the Russian Embassy, the 'hunger-marchers' who had designs on the British Museum – all were sure of respectful and tender handling. He had announced, more than once, amid tumultuous cheering, that he would never be the means of branding earnestness, however mistaken, with the badge of the felon.

He was talking, as I recall the scene, to Lady Lavinia Dobson, renowed in two hemispheres for her advocacy of women's rights. And this was what I heard him say. His face had grown suddenly flushed and his eye bright, so that he looked liker than ever to a bookmaker who had had a good meeting. 'No, no, my dear lady, I have been a lawyer, and it is my duty in office to see that the law, the palladium of British liberties, is kept sacrosanct. The law is no respecter of persons, and I intend that it shall be no respecter of creeds. If men or women break the laws, to jail they shall go, though their intentions were those of the Apostle Paul. We don't punish them for being Socialists or Suffragists, but for breaking the peace. Why, goodness me, if we didn't, we should have every malefactor in Britain claiming preferential treatment because he was a Christian Scientist or a Pentecostal Dancer.'

'Mr Cargill, do you realize what you are saying?' said Lady Lavinia with a scared face.

'Of course I do. I am a lawyer, and may be presumed to know the law. If any other doctrine were admitted, the Empire would burst up in a fortnight.'

'That I should live to hear you name that accursed name!'* cried the outraged lady. 'You are denying your gods, Mr Cargill. You are forgetting the principles of a lifetime.'

Mr Cargill was becoming excited, and exchanging his ordinary Edinburgh-English for a broader and more effective dialect.

'Tut, tut, my good wumman, I may be allowed to know my own principles best. I tell ye I've always maintained these views from the day when I first walked the floor of the Parliament House. Besides, even if I hadn't, I'm surely at liberty to change if I get more light. Whoever makes a fetich of consistency is a trumpery body and little use to God or man. What ails ye at the Empire, too? Is it not better to have a big country than a kailyard*, or a house in Grosvenor Square than a but-and-ben* in Balham?'

Lady Lavinia folded her hands. 'We slaughter our black fellow-citizens, we fill South Africa with yellow slaves*, we crowd the Indian prisons with the noblest and most enlightened of the Indian race, and we call it Empire-building?'

'No, we don't,' said Mr Cargill stoutly, 'we call it common sense. That is the penal and repressive side of any great activity. D'ye mean to tell me that you never give your maid a good hearing? But would you like it to be said that you spent the whole of your days swearing at the wumman?'

'I never swore in my life,' said Lady Lavinia.

'I spoke metaphorically,' said Mr Cargill. 'If ye cannot understand a simple metaphor, ye cannot understand the rudiments of politics.'

Picture to yourself a prophet who suddenly discovers that his God is laughing at him, a devotee whose saint winks and tells him that the devotion of years has been a farce, and you will get some idea of Lady Lavinia's frame of mind. Her sallow face flushed, her lip trembled, and she slewed round as far as her chair would permit her.

Meanwhile Mr Cargill, redder than before, went on contentedly with his dinner.

I was glad when my aunt gave the signal to rise. The atmosphere was electric, and all were conscious of it save the three Ministers, Deloraine, and Miss Claudia. Vennard seemed to be behaving very badly. He was arguing with Caerlaverock down the table, and the ex-Viceroy's face was slowly getting purple. When the ladies had gone, we remained oblivious to wine and cigarettes, listening to this heated controversy which threatened any minute to end in a quarrel.

The subject was India, and Vennard was discoursing on the follies of all Viceroys.

'Take this idiot we've got now,' he declared. 'He expects me to be a sort of wet-nurse to the Government of India and do all their dirty work for them. They know local conditions, and they have ample powers if they would only use them, but they won't take an atom of responsibility. How the deuce am I to decide for them, when in the nature of things I can't be half as well informed about the facts!'

'Do you maintain,' said Caerlaverock, stuttering in his wrath, 'that the British Government should divest itself of responsibility for the government of our great Indian Dependency?'

'Not a bit,' said Vennard impatiently; 'of course we are responsible, but that is all the more reason why the fellows who know the business at first hand should do their duty. If I am the head of a bank I am responsible for its policy, but that doesn't mean that every local bank manager should consult me about the solvency of clients I never heard of. Faversham keeps bleating to me that the state of India is dangerous. Well, for God's sake let him suppress every native paper, shut up the schools, and send every agitator to the Andamans*. I'll back him up all right. But don't let him ask me what to do, for I don't know.'

'You think such a course would be popular?' asked a large, grave man, a newspaper editor.

'Of course it would,' said Vennard cheerily. 'The British public hates the idea of letting India get out of hand. But they want a lead. They can't be expected to start the show any more than I can.'

Lord Caerlaverock rose to join the ladies with an air of outraged dignity. Vennard pulled out his watch and announced that he must get back to the House.

'Do you know what I am going to do?' he asked. 'I am going down to tell Simpson what I think of him. He gets up and prates of having been forty years in India. Well, I am going to tell him that it is to him and his forty-year lot that all this muddle is due. Oh, I assure you, there's going to be a row,' said Vennard, as he struggled into his coat.

Mulross had been sitting next to me, and I asked him if he was leaving town. 'I wish I could,' he said, 'but I fear I must stick on over the Twelfth. I don't like the way that fellow von Kladow* has been talking. He's up to no good, and he's going to get a flea in his ear before he is very much older.'

Cheerfully, almost hilariously, the three Ministers departed. Vennard and Cargill in a hansom, and Mulross on foot. I can only describe the condition of those left behind as nervous prostration. We looked furtively at each other, each afraid to hint his suspicions, but all convinced that a surprising judgement had befallen at least two members of His Majesty's Government. For myself I put the number at three, for I did not like to hear a respected Whig Foreign Secretary talk about giving the Chancellor of a friendly but jealous Power a flea in his ear.

The only unperplexed face was Deloraine's. He whispered to me that Miss Barriton was going on to the Alvanleys' ball, and had warned him to be there. 'She hasn't been to a dance for months, you know,' he said. 'I really think things are beginning to go a little better, old man.'

III

When I opened my paper next morning I read two startling pieces of news. Lord Mulross had been knocked down by a taxi-cab on his way home the night before, and was now in bed suffering from a bad shock and a bruised ankle. There was no cause for anxiety, said the report, but his lordship must keep his room for a week or two.

The second item, which filled leading articles and overflowed into 'Political Notes', was Mr Vennard's speech. The Secretary for India had gone down about eleven o'clock to the House, where an Indian debate was dragging out its slow length*. He sat himself on the Treasury Bench and took notes, and the House soon filled in anticipation of his reply. His 'tail' – progressive young men like himself – were there in full strength, ready to cheer every syllable which fell from their idol. Somewhere about half-past twelve he rose to wind up the debate, and the House was treated to an unparalleled sensation. He began with his critics, notably the unfortunate Simpson, and, pretty much in Westbury's language to the herald*, called them silly old men who did not understand their silly old business. But it was the reasons he gave for this abuse which left his followers aghast. He attacked his critics not for being satraps* and reactionaries, but because they had dared to talk second-rate Western politics in connection with India. 'Have you lived for forty years with your eyes shut,' he cried, 'that you cannot see the differences between a Bengali, married at fifteen and worshipping a pantheon of savage gods, and the university-extension young Radical at home? There is a thousand years between them, and you dream of annihilating the centuries with a little dubious popular science!' Then he turned to the other critics of Indian administration – his quondam supporters. He analysed the character of these 'members for India' with a vigour and acumen which deprived them of speech. The East, he said, had had its revenge upon the West by making certain Englishmen babus*. His honourable friends had the same slip-shod minds, and they talked the same pigeon-English, as the patriots of Bengal. Then his mood changed, and he delivered a solemn warning against what he called 'the treason begotten of restless vanity and proved incompetence'. He sat down, leaving a House deeply impressed and horribly mystified.

The Times did not know what to make of it at all. In a weighty leader it welcomed Mr Vennard's conversion, but hinted that with a convert's zeal he had slightly overstated his case. The *Daily Chronicle* talked of 'nervous breakdown', and suggested 'kindly forgetfulness' as the best treatment. The *Daily News*, in a spirited article called 'The Great Betrayal', washed its hands of Mr Vennard unless he donned the white sheet of the penitent. Later in the day I got the *Westminster Gazette*, and found an ingenious leader which proved that the speech in no way conflicted with Liberal principles, and was capable of a quite ordinary explanation. Then I went to see Lady Caerlaverock.

I found my aunt almost in tears.

'What has happened?' she cried. 'What have we done

that we should be punished in this awful way? And to think that the blow fell in this house? Caerlaverock – we all – thought Mr Vennard so strange last night, and Lady Lavinia told me that Mr Cargill was perfectly horrible. I suppose it must be the heat and the strain of the session. And that poor Lord Mulross, who was always so wise, should be stricken down at this crisis!'

I did not say that I thought Mulross's accident a merciful dispensation. I was far more afraid of him than of all the others, for if with his reputation for sanity he chose to run amok, he would be taken seriously. He was better in bed than affixing a flea to von Kladow's ear.

'Caerlaverock was with the Prime Minister this morning,' my aunt went on. 'He is going to make a statement in the Lords tomorrow to try to cover Mr Vennard's folly. They are very anxious about what Mr Cargill will do today. He is addressing the National Convention of Young Liberals at Oldham this afternoon, and though they have sent him a dozen telegrams they can get no answer. Caerlaverock went to Downing Street an hour ago to get news.'

There was the sound of an electric brougham stopping in the square below, and we both listened with a premonition of disaster. A minute later Caerlaverock entered the room, and with him the Prime Minister. The cheerful, eupeptic countenance of the latter was clouded with care. He shook hands dismally with my aunt, nodded to me, and flung himself down on a sofa.

'The worst has happened,' Caerlaverock boomed solemnly. 'Cargill has been incredibly and infamously silly.' He tossed me an evening paper.

One glance convinced me that the Convention of Young Liberals had had a waking-up. Cargill had addressed them on what he called the true view of citizenship.

He had dismissed manhood suffrage as an obsolete folly. The franchise, he maintained, should be narrowed and given only to citizens, and his definition of citizenship was military training combined with a fairly high standard of rates and taxes. I do not know how the Young Liberals received this creed, but it had no sort of success with the Prime Minister.

'We must disavow him,' said Caerlaverock.

'He is too valuable a man to lose,' said the Prime Minister. 'We must hope that it is only a temporary aberration. I simply cannot spare him in the House.'

'But this is flat treason.'

'I know. I know. It is all too horrible, and utterly unexpected. But the situation wants delicate handling, my dear Caerlaverock. I see nothing for it but to give out that he was ill.'

'Or drunk?' I suggested.

The Prime Minister shook his head sadly. 'I fear it will be the same thing. What we call illness the ordinary man will interpret as intoxication. It is a most regrettable necessity, but we must face it.'

The harassed leader rose, seized the evening paper, and departed as swiftly as he had come. 'Remember, illness,' were his parting words. 'An old heart trouble, which is apt to affect his brain. His friends have always known about it.'

I walked home, and looked in at the Club on my way. There I found Deloraine devouring a hearty tea and looking the picture of virtuous happiness.

'Well, this is tremendous news,' I said, as I sat down beside him.

'What news?' he asked with a start.

'This row over Vennard and Cargill.'

'Oh, that! I haven't seen the papers today. What's it all about?' His tone was devoid of interest.

Then I knew that something of great private moment had happened to Tommy.

'I hope I may congratulate you,' I said.

Deloraine beamed on me affectionately. 'Thanks very much, old man. Things came all right, quite suddenly, you know. We spent most of the time at the Alvanleys' together, and this morning in the Park she accepted me. It will be in the papers next week, but we mean to keep it quiet for a day or two. However, it was your right to be told – and besides, you guessed.'

I remember wondering, as I finished my walk home, whether there could not be some connection between the stroke of Providence which had driven three Cabinet Ministers demented and that gentler touch which had restored Miss Claudia Barriton to good sense and a reasonable marriage.

IV

The next week was an epoch in my life. I seemed to live in the centre of a Mad Tea-party, where everyone was convinced of the madness, and yet resolutely protested that nothing had happened. The public events of those days were simple enough. While Lord Mulross's ankle approached convalescence, the hives of politics were humming with rumours. Vennard's speech had dissolved his party into its parent elements, and the Opposition, as nonplussed as the Government, did not dare as yet to claim the recruit. Consequently he was left alone till he should see fit to take a further step. He refused to be interviewed, using blasphemous language about our free Press; and mercifully he showed no desire to make speeches. He went down to golf at Littlestone, and rarely showed himself in the House. The earnest young reformer seemed to have adopted not only the creed but the habits of his enemies.

Mr Cargill's was a hard case. He returned from Oldham, delighted with himself and full of fight, to find awaiting him an urgent message from the Prime Minister. His chief was sympathetic and kindly. He had long noticed that the Home Secretary looked fagged and ill. There was no Home Office Bill very pressing, and his assistance in general debate could be dispensed with for a little. Let him take a fortnight's holiday – fish, golf, yacht – the Prime Minister was airily suggestive. In vain Mr Cargill declared he was perfectly well. His chief gently but firmly overbore him, and insisted on sending him his own doctor. That eminent specialist, having been well coached, was vaguely alarming, and advised a change. Then Mr Cargill began to suspect, and asked the Prime Minister point-blank if he objected to his Oldham speech. He was told that there was no objection – a little strong meat, perhaps, for Young Liberals, a little daring, but full of Mr Cargill's old intellectual power. Mollified and reassured, the Home Secretary agreed to a week's absence, and departed for a little salmon fishing in Scotland. His wife had meantime been taken into the affair, and privately assured by the Prime Minister that she would greatly ease the mind of the Cabinet if she could induce her husband to take a longer holiday – say three weeks. She promised to do her best and to keep her instructions secret, and the Cargills duly departed for the North. 'In a fortnight,' said the Prime Minister to my aunt, 'he will have forgotten all this nonsense; but of course we shall have to watch him very carefully in the future.'

The Press was given its cue, and announced that Mr

Cargill had spoken at Oldham while suffering from severe nervous breakdown, and that the remarkable doctrines of that speech need not be taken seriously. As I expected, the public put its own interpretation upon this tale. Men took each other aside in clubs, women gossiped in drawing-rooms, and in a week the Cargill scandal had assumed amazing proportions. The popular version was that the Home Secretary had got very drunk at Caerlaverock House, and still under the influence of liquor had addressed the Young Liberals at Oldham. He was now in an Inebriates' Home, and would not return to the House that session. I confess I trembled when I heard this story, for it was altogether too libellous to pass unnoticed. I believed that soon it would reach the ear of Cargill, fishing quietly at Tomandhoul, and that then there would be the deuce to pay.

Nor was I wrong. A few days later I went to see my aunt to find out how the land lay. She was very bitter, I remember, about Claudia Barriton. 'I expected sympathy and help from her, and she never comes near me. I can understand her being absorbed in her engagement, but I cannot understand the frivolous way she spoke when I saw her yesterday. She had the audacity to say that both Mr Vennard and Mr Cargill had gone up in her estimation. Young people can be so heartless.'

I would have defended Miss Barriton, but at this moment an astonishing figure was announced. It was Mrs Cargill in travelling dress, with a purple bonnet and a green motor veil. Her face was scarlet, whether from excitement or the winds of Tomandhoul, and she charged down on us like a young bull.

'We have come back,' she said, 'to meet our accusers.'

'Accusers!' cried my aunt.

'Yes, accusers!' said the lady. 'The abominable rumour

about Alexander has reached our ears. At this moment he is with the Prime Minister, demanding an official denial. I have come to you, because it was here, at your table, that Alexander is said to have fallen.'

'I really don't know what you mean, Mrs Cargill.'

'I mean that Alexander is said to have become drunk while dining here, to have been drunk when he spoke at Oldham, and to be now in a Drunkards' Home.' The poor lady broke down. 'Alexander,' she cried, 'who has been a teetotaller from his youth, and for thirty years an elder in the UP Church*! No form of intoxicant has ever been permitted at our table. Even in illness the thing has never passed our lips.'

My aunt by this time had pulled herself together. 'If this outrageous story is current, Mrs Cargill, there was nothing for it but to come back. Your friends know that it is a gross libel. The only denial necessary is for Mr Cargill to resume his work. I trust his health is better.'

'He is well, but heartbroken. His is a sensitive nature, Lady Caerlaverock, and he feels a stain like a wound.'

'There is no stain,' said my aunt briskly. 'Every public man is a target for scandals, but no one but a fool believes them. They will die a natural death when he returns to work. An official denial would make everybody look ridiculous, and encourage the ordinary person to think that there may have been something in them. Believe me, dear Mrs Cargill, there is nothing to be anxious about now that you are back in London again.'

On the contrary, I thought, there was more cause for anxiety than ever. Cargill was back in the House, and the illness game could not be played a second time. I went home that night acutely sympathetic towards the worries of the Prime Minister. Mulross would be abroad in a day or two, and Vennard and Cargill were volcanoes in eruption. The Government was in a parlous state, with three demented Ministers on the loose.

The same night I first heard the story of *the* Bill. Vennard had done more than play golf at Littlestone. His active mind – for his bitterest enemies never denied his intellectual energy – had been busy on a great scheme. At that time, it will be remembered, a serious shrinkage of unskilled labour existed not only in the Transvaal, but in the new copper fields of East Africa. Simultaneously a famine was scourging Behar, and Vennard, to do him justice, had made manful efforts to cope with it. He had gone fully into the question, and had been slowly coming to the conclusion that Behar was hopelessly overcrowded. In his new frame of mind – unswervingly logical, utterly unemotional, and wholly unbound by tradition – he had come to connect the African and Indian troubles, and to see in one the relief of the other. The first fruit of his meditations was a letter to *The Times*. In it he laid down a new theory of emigration. The peoples of the Empire, he said, must be mobile, shifting about to suit economic conditions. But if this was true for the white man, it was equally true for the dark races under our tutelage. He referred to the famine, and argued that the recurrence of such disasters was inevitable, unless we assisted the poverty-stricken ryot* to emigrate and sell his labour to advantage. He proposed indentures and terminable contracts, for he declared he had no wish to transplant for good. All that was needed was a short season of wage-earning abroad, that the labourer might return home with savings which would set him for the future on a higher economic plane. The letter was temperate and academic in phrasing, the speculation of a publicist rather than the declaration of a Minister. But in Liberals, who remembered the pandemonium raised over the Chinese in South Africa, it stirred up the gloomiest forebodings.

Then, whispered from mouth to mouth, came the news of the Great Bill. Vennard, it was said, intended to bring in a measure at the earliest possible date to authorize a scheme of enforced and State-aided emigration to the African mines. It would apply at first only to the famine districts, but power would be given to extend its working by proclamation to other areas. Such was the rumour, and I need not say it was soon magnified. Questions were asked in the House which the Speaker ruled out of order. Furious articles, inviting denial, appeared in the Liberal press; but Vennard took not the slightest notice. He spent his time between his office in Whitehall and the links at Littlestone, dropping into the House once or twice for half an hour's slumber while a colleague was speaking. His Under Secretary in the Lords – a young gentleman who had joined the party for a bet, and to his immense disgust had been immediately rewarded with office – lost his temper under cross-examination, and swore audibly at the Opposition. In a day or two the story universally believed was that the Secretary for India was about to transfer the bulk of the Indian people to work as indentured labourers for South African Jews.

It was this popular version, I fancy, which reached the ears of Ram Singh, and the news came on him like a thunderclap. He thought that what Vennard proposed Vennard could do. He saw his native province stripped of its people, his fields left unploughed, and his cattle untended; nay, it was possible, his own worthy and honourable self sent to a far country to dig in a hole. It was a grievous and intolerable prospect. He walked home to Gloucester Road in heavy preoccupation, and the first thing he did was to get out the mysterious brass box in which he kept his valuables. From a pocket-book he took a small silk packet, opened it, and spilled a few clear grains on his hand. It was the antidote.

He waited two days, while on all sides the rumour of the Bill grew stronger and its provisions more stringent. Then he hesitated no longer, but sent for Lord Caerlaverock's cook.

V

I conceived that the drug did not create new opinions, but elicited those which had hitherto lain dormant. Every man has a creed, but in his soul he knows that that creed has another side, possibly not less logical, which it does not suit him to produce. Our most honest convictions are not the children of pure reason, but of temperament, environment, necessity, and interest. Most of us take sides in life and forget the one we reject. But our conscience tells us it is there, and we can on occasion state it with a fairness and fullness which proves that it is not wholly repellent to our reason. During the crisis I write of, the attitude of Cargill and Vennard was not that of roysterers out for irresponsible mischief. They were eminently reasonable and wonderfully logical, and in private conversation they gave their opponents a very bad time. Cargill, who had hitherto been the hope of the extreme Free-traders, wrote an article for the *Quarterly* on Tariff Reform*. It was set up, but long before it could be used it was cancelled and the type scattered. I have seen a proof of it, however, and I confess I have never read a more brilliant defence of a doctrine which the author had hitherto described as a childish heresy. Which proves my contention – that Cargill all along knew that there was a case against Free Trade, but naturally did not choose to admit it, his allegiance being vowed elsewhere. The drug altered temperament, and with it the creed which is based mainly on temperament. It scattered current convictions, roused dormant speculations, and without damaging the reason switched it on to a new track.

I can see all this now, but at the time I saw only stark madness and the horrible ingenuity of the lunatic. While Vennard was ruminating on his Bill, Cargill was going about London arguing like a Scotch undergraduate. The Prime Minister had seen from the start that the Home Secretary was the worse danger. Vennard might talk of his preposterous Bill, but the Cabinet would have something to say before its introduction, and he was mercifully disinclined to go near St Stephen's. But Cargill was assiduous in his attendance at the House, and at any moment might blow the Government sky-high. His colleagues were detailed in relays to watch him. One would hale him to luncheon, and keep him till question time was over. Another would insist on taking him for a motor ride, which would end in a breakdown about Brentford. Invitations to dinner were showered upon him, and Cargill, who had been unknown in society, found the whole social machinery of his party set at work to make him a lion. The result was that he was prevented from speaking in public, but given far too much encouragement to talk in private. He talked incessantly, before, at, and after dinner, and he did enormous harm. He was horribly clever, too, and usually got the best of an argument, so that various eminent private Liberals had their tempers ruined by his dialectic. In his rich and unabashed accent – he had long discarded his Edinburgh-English – he dissected their arguments and ridiculed their character. He had once been famous for his soapy manners: now he was as rough as a Highland stot*.

Things could not go on in this fashion: the risk was too great. It was just a fortnight, I think, after the Caerlaverock dinner-party, when the Prime Minister resolved to bring matters to a head. He could not afford to wait for ever on a return of sanity. He consulted Caerlaverock, and it was agreed that Vennard and Cargill should be asked, or rather commanded, to dine on the following evening at Caerlaverock House. Mulross, whose sanity was not suspected, and whose ankle was now well again, was also invited, as were three other members of the Cabinet, and myself as *amicus curiæ**. It was understood that after dinner there would be a settling-up with the two rebels. Either they should recant and come to heel, or they should depart from the fold to swell the wolf-pack of the Opposition. The Prime Minister did not conceal the loss which his party would suffer, but he argued very sensibly that anything was better than a brace of vipers in its bosom.

I have never attended a more lugubrious function. When I arrived I found Caerlaverock, the Prime Minister, and the three other members of the Cabinet standing round a small fire in attitudes of nervous dejection. I remember it was a raw, wet evening, but the gloom out of doors was sunshine compared to the gloom within. Caerlaverock's viceregal air had sadly altered. The Prime Minister, once famous for his genial manners, was pallid and preoccupied. We exchanged remarks about the weather and the duration of the session. Then we fell silent till Mulross arrived.

He did not look as if he had come from a sick bed. He came in as jaunty as a boy, limping just a little from his accident. He was greeted by his colleagues with tender solicitude – solicitude, I fear, completely wasted on him.

'Devilish silly thing to do to get run over,' he said. 'I was in a brown study when a cab came round a corner. But I don't regret it, you know. During the past fortnight I have had leisure to go into this Bosnian Succession* business, and I see now that von Kladow has been playing one big game of bluff. Very well; it has got to stop. I am going to prick the bubble before I am many days older.'

The Prime Minister looked anxious. 'Our policy towards Bosnia has been one of non-interference. It is not for us, I should have thought, to read Germany a lesson.'

'Oh, come now,' Mulross said, slapping – yes, actually slapping – his leader on the back; 'we may drop that nonsense when we are alone. You know very well that there are limits to our game of non-interference. If we don't read Germany a lesson, she will read us one – and a damned long unpleasant one too. The sooner we give up all this milk-blooded, blue-spectacled, pacificist talk the better. However, you will see what I have got to say tomorrow in the House.'

The Prime Minister's face lengthened. Mulross was not the pillar he had thought him, but a splintering reed. I saw that he agreed with me that this was the most dangerous of the lot.

Then Cargill and Vennard came in together. Both looked uncommonly fit, younger, trimmer, cleaner. Vennard, instead of his sloppy clothes and shaggy hair, was groomed like a guardsman; had a large pearl-and-diamond solitaire in his shirt, and a white waistcoat with jewelled buttons. He had lost all his self-consciousness, grinned cheerfully at the others, warmed his hands at the fire, and cursed the weather. Cargill, too, had lost his sanctimonious look. There was a bloom of rustic health on his cheek, and a sparkle in his eye, so that he had the appearance of some rosy Scotch laird of Raeburn's painting. Both men wore an air of purpose and contentment.

Vennard turned at once on the Prime Minister. 'Did you get my letter?' he asked. 'No? Well, you'll find it waiting when you get home. We're all friends here, so I can tell you its contents. We *must* get rid of this ridiculous Radical "tail". They think they have the whip-hand of us; well, we have got to prove that we can do very well without them. They are a collection of confounded, treacherous, complacent prigs, but they have no grit in them, and will come to heel if we tackle them firmly. I respect an honest fanatic, but I do not respect those sentiment-mongers. They have the impudence to say that the country is with them. I tell you it is rank nonsense. If you take a strong hand with them, you'll double your popularity, and we'll come back next year with an increased majority. Cargill agrees with me.'

The Prime Minister looked grave. 'I am not prepared to discuss any policy of ostracism. What you call our "tail" is a vital section of our party. Their creed may be one-sided, but it is none the less part of our mandate from the people.'

'I want a leader who governs as well as reigns,' said Vennard. 'I believe in discipline, and you know as well as I do that the Rump is infernally out of hand.'

'They are not the only members who fail in discipline.'

Vennard grinned. 'I suppose you mean Cargill and myself. But we are following the central lines of British policy. We are on your side, and we want to make your task easier.'

Cargill suddenly began to laugh. 'I don't want any ostracism. Leave them alone, and Vennard and I will undertake to give them such a time in the House that they will wish they had never been born. We'll make them resign in batches.'

Dinner was announced, and, laughing uproariously, the two rebels went arm-in-arm into the dining-room.

Cargill was in tremendous form. He began to tell Scotch stories, memories of his old Parliament House days. He told them admirably, with a raciness of idiom which I had thought beyond him. They were long tales, and some were as broad as they were long, but Mr Cargill disarmed criticism. His audience, rather scandalized at the start, were soon captured, and political troubles were forgotten in old-fashioned laughter. Even the Prime Minister's anxious face relaxed.

This lasted till the *entrée*, the famous Caerlaverock curry.

As I have said, I was not in the secret, and did not detect the transition. As I partook of the dish, I remember feeling a sudden giddiness and a slight nausea. The antidote, to those who had not taken the drug, must have been, I suppose, in the nature of a mild emetic. A mist seemed to obscure the faces of my fellow-guests, and slowly the tide of conversation ebbed away. First Vennard, then Cargill, became silent. I was feeling rather sick, and I noticed with some satisfaction that all our faces were a little green. I wondered casually if I had been poisoned.

The sensation passed, but the party had changed. More especially I was soon conscious that something had happened to the three Ministers. I noticed Mulross particularly, for he was my neighbour. The look of keenness and vitality had died out of him, and suddenly he seemed a rather old, rather tired man, very weary about the eyes.

I asked him if he felt seedy.

'No, not specially,' he replied, 'but that accident gave me a nasty shock.'

'You should go off for a change,' I said.

'I almost think I will,' was the answer. 'I had not meant to leave town till just before the Twelfth, but I think I had better get away to Marienbad* for a fortnight. There is nothing doing in the House, and work at the Office is at a standstill. Yes, I fancy I'll go abroad before the end of the week.'

I caught the Prime Minister's eye and saw that he had forgotten the purpose of the dinner, being dimly conscious that that purpose was now idle. Cargill and Vennard had ceased to talk like rebels. The Home Secretary had subsided into his old suave, phrasing self. The humour had gone out of his eye, and the looseness had returned to his lips. He was an older and more commonplace man, and harmless, quite harmless. Vennard, too, wore a new air, or rather had recaptured his old one. He was saying little, but his voice had lost its crispness and recovered its half-plaintive unction; his shoulders had a droop in them; once more he bristled with self-consciousness.

We others were still shaky from that detestable curry, and were so puzzled as to be acutely uncomfortable. Relief would come later, no doubt, for the present we were uneasy at this weird transformation. I saw the Prime Minister examining the two faces intently, and the result seemed to satisfy him. He sighed and looked at Caerlaverock, who smiled and nodded.

'What about that Bill of yours, Vennard?' he asked. 'There have been a lot of stupid rumours.'

'Bill?' Vennard said. 'I know of no Bill. Now that my departmental work is over, I can give my whole soul to Cargill's Small Holdings. Do you mean that?'

'Yes, of course. There was some confusion in the popular mind, but the old arrangement holds. You and Cargill will put it through between you.'

They began to talk about those weariful small holdings, and I ceased to listen. We left the dining-room and drifted to the library, where a fire tried to dispel the gloom of the weather. There was a feeling of deadly depression abroad, so that, for all its awkwardness, I would really have preferred the former Caerlaverock dinner. The Prime Minister was whispering to his host. I heard him say something about there being 'the devil of a lot of explaining' before him.

Vennard and Cargill came last to the library, arm-in-arm as before.

'I should count it a great honour,' Vennard was saying, 'to sweeten the lot of one toiler in England than to add a million miles to our territory. While one English household falls below the minimum scale of civic wellbeing, all talk of Empire is sin and folly.'

'Excellent!' said Mr Cargill.

Then I knew for certain that at last peace had descended upon the vexed tents of Israel*.

The Lemnian

'The Lemnian' is the short story with which Buchan was most satisfied. Sir Arthur Quiller-Couch described it as a story which 'any man in my generation might be proud to sign'. It first appeared simultaneously in Blackwood's *and* the Atlantic Monthly *in January 1911, and then in* The Moon Endureth *in 1912.*

Fifteen years or so earlier, when Buchan had been an undergraduate at Glasgow University, his young professor Gilbert Murray had awakened his interest in the so-called 'Ionian migration' which in prehistoric times sent great movements of peoples across the Aegean to colonize Ionia, the western coast of Asia Minor. Arising from that interest, and from John and Susan Buchan's cruise among the islands of the Aegean in the spring of 1910, Gilbert Murray's The Rise of the Greek Epic* *in hand, came this story about the seafarer from the island of Lemnos who was blown far into the mainland of Greece at a crucial moment in the fifth century* BC.

Buchan's gift for getting the 'feel' of a situation, and particularly landscape, however remote in time or place, comes over well. The military historian in him both understands, and communicates, the topography of a particular kind of lonely conflict.

The Lemnian

He pushed the matted locks from his brow as he peered into the mist. His hair was thick with salt, and his eyes smarted from the green-wood fire on the poop. The four slaves who crouched beside the thwarts – Carians* with thin birdlike faces – were in a pitiable case, their hands blue with oar-weals and the lash marks on their shoulders beginning to gape from sun and sea. The Lemnian himself bore marks of ill-usage. His cloak was still sopping, his eyes heavy with watching, and his lips black and cracked with thirst. Two days before the storm had caught him and swept his little craft into mid-Aegean. He was a sailor, come of sailor stock, and he had fought the gale manfully and well. But the sea had burst his water-jars, and the torments of drought had been added to his toil. He had been driven south almost to Scyros, but had found no harbour. Then a weary day with the oars had brought him close to the Eubœan shore, when a freshet of storm drove him seaward again. Now at last in this northerly creek of Sciathos he had found shelter and a spring. But it was a perilous place, for there were robbers in the bushy hills – mainland men who loved above all things to rob an islander; and out at sea, as he looked towards Pelion, there seemed something adoing which boded little good. There was deep water beneath a ledge of cliff, half covered by a tangle of wildwood. So Atta lay in the bows, looking through the trails of vine at the racing tides now reddening in the dawn.

The storm had hit others besides him, it seemed. The

channel was full of ships, aimless ships that tossed between tide and wind. Looking closer, he saw that they were all wreckage. There had been tremendous doings in the north, and a navy of some sort had come to grief. Atta was a prudent man, and knew that a broken fleet might be dangerous. There might be men lurking in the maimed galleys who would make short work of the owner of a battered but navigable craft. At first he thought that the ships were those of the Hellenes. The troublesome fellows were everywhere in the islands, stirring up strife and robbing the old lords. But the tides running strongly from the east were bringing some of the wreckage in an eddy into the bay. He lay closer and watched the spars and splintered poops as they neared him. These were no galleys of the Hellenes. Then came a drowned man, swollen and horrible: then another – swarthy, hook-nosed fellows, all yellow with the sea. Atta was puzzled. They must be the men from the East about whom he had been hearing. Long ere he left Lemnos there had been news about the Persians. They were coming like locusts out of the dawn, swarming over Ionia and Thrace, men and ships numerous beyond telling. They meant no ill to honest islanders; a little earth and water were enough to win their friendship. But they meant death to the $\hat{v}\beta\rho\iota\varsigma$* of the Hellenes. Atta was on the side of the invaders; he wished them well in their war with his ancient foes. They would eat them up, Athenians, Lacedæmonians, Corinthians, Æginetans, men of Argos and Elis, and none would be left to trouble him. But in the meantime something had gone wrong. Clearly there had been no battle. As the bodies butted against the side of the galley he hooked up one or two and found no trace of a wound. Poseidon had grown cranky, and had claimed victims. The god would be appeased by this time, and all would go well.

Danger being past, he bade the men get ashore and fill the water-skins. 'God's curse on all Hellenes,' he said, as he soaked up the cold water from the spring in the thicket.

About noon he set sail again. The wind sat in the north-east, but the wall of Pelion turned it into a light stern breeze which carried him swiftly westward. The four slaves, still leg-weary and arm-weary, lay like logs beside the thwarts. Two slept; one munched some salty figs; the fourth, the headman, stared wearily forward, with ever and again a glance back at his master. But the Lemnian never looked his way. His head was on his breast, as he steered, and he brooded on the sins of the Hellenes. He was of the old Pelasgian* stock, the first lords of the land, who had come out of the soil at the call of God. The pillaging northmen had crushed his folk out of the mainlands and most of the islands, but in Lemnos they had met their match. It was a family story how every grown male had been slain, and how the women long after had slaughtered their conquerors in the night. 'Lemnian deeds,' said the Hellenes, when they wished to speak of some shameful thing: but to Atta the shame was a glory to be cherished for ever. He and his kind were the ancient people, and the gods loved old things, as those new folk would find. Very especially he hated the men of Athens. Had not one of their captains, Miltiades, beaten the Lemnians, and brought the island under Athenian sway? True, it was a rule only in name, for any Athenian who came alone to Lemnos would soon be cleaving the air from the highest clifftop. But the thought irked his pride, and he gloated over the Persians' coming. The Great King from beyond the deserts would smite those outrageous upstarts. Atta would willingly give earth and water. It was the whim of a fantastic barbarian, and would be well repaid if the bastard Hellenes were destroyed. They spoke his own tongue, and worshipped his own gods, and yet did evil. Let the nemesis of Zeus devour them!

The wreckage pursued him everywhere. Dead men shouldered the sides of the galley, and the straits were stuck full of things like monstrous buoys, where tall ships had foundered. At Artemision he thought he saw signs of an anchored fleet with the low poops of the Hellenes, and sheered off to the northern shores. There, looking towards Œta and the Malian Gulf, he found an anchorage at sunset. The waters were ugly and the times ill, and he had come on an enterprise bigger than he had dreamed. The Lemnian was a stout fellow, but he had no love for needless danger. He laughed mirthlessly as he thought of his errand, for he was going to Hellas, to the shrine of the Hellenes.

It was a woman's doing, like most crazy enterprises. Three years ago his wife had laboured hard in childbirth, and had had the whims of labouring women. Up in the keep of Larisa, on the windy hillside, there had been heart-searching and talk about the gods. The little olive-wood Hermes, the very private and particular god of Atta's folk, was good enough in simple things like a lambing or a harvest, but he was scarcely fit for heavy tasks. Atta's wife declared that her lord lacked piety. There were mainland gods who repaid worship, but his scorn of all Hellenes made him blind to the merits of those potent divinities. At first Atta resisted. There was Attic blood in his wife, and he strove to argue with her unorthodox craving. But the woman persisted, and a Lemnian wife, as she is beyond other wives in virtue and comeliness, excels them in stubbornness of temper. A second time she was with child, and nothing would content her but that Atta should make his prayers to the stronger gods. Dodona was far away, and long ere he reached it his throat would be cut in the hills. But Delphi was but two days' journey from the Malian coast, and the god of Delphi, the Far-Darter*, had surprising gifts, if one were to credit travellers' tales. Atta yielded with an ill grace, and out of his wealth devised an offering to Apollo. So on this July day he found himself looking across the gulf to Kallidromos, bound for a Hellenic shrine, but hating all Hellenes in his soul. A verse of Homer consoled him – the words which Phocion spoke to Achilles. 'Verily even the gods may be turned, they whose excellence and honour and strength are greater than thine; yet even these do men, when they pray, turn from their purpose with offerings of incense and pleasant vows.'* The Far-Darter must hate the ὕβρις of those Hellenes, and be the more ready to avenge it since they dared to claim his countenance. 'No race has ownership in the gods,' a Lemnian song-maker* had said when Atta had been questioning the ways of Poseidon.

The following dawn found him coasting past the north end of Eubœa in the thin fog of a windless summer morn. He steered by the peak of Othrys and a spur of Œta, as he had learned from a slave who had travelled the road. Presently he was in the muddy Malian waters, and the sun was scattering the mist on the landward side. And then he became aware of a greater commotion than Poseidon's play with the ships off Pelion. A murmur like a winter's storm came seawards. He lowered the sail, which he had set to catch a chance breeze, and bade the men rest on their oars. An earthquake seemed to be tearing at the roots of the hills.

The mist rolled up, and his hawk eyes saw a strange sight. The water was green and still around him, but shoreward it changed its colour. It was a dirty red, and things bobbed about in it like the Persians in the creek of

Sciathos. On the strip of shore, below the sheer wall of Kallidromos, men were fighting – myriads of men, for away towards Locris they stretched in ranks and banners and tents till the eye lost them in the haze. There was no sail on the queer, muddy, red-edged sea; there was no man on the hills: but on that one flat ribbon of sand all the nations of the earth were warring. He remembered about the place: Thermopylæ* they called it, the Gate of the Hot Springs. The Hellenes were fighting the Persians in the pass for their fatherland.

Atta was prudent and loved not other men's quarrels. He gave the word to the rowers to row seaward. In twenty strokes they were in the mist again . . .

Atta was prudent, but he was also stubborn. He spent the day in a creek on the northern shore of the gulf, listening to the weird hum which came over the waters out of the haze. He cursed the delay. Up on Kallidromos would be clear dry air and the path to Delphi among the oak woods. The Hellenes could not be fighting everywhere at once. He might find some spot on the shore, far in their rear, where he could land and gain the hills. There was danger indeed, but once on the ridge he would be safe; and by the time he came back the Great King would have swept the defenders into the sea, and be well on the road for Athens. He asked himself if it were fitting that a Lemnian should be stayed in his holy task by the struggles of Hellene and Barbarian. His thoughts flew to his steading at Larisa, and the dark-eyed wife who was awaiting his home-coming. He could not return without Apollo's favour: his manhood and the memory of his lady's eyes forbade it. So late in the afternoon he pushed off again and steered his galley for the south.

About sunset the mist cleared from the sea; but the dark falls swiftly in the shadow of the high hills, and Atta had no fear. With the night the hum sank to a whisper; it seemed that the invaders were drawing off to camp, for the sound receded to the west. At the last light the Lemnian touched a rock point well to the rear of the defence. He noticed that the spume at the tide's edge was reddish and stuck to his hands like gum. Of a surety much blood was flowing on that coast.

He bade his slaves return to the north shore and lie hidden to await him. When he came back he would light a signal fire on the topmost bluff of Kallidromos. Let them watch for it and come to take him off. Then he seized his bow and quiver, and his short hunting-spear, buckled his cloak about him, saw that the gift to Apollo was safe in the folds of it, and marched sturdily up the hillside.

The moon was in her first quarter, a slim horn which at her rise showed only the faint outline of the hill. Atta plodded steadfastly on, but he found the way hard. This was not like the crisp sea-turf of Lemnos, where, among the barrows of the ancient dead, sheep and kine could find sweet fodder. Kallidromos ran up as steep as the roof of a barn. Cytisus and thyme and juniper grew rank, but above all the place was strewn with rocks, leg-twisting boulders, and great cliffs where eagles dwelt. Being a seaman, Atta had his bearings. The path to Delphi left the shore road near the Hot Springs, and went south by a rift of the mountain. If he went up the slope in a beeline he must strike it in time and find better going. Still it was an eerie place to be tramping after dark. The Hellenes had strange gods of the thicket and hillside, and he had no wish to intrude upon their sanctuaries. He told himself that next to the Hellenes he hated this country of theirs, where a man sweltered in hot jungles or tripped among hidden crags. He sighed for the cool beaches below Larisa, where the surf was white as the snows of Samothrace, and the fisherboys sang round their smoking broth-pots.

Presently he found a path. It was not the mule road, worn by many feet, that he had looked for, but a little track which twined among the boulders. Still it eased his feet, so he cleared the thorns from his sandals, strapped his belt tighter, and stepped out more confidently. Up and up he went, making odd detours among the crags. Once he came to a promontory, and, looking down, saw lights twinkling from the Hot Springs. He had thought the course lay more southerly, but consoled himself by remembering that a mountain path must have many windings. The great matter was that he was ascending, for he knew that he must cross the ridge of Œta before he struck the Locrian glens that led to the Far-Darter's shrine.

At what seemed the summit of the first ridge he halted for breath, and, prone on the thyme, looked back to sea. The Hot Springs were hidden, but across the gulf a single light shone from the far shore. He guessed that by this time his galley had been beached and his slaves were cooking supper. The thought made him homesick. He had beaten and cursed these slaves of his times without number, but now in this strange land he felt them kinsfolk, men of his own household. Then he told himself he was no better than a woman. Had he not gone sailing to Chalcedon and distant Pontus, many months' journey from home, while this was but a trip of days? In a week he would be welcomed by a smiling wife, with a friendly god behind him.

The track still bore west, though Delphi lay in the south. Moreover, he had come to a broader road running through a little tableland. The highest peaks of Œta were dark against the sky, and around him was a flat glade where oaks whispered in the night breezes. By this time he judged from the stars that midnight had passed, and he began to consider whether, now that he was beyond the fighting, he should not sleep and wait for dawn. He made up his mind to find a shelter, and, in the aimless way of the night traveller, pushed on and on in the quest of it. The truth is his mind was on Lemnos, and a dark-eyed, white-armed dame spinning in the evening by the threshold. His eyes roamed among the oak trees, but vacantly and idly, and many a mossy corner was passed unheeded. He forgot his ill-temper, and hummed cheerfully the song his reapers sang in the barley-fields below his orchard. It was a song of seamen turned husbandmen, for the gods it called on were the gods of the sea . . .

Suddenly he found himself crouching among the young oaks, peering and listening. There was something coming from the west. It was like the first mutterings of a storm in a narrow harbour, a steady rustling and whispering. It was not wind; he knew winds too well to be deceived. It was the tramp of light-shod feet among the twigs – many feet, for the sound remained steady, while the noise of a few men will rise and fall. They were coming fast and coming silently. The war had reached far up Kallidromos.

Atta had played this game often in the little island wars. Very swiftly he ran back and away from the path up the slope which he knew to be the first ridge of Kallidromos. The army, whatever it might be, was on the Delphian road. Were the Hellenes about to turn the flank of the Great King?

A moment later he laughed at his folly. For the men began to appear, and they were crossing to meet him, coming from the west. Lying close in the brushwood he could see them clearly. It was well he had left the road, for

they stuck to it, following every winding – crouching, too,
like hunters after deer. The first man he saw was a
Hellene, but the ranks behind were no Hellenes. There
was no glint of bronze or gleam of fair skin. They were
dark, long-haired fellows, with spears like his own, and
round Eastern caps, and egg-shaped bucklers. Then Atta
rejoiced. It was the Great King who was turning the flank
of the Hellenes. They guarded the gate, the fools, while
the enemy slipped through the roof.

He did not rejoice long. The van of the army was
narrow and kept to the path, but the men behind were
straggling all over the hillside. Another minute and he
would be discovered. The thought was cheerless. It was
true that he was an islander and friendly to the Persian,
but up on the heights who would listen to his tale? He
would be taken for a spy, and one of those thirsty spears
would drink his blood. It must be farewell to Delphi for
the moment, he thought, or farewell to Lemnos for ever.
Crouching low, he ran back and away from the path to the
crest of the sea-ridge of Kallidromos.

The men came no nearer him. They were keeping
roughly to the line of the path, and drifted through the
oak wood before him, an army without end. He had
scarcely thought there were so many fighting men in the
world. He resolved to lie there on the crest, in the hope
that ere the first light they would be gone. Then he would
push on to Delphi, leaving them to settle their quarrels
behind him. These were the hard times for a pious
pilgrim.

But another noise caught his ear from the right. The
army had flanking squadrons, and men were coming along
the ridge. Very bitter anger rose in Atta's heart. He had
cursed the Hellenes, and now he cursed the Barbarians no
less. Nay, he cursed all war, that spoiled the errands of

peaceful folk. And then, seeking safety, he dropped over the crest on to the steep shoreward face of the mountain.

In an instant his breath had gone from him. He slid down a long slope of screes, and then with a gasp found himself falling sheer into space. Another second and he was caught in a tangle of bush, and then dropped once more upon screes, where he clutched desperately for handhold. Breathless and bleeding he came to anchor on a shelf of greensward and found himself blinking up at the crest which seemed to tower a thousand feet above. There were men on the crest now. He heard them speak and felt that they were looking down.

The shock kept him still till the men had passed. Then the terror of the place gripped him, and he tried feverishly to retrace his steps. A dweller all his days among gentle downs, he grew dizzy with the sense of being hung in space. But the only fruit of his efforts was to set him slipping again. This time he pulled up at a root of gnarled oak which overhung the sheerest cliff on Kallidromos. The danger brought his wits back. He sullenly reviewed his case, and found it desperate.

He could not go back, and, even if he did, he would meet the Persians. If he went on he would break his neck, or at the best fall into the Hellenes' hands. Oddly enough he feared his old enemies less than his friends. He did not think that the Hellenes would butcher him. Again, he might sit perched in his eyrie till they settled their quarrel, or he fell off. He rejected this last way. Fall off he should for certain, unless he kept moving. Already he was retching with the vertigo of the heights. It was growing lighter. Suddenly he was looking not into a black world, but to a pearl-grey floor far beneath him. It was the sea, the thing he knew and loved. The sight screwed up his courage. He remembered that he was a Lemnian and a seafarer. He would be conquered neither by rock, nor by Hellene, nor by the Great King. Least of all by the last, who was a barbarian. Slowly, with clenched teeth and narrowed eyes, he began to clamber down a ridge which flanked the great cliff of Kallidromos. His plan was to reach the shore and take the road to the east before the Persians completed their circuit. Some instinct told him that a great army would not take the track he had mounted by. There must be some longer and easier way debouching farther down the coast. He might yet have the good luck to slip between them and the sea.

The two hours which followed tried his courage hard. Thrice he fell, and only a juniper root stood between him and death. His hands grew ragged, and his nails were worn to the quick. He had long ago lost his weapons; his cloak was in shreds, all save the breast-fold which held the gift to Apollo. The heavens brightened, but he dared not look around. He knew he was traversing awesome places, where a goat could scarcely tread. Many times he gave up hope of life. His head was swimming, and he was so deadly sick that often he had to lie gasping on some shoulder of rock less steep than the rest. But his anger kept him to his purpose. He was filled with fury at the Hellenes. It was they and their folly that had brought him these mischances. Some day . . .

He found himself sitting blinking on the shore of the sea. A furlong off the water was lapping on the reefs. A man, larger than human in the morning mist, was standing above him.

'Greeting, stranger,' said the voice. 'By Hermes, you choose the difficult roads to travel.'

Atta felt for broken bones, and, reassured, struggled to his feet.

'God's curse upon all mountains,' he said. He staggered to the edge of the tide and laved his brow. The savour of salt revived him. He turned to find the tall man at his elbow, and noted how worn and ragged he was, and yet how upright.

'When a pigeon is flushed from the rocks there is a hawk near,' said the voice.

Atta was angry. 'A hawk?' he cried. 'Nay, an army of eagles. There will be some rare flushing of Hellenes before evening.'

'What frightened you, Islander?' the stranger asked. 'Did a wolf bark up on the hillside?'

'Ay, a wolf. The wolf from the East with a multitude of wolflings. There will be fine eating soon in the pass.'

The man's face grew dark. He put his hand to his mouth and called. Half a dozen sentries ran to join him. He spoke to them in the harsh Lacedæmonian speech which made Atta sick to hear. They talked with the back of the throat, and there was not an 's' in their words.

'There is mischief in the hills,' the first man said. 'This islander has been frightened down over the rocks. The Persian is stealing a march on us.'

The sentries laughed. One quoted a proverb about island courage. Atta's wrath flared and he forgot himself. He had no wish to warn the Hellenes, but it irked his pride to be thought a liar. He began to tell his story hastily, angrily, confusedly; and the men still laughed.

Then he turned eastward and saw the proof before him. The light had grown and the sun was coming up over Pelion. The first beam fell on the eastern ridge of Kallidromos, and there, clear on the sky-line, was the proof. The Persian was making a wide circuit, but moving shoreward. In a little while he would be at the coast, and by noon at the Hellenes' rear.

His hearers doubted no more. Atta was hurried forward through the lines of the Greeks to the narrow throat of the pass, where behind a rough rampart of stones lay the Lacedæmonian headquarters. He was still giddy from the heights, and it was in a giddy dream that he traversed the misty shingles of the beach amid ranks of sleeping warriors. It was a grim place, for there were dead and dying in it, and blood on every stone. But in the lee of the wall little fires were burning and slaves were cooking breakfast. The smell of roasting flesh came pleasantly to his nostrils, and he remembered that he had had no meal since he crossed the gulf.

Then he found himself the centre of a group who had the air of kings. They looked as if they had been years in war. Never had he seen faces so worn and so terribly scarred. The hollows in their cheeks gave them the air of smiling, and yet they were grave. Their scarlet vests were torn and muddied, and the armour which lay near was dinted like the scrap-iron before a smithy door. But what caught his attention were the eyes of the men. They glittered as no eyes he had ever seen before glittered. The sight cleared his bewilderment and took the pride out of his heart. He could not pretend to despise a folk who looked like Ares* fresh from the wars of the Immortals.

They spoke among themselves in quiet voices. Scouts came and went, and once or twice one of the men, taller than the rest, asked Atta a question. The Lemnian sat in the heart of the group, sniffing the smell of cooking, and looking at the rents in his cloak and the long scratches on his legs. Something was pressing on his breast, and he found that it was Apollo's gift. He had forgotten all about it. Delphi seemed beyond the moon, and his errand a child's dream.

Then the King, for so he thought of the tall man, spoke.

'You have done us a service, Islander. The Persian is at our back and front, and there will be no escape for those who stay. Our allies are going home, for they do not share our vows. We of Lacedæmon wait in the pass. If you go with the men of Corinth you will find a place of safety before noon. No doubt in the Euripus there is some boat to take you to your own land.'

He spoke courteously, not in the rude Athenian way; and somehow the quietness of his voice and his glittering eyes roused wild longings in Atta's heart. His island pride was face to face with a greater – greater than he had ever dreamed of.

'Bid yon cooks give me some broth,' he said gruffly. 'I am faint. After I have eaten I will speak with you.'

He was given food, and as he ate he thought. He was on trial before these men of Lacedæmon. More, the old faith of the islands, the pride of the first masters, was at stake in his hands. He had boasted that he and his kind were the last of the men; now these Hellenes of Lacedæmon were preparing a great deed, and they deemed him unworthy to share in it. They offered him safety. Could he brook the insult? He had forgotten that the cause of the Persian was his; that the Hellenes were the foes of his race. He saw only that the last test of manhood was preparing, and the manhood in him rose to greet the trial. An odd wild ecstasy surged in his veins. It was not the lust of battle, for he had no love of slaying, or hate of the Persian, for he was his friend. It was the joy of proving that the Lemnian stock had a starker pride than these men of Lacedæmon. They would die for their fatherland, and their vows; but he, for a whim, a scruple, a delicacy of honour. His mind was so clear that no other course occurred to him. There was only one way for a man. He, too, would be dying for his fatherland, for through him the island race would be ennobled in the eyes of gods and men.

Troops were filing fast to the east – Thebans, Corinthians.

'Time flies, Islander,' said the King's voice. 'The hours of safety are slipping past.'

Atta looked up carelessly. 'I will stay,' he said. 'God's curse on all Hellenes! Little I care for your quarrels. It is nothing to me if your Hellas is under the heel of the East. But I care much for brave men. It shall never be said that a man of Lemnos, a son of the old race, fell back when Death threatened. I stay with you, men of Lacedæmon.'

The King's eyes glittered; they seemed to peer into his heart.

'It appears they breed men in the islands,' he said. 'But you err. Death does not threaten. Death awaits us.'

'It is all one,' said Atta. 'But I crave a boon. Let me fight my last fight by your side. I am of older stock than you, and a king in my own country. I would strike my last blow among kings.'

There was an hour of respite before battle was joined, and Atta spent it by the edge of the sea. He had been given arms, and in girding himself for the fight he had found Apollo's offering in his breastfold. He was done with the gods of the Hellenes. His offering should go to the gods of his own people. So, calling upon Poseidon, he flung the little gold cup far out to sea. It flashed in the sunlight, and then sank in the soft green tides so noiselessly that it seemed as if the hand of the Sea-god had been stretched to take it. 'Hail, Poseidon!' the Lemnian cried. 'I am bound this day for the Ferryman. To you only I make prayer, and to the little Hermes of Larisa. Be kind to my kin when they travel the sea, and keep them islanders and seafarers for ever. Hail and farewell. God of my own folk!'

Then, while the little waves lapped on the white sand, Atta made a song. He was thinking of the homestead far up in the green downs, looking over to the snows of Samothrace. At this hour in the morning there would be a tinkle of sheep-bells as the flocks went down to the low pastures. Cool wind would be blowing, and the noise of the surf below the cliffs would come faint to the ear. In the hall the maids would be spinning, while their dark-haired mistress would be casting swift glances to the doorway, lest it might be filled any moment by the form of her returning lord. Outside in the chequered sunlight of the orchard the child would be playing with his nurse, crooning in childish syllables the chanty his father had taught him. And at the thought of his home a great passion welled up in Atta's heart. It was not regret, but joy and pride and aching love. In his antique island creed the death he was awaiting was not other than a bridal. He was dying for the things he loved, and by his death they would be blessed eternally. He would not have long to wait before bright eyes came to greet him in the House of Shadows.

So Atta made the Song of Atta, and sang it then, and later in the press of battle. It was a simple song, like the lays of seafarers. It put into rough verse the thought which cheers the heart of all adventurers – nay, which makes adventure possible for those who have much to leave. It spoke of the shining pathway of the sea which is the Great Uniter. A man may lie dead in Pontus or beyond the Pillars of Herakles, but if he dies on the shore there is nothing between him and his fatherland. It spoke of a battle all the long dark night in a strange place – a place of marshes and black cliffs and shadowy terrors.

'In the dawn the sweet light comes,' said the song, *'and the salt winds and the tides will bear me home . . .'*

When in the evening the Persians took toll of the dead, they found one man who puzzled them. He lay among the tall Lacedæmonians, on the very lip of the sea, and around him were swathes of their countrymen. It looked as if he had been fighting his way to the water, and had been overtaken by death as his feet reached the edge. Nowhere in the pass did the dead lie so thick, and yet he was no Hellene. He was torn like a deer that the dogs have worried, but the little left of his garments and his features spoke of Eastern race. The survivors could tell nothing except that he had fought like a god and had been singing all the while.

The matter came to the ear of the Great King, who was sore enough at the issue of the day. That one of his men had performed feats of valour beyond the Hellenes was a pleasant tale to tell. And so his captains reported it. Accordingly when the fleet from Artemision arrived next morning, and all but a few score Persians were shovelled into holes, that the Hellenes might seem to have been conquered by a lesser force, Atta's body was laid out with pomp in the midst of the Lacedæmonians. And the seamen rubbed their eyes and thanked their strange gods that one man of the East had been found to match those terrible warriors whose name was a nightmare. Further, the Great King gave orders that the body of Atta should be embalmed and carried with the army, and that his name and kin should be sought out and duly honoured. This latter was a task too hard for the staff, and no more was heard of it till months later, when the King, in full flight after Salamis, bethought him of the one man who had not played him false. Finding that his lieutenants had nothing to tell him, he eased five of them of their heads.

* * *

As it happened, the deed was not quite forgotten. An islander, a Lesbian and a cautious man, had fought at Thermopylæ in the Persian ranks, and had heard Atta's singing and seen how he fell. Long afterwards some errand took this man to Lemnos, and in the evening, speaking with the Elders, he told his tale and repeated something of the song. There was that in the words which gave the Lemnians a clue, the mention, I think, of the olive-wood Hermes and the snows of Samothrace. So Atta came to great honour among his own people, and his memory and his words were handed down to the generations. The song became a favourite island lay, and for centuries throughout the Aegean seafaring men sang it when they turned their prows to wild seas. Nay, it travelled farther, for you will find part of it stolen by Euripides and put in a chorus of the *Andromache*. There are echoes of it in some of the epigrams of the *Anthology*; and, though the old days have gone, the simple fisherfolk still sing snatches in their barbarous dialect. The Klephts* used to make a catch of it at night round their fires in the hills, and only the other day I met a man in Scyros who had collected a dozen variants, and was publishing them in a dull book on island folklore.

In the centuries which followed the great fight, the sea fell away from the roots of the cliffs and left a mile of marshland. About fifty years ago a peasant, digging in a rice-field, found the cup which Atta had given to Poseidon. There was much talk about the discovery, and scholars debated hotly about its origin. Today it is in the Berlin Museum, and according to the new fashion in archæology it is labelled 'Minoan', and kept in the Cretan Section. But any one who looks carefully will see behind the rim a neat little carving of a dolphin; and I happen to know that that was the private badge of Atta's house.

Fullcircle

After the First World War Buchan and his family settled with profound and active contentment into Cotswold life, in a house which had associations with Dr Johnson at Elsfield, near Oxford; (he wrote about the house in the novel Midwinter). The old Cotswold mixture of wildness and elegant habitation touched him deeply, and the fifteen years he spent in the house were among the most productive of his extraordinary life. Nearly fifty books, and so far uncounted other writing, were written at Elsfield: and he was at that time publisher, Director of Reuters, Member of Parliament, Curator of Oxford University Chest, Lord High Commissioner to the General Assembly of the Church of Scotland, family man, fisherman, walker and friend.

'Fullcircle', after appearing simultaneously in Blackwood's and the Atlantic Monthly in January 1920, appeared again in The Runagates Club of 1928, now with the narrator identified as 'Peckwether the historian', one of Buchan's most shadowy figures. He is, of course, mainly a distancing device, making a series of gates to the house, as if its influence had to be isolated a little, made accessible only through ceremony. So Buchan introduces Peckwether who tells of Leithen who introduces the Giffens who then tell of the house, which is active at the heart of the story. Each of the three visits, in October, June and November, has a scene-setting before it, a transition passage. In the house itself, the chapel is only approachable through the effects of other changes.

It is Leithen's story. This quiet lawyer is used as narrator by Buchan with some subtlety in one or two other stories and in five novels – The Power House *(Buchan's first 'shocker', written before the first Hannay story,* The Thirty-Nine Steps*),* John Macnab, The Dancing Floor, The Gap in the Curtain *and* Sick Heart River. *All these are marked by a certain obliqueness of narrative, by strongly visionary experiences (which the indirectness of the narrative helps to establish), and by a sense of the importance, even in times of the greatest stress, of what Wordsworth called 'a wise passiveness'. All these features make him Richard Hannay's opposite.*

Fullcircle

Between the Windrush and the Colne
I found a little house of stone –
A little wicked house of stone.

Peckwether, the historian, whose turn for story-telling came at our last dinner before the summer interregnum, apologized for reading his narrative. He was not good, he said, at impromptu composition. He also congratulated himself on Leithen's absence. 'He comes into the story, and I should feel rather embarrassed talking about him to his face. But he has read my manuscript and approved it, so you have two reliable witnesses to a queerish tale.'

In his precise academic voice he read what follows.

The October day was brightening towards late afternoon when Leithen and I climbed the hill above the stream and came in sight of the house. All morning a haze with the sheen of pearl in it had lain on the folds of downland, and the vision of far horizons, which is the glory of Cotswold, had been veiled, so that every valley seemed a place enclosed and set apart. But now a glow had come into the air, and for a little the autumn lawns had the tints of summer. The gold of sunshine was warm on the grasses, and only the riot of colour in the berry-laden edges of the fields and the slender woodlands told of the failing year.

We were looking into a green cup of the hills, and it was all a garden. A little place, bounded by slopes that defined its graciousness with no hint of barrier, so that a dweller there, though his view was but half a mile on any side, would yet have the sense of dwelling on uplands and commanding the world. Round the top edge ran an old wall of stones, beyond which the October bracken flamed to the skyline. Inside were folds of ancient pasture with here and there a thornbush, falling to rose gardens, and, on one side, to the smooth sward of a terrace above a tiny lake. At the heart of it stood the house, like a jewel well set. It was a miniature, but by the hand of a master. The style was late seventeenth-century, when an agreeable classic convention had opened up to sunlight and comfort the dark magnificence of the Tudor fashion. The place had the spacious air of a great mansion, and was finished in every detail with a fine scrupulousness. Only when the eye measured its proportions with the woods and the hillside did the mind perceive that it was a small dwelling. The stone of Cotswold takes curiously the colour of the weather. Under thunder-clouds it will be as dark as basalt; on a grey day it is grey like lava; but in sunshine it absorbs the sun. At the moment the little house was pale gold, like honey.

Leithen swung a long leg across the stile.

'Pretty good, isn't it?' he said. 'It's pure authentic Sir Christopher Wren. The name is worthy of it, too. It is called Fullcircle.'

He told me its story. It had been built after the Restoration by the Carteron family, whose wide domains ran into these hills. The Lord Carteron of the day was a friend of the Merry Monarch, but it was not as a sanctuary for orgies that he built the house. Perhaps he was tired of the gloomy splendour of Minster Carteron, and wanted a home of his own and not of his ancestors' choosing. He had an elegant taste in letters, as we can learn from his neat imitations of Martial*, his pretty *Bucolics**, and the more than respectable Latin hexameters of his *Ars Vivendi**. Being a great nobleman, he had the best skill of the day to construct his hermitage, and here he would retire for months at a time with like-minded friends to a world of books and gardens. He seems to have had no ill-wishers; contemporary memoirs speak of him charitably, and Dryden spared him four lines of encomium. 'A selfish old dog,' Leithen called him. 'He had the good sense to eschew politics and enjoy life. His soul is in that little house. He only did one rash thing in his career – he anticipated the King, his master, by some years in turning Papist.'

I asked about its later history.

'After his death it passed to a younger branch of the Carterons. It left them in the eighteenth century, and the Applebys got it. They were a jovial lot of hunting squires, and let the library go to the dogs. Old Colonel Appleby was still alive when I came to Borrowby. Something went wrong in his inside when he was nearly seventy, and the doctors knocked him off liquor. Not that he drank too much, though he did himself well. That finished the poor old boy. He told me that it revealed to him the amazing truth that during a long and, as he hoped, publicly useful life he had never been quite sober. He was a good fellow, and I missed him when he died . . . The place went to a remote cousin called Giffen.'

Leithen's eyes, as they scanned the prospect, seemed amused.

'Julian and Ursula Giffen . . . I daresay you know the names. They always hunt in couples, and write books about sociology and advanced ethics and psychics – books called either "The New This or That", or "Towards Something or Other". You know the sort of thing. They're deep in all the pseudo-sciences . . . Decent souls, but you can guess the type. I came across them in a case I had at the Old Bailey – defending a ruffian who was charged with murder. I hadn't a doubt he deserved hanging on twenty counts, but there wasn't enough evidence to convict him on this one. Dodderidge was at his worst – it was just before they induced him to retire – and his handling of the jury was a masterpiece of misdirection. Of course there was a shindy. The thing was a scandal, and it stirred up all the humanitarians, till the murderer was almost forgotten in the iniquities of old Dodderidge. You must remember the case. It filled the papers for weeks. Well, it was in that connection that I fell in with the Giffens. I got rather to like them, and I've been to see them at their house in Hampstead. Golly, what a place! Not a chair fit to sit down on, and colours that made you want to weep. I never met people with heads so full of feathers.'

I said something about that being an odd milieu for him.

'Oh, I like human beings – all kinds. It's my profession to study them, for without that the practice of the law would be a lean affair. There are hordes of people like the Giffens – only not so good, for they really have hearts of gold. They are the rootless stuff in the world today – in revolt against everything and everybody with any ancestry. A kind of innocent self-righteousness – wanting to be the people with whom wisdom begins and ends. They are mostly sensitive and tender-hearted, but they wear themselves out in an eternal dissidence. Can't build, you know, for they object to all tools, but very ready to crab*. They scorn any form of Christianity, but they'll walk miles to patronize some wretched sect that has the merit of being brand-new. "Pioneers" they call themselves – funny little unclad people adventuring into the cold desert with no maps. Giffen once described himself and his friends to me as "forward-looking", but that, of course, is just what they are not. To tackle the future you must have a firm grip of the past, and for them the past is only a pathological curiosity. They're up to their necks in the mud of the present . . . But good, after a fashion; and innocent – sordidly innocent. Fate was in an ironical mood when she saddled them with that wicked little house.'

'Wicked' did not seem to me to be a fair word. It sat honey-coloured among its gardens with the meekness of a dove. The sound of a bicycle on the road behind made us turn round, and Leithen advanced to meet a dismounting rider.

He was a tallish fellow, some forty years old perhaps, with one of those fluffy blond beards that have never been shaved. Short-sighted, of course, and wore glasses. Biscuit-coloured knickerbockers and stockings clad his lean limbs.

Leithen introduced me. 'We are walking to Borrowby, and stopped to admire your house. Could we have just a glimpse inside? I want Peckwether to see the staircase.'

Mr Giffen was very willing. 'I've been over to Clyston to send a telegram. We have some friends for the weekend who might interest you. Won't you stay to tea?'

There was a gentle formal courtesy about him, and his voice had the facile intonations of one who loves to talk. He led us through a little gate, and along a shorn green walk among the bracken to a postern which gave entrance to the garden. Here, though it was October, there was still a bright show of roses, and the jet of water from the leaden Cupid dripped noiselessly among fallen petals. And then we stood before the doorway, above which the old Carteron had inscribed a line of Horace.

I have never seen anything quite like the little hall. There were two, indeed, separated by a staircase of a wood that looked like olive. Both were paved with black and white marble, and the inner was oval in shape, with a gallery supported on slender walnut pillars. It was all in miniature, but it had a spaciousness which no mere size could give. Also it seemed to be permeated by the quintessence of sunlight. Its air was of long-descended, confident, equable happiness.

There were voices on the terrace beyond the hall. Giffen led us into a room on the left. 'You remember the house in Colonel Appleby's time, Leithen. This was the chapel. It had always been the chapel. You see the change we have made . . . I beg your pardon, Mr Peckwether. You're not by any chance a Roman Catholic?'

The room had a white panelling, and on two sides deep windows. At one end was a fine Italian shrine of marble, and the floor was mosaic, blue and white, in a quaint Byzantine pattern. There was the same air of sunny cheerfulness as in the rest of the house. No mystery could find a lodgment here. It might have been a chapel for three centuries, but the place was pagan. The Giffens' changes were no sort of desecration. A green-baize table filled most of the floor, surrounded by chairs like a committee room. On new raw-wood shelves were files of papers and stacks of blue-books* and those desiccated works into which reformers of society torture the English tongue. Two typewriters stood on a side-table.

'It is our workroom,' Giffen explained, 'where we hold our Sunday moots*. Ursula thinks that a weekend is wasted unless it produces some piece of real work. Often a quite valuable committee has its beginning here. We try to make our home a refuge for busy workers, where they need not idle but can work under happy conditions.'

'"A college situate in a clearer air,"' Leithen quoted. But Giffen did not respond except with a smile; he had probably never heard of Lord Falkland*.

A woman entered the room, a woman who might have been pretty if she had taken a little pains. Her reddish hair was drawn tightly back and dressed in a hard knot, and her clothes were horribly incongruous in a remote manor-house. She had bright eager eyes, like a bird, and hands that fluttered nervously. She greeted Leithen with warmth.

'We have settled down marvellously,' she told him. 'Julian and I feel as if we had always lived here, and our life has arranged itself so perfectly. My Mothers' Cottages in the village will soon be ready, and the Club is to be opened next week. Julian and I will carry on the classes ourselves for the first winter. Next year we hope to have a really fine programme . . . And then it is so pleasant to be able to entertain one's friends . . . Won't you stay to tea? Dr Swope is here, and Mary Elliston, and Mr Percy Blaker – you know, the Member of Parliament. Must you hurry off? I'm so sorry . . . What do you think of our workroom? It was utterly terrible when we first came here – a sort of decayed chapel, like a withered tuberose. We have let the air of heaven into it.'

I observed that I had never seen a house so full of space and light.

'Ah, you notice that? It is a curiously happy place to live in. Sometimes I'm almost afraid to feel so light-hearted. But we look on ourselves as only trustees. It is a trust we have to administer for the common good. You know, it's a house on which you can lay your own impress. I can imagine places which dominate the dwellers, but Fullcircle is plastic, and we can make it our own just as much as if we had planned and built it. That's our chief piece of good fortune.'

We took our leave, for we had no desire for the company of Dr Swope and Mr Percy Blaker. When we reached the highway we halted and looked back on the little jewel. Shafts of the westering sun now caught the stone and turned the honey to ripe gold. Thin spires of amethyst smoke rose into the still air. I thought of the well-meaning restless couple inside its walls, and somehow they seemed out of the picture. They simply did not matter. The house was the thing, for I had never met in inanimate stone such an air of gentle masterfulness. It had a personality of its own, clean-cut and secure, like a high-born old dame among the females of profiteers. And Mrs Giffen claimed to have given it her impress!

That night in the library at Borrowby, Leithen discoursed of the Restoration. Borrowby, of which, by the expenditure of much care and a good deal of money, he had made a civilized dwelling, is a Tudor manor of the Cotswold type, with high-pitched narrow roofs and tall stone chimneys, rising sheer from the meadows with something of the massiveness of a Border keep. He nodded towards the linen-fold panelling and the great carven chimney-piece.

'In this kind of house you have the mystery of the elder England. What was Raleigh's phrase? "High thoughts and divine contemplations."* The people who built this sort of thing lived close to another world, and they thought bravely of death. It doesn't matter who they were – Crusaders or Elizabethans or Puritans – they all had poetry in them, and the heroic, and a great unworldliness. They had marvellous spirits, and plenty of joys and triumphs; but they had also their hours of black gloom. Their lives were like our weather – storm and sun. One thing they never feared – death. He walked too near them all their days to be a bogy.

'But the Restoration was a sharp break. It brought paganism into England – paganism and the art of life. No people have ever known better the secret of a bland happiness. Look at Fullcircle. There are no dark corners there. The man that built it knew all there was to be known about how to live . . . The trouble was that they did not know how to die. That was the one shadow on the glass. So they provided for it in the pagan way. They tried magic. They never became true Catholics – they were always pagan to the end, but they smuggled a priest into their lives. He was a kind of insurance premium against unwelcome mystery.'

It was not till nearly two years later that I saw the Giffens again. The May-fly season was near its close, and I had snatched a day on a certain limpid Cotswold river. There was another man on the same beat, fishing from the opposite bank, and I watched him with some anxiety, for a duffer would have spoilt my day. To my relief I recognized Giffen. With him it was easy to come to terms, and presently the water was parcelled out between us.

We foregathered for luncheon, and I stood watching while he nearly stalked, rose and landed a trout. I confessed to some surprise – first that Giffen should be a fisherman at all, for it was not in keeping with my old notion of him; and second, that he should cast such a workman-like line. As we lunched together, I observed several changes. He had shaved his fluffy beard, and his face was notably less lean, and had the clear even sunburn of the countryman. His clothes, too, were different. They also were workman-like, and looked as if they belonged to him – no more the uneasy knickerbockers of the Sunday golfer.

'I'm desperately keen,' he told me. 'You see it's only my second May-fly season, and last year I was no better than a beginner. I wish I had known long ago what good fun fishing was. Isn't this a blessed place?' And he looked up through the canopy of flowering chestnuts to the June sky.

'I'm glad you've taken to sport,' I said. 'Even if you only come here for the weekends, sport lets you into the secrets of the countryside.'

'Oh, we don't go much to London now,' was his answer. 'We sold our Hampstead house a year ago. I can't think how I ever could stick that place. Ursula takes the same view . . . I wouldn't leave Oxfordshire just now for a thousand pounds. Do you smell the hawthorn? Last week this meadow was scented like Paradise. D'you know, Leithen's a queer fellow?'

I asked why.

'He once told me that this countryside in June made him sad. He said it was too perfect a thing for fallen humanity. I call that morbid. Do you see any sense in it?'

I knew what Leithen meant, but it would have taken too long to explain.

'I feel warm and good and happy here,' he went on. 'I used to talk about living close to nature. Rot! I didn't know what nature meant. Now – ' He broke off. 'By Jove, there's a kingfisher. That is only the second I've seen this year. They're getting uncommon with us.'

'With us' – I liked the phrase. He was becoming a true countryman.

We had a good day – not extravagantly successful, but satisfactory, and he persuaded me to come home with him to Fullcircle for the night, explaining that I could catch an early train next morning at the junction. So we extricated a little two-seater from a thicket of lilacs, and he drove me through four miles of sweet-scented dusk, with nightingales shouting in every thicket. I changed into a suit of his flannels in a bedroom looking out on the little lake where trout were rising, and I remember that I whistled from pure light-heartedness. In that adorable house one seemed to be still breathing the air of the spring meadows.

Dinner was my first big surprise. It was admirable – plain but perfectly cooked, and with that excellence of basic material which is the glory of a well-appointed country house. There was wine too, which, I am certain, was a new thing. Giffen gave me a bottle of sound claret, and afterwards some more than decent port. My second surprise was my hostess. Her clothes, like her husband's, must have changed, for I did not notice what she was wearing, and I had noticed it only too clearly the last time we met. More remarkable still was the difference in her face. For the first time I realized that she was a pretty woman. The contours had softened and rounded, and there was a charming well-being in her eyes very different from the old restlessness. She looked content – infinitely content.

I asked about her Mothers' Cottages. She laughed cheerfully.

'I gave them up after the first year. They didn't mix well with the village people. I'm quite ready to admit my mistake, and it was the wrong kind of charity. The Londoners didn't like it – felt lonesome and sighed for the fried-fish shop; and the village women were shy of them – afraid of infectious complaints, you know. Julian and I have decided that our business is to look after our own people.'

It may have been malicious, but I said something about the wonderful scheme of village education.

'Another relic of Cockneyism,' laughed the lady; but Giffen looked a trifle shy.

'I gave it up because it didn't seem worth while. What is the use of spoiling a perfectly wholesome scheme of life by introducing unnecessary complications? Medicine is no good unless a man is sick, and these people are not sick. Education is the only cure for certain diseases the modern world has engendered, but if you don't find the disease the remedy is superfluous. The fact is, I hadn't the face to go on with the thing. I wanted to be taught rather than to teach. There's a whole world round me of which I know very little, and my first business is to get to understand it. Any village poacher can teach me more of the things that matter than I have to tell him.'

'Besides, we have so much to do,' his wife added. 'There's the house and the garden, and the home-farm and the property. It isn't large, but it takes a lot of looking after.'

The dining-room was long and low-ceilinged, and had a white panelling in bold relief. Through the windows came odours of the garden and a faint tinkle of water. The dusk was deepening, and the engravings in their rosewood frames were dim, but sufficient light remained to reveal the picture above the fireplace. It showed a middle-aged man in the clothes of the later Carolines. The plump tapering fingers of one hand held a book, the other was hidden in the folds of a flowered waistcoat. The long, curled wig framed a delicate face, with something of the grace of youth left to it. There were quizzical lines about the mouth, and the eyes smiled pleasantly yet very wisely. It was the face of a man I should have liked to dine with. He must have been the best of company.

Giffen answered my question.

'That's the Lord Carteron who built the house. No. No relation. Our people were the Applebys, who came in 1753. We've both fallen so deep in love with Fullcircle that we wanted to see the man who conceived it. I had some trouble getting it. It came out of the Minster Carteron sale, and I had to give a Jew dealer twice what he paid for it. It's a jolly thing to live with.'

It was indeed a curiously charming picture. I found my eyes straying to it till the dusk obscured the features. It was the face of one wholly at home in a suave world, learned in all the urbanities. A good friend, I thought, the old lord must have been, and a superlative companion. I could imagine neat Horatian tags coming ripely from his lips. Not a strong face, but somehow a dominating one. The portrait of the long-dead gentleman had still the atmosphere of life. Giffen raised his glass of port to him as we rose from the table, as if to salute a comrade.

We moved to the room across the hall, which had once been the Giffens' workroom, the cradle of earnest committees and weighty memoranda. This was my third surprise. Baize-covered table and raw-wood shelves had disappeared. The place was now half smoking-room, half library. On the walls hung a fine collection of coloured sporting prints, and below them were ranged low Hepplewhite bookcases. The lamplight glowed on the ivory walls, and the room, like everything else in the house, was radiant. Above the mantelpiece was a stag's head – a fair eleven-pointer.

Giffen nodded proudly towards it. 'I got that last year at Machray. My first stag.'

There was a little table with an array of magazines and weekly papers. Some amusement must have been visible in my face as I caught sight of various light-hearted sporting journals, for he laughed apologetically. 'You mustn't think that Ursula and I take in that stuff for ourselves. It amuses our guests, you know.'

I dared say it did, but I was convinced that the guests were no longer Dr Swope and Mr Percy Blaker.

One of my failings is that I can never enter a room

containing books without scanning the titles. Giffen's collection won my hearty approval. There were the very few novelists I can read myself – Miss Austen and Sir Walter and the admirable Marryat; there was a shelf full of memoirs, and a good deal of seventeenth- and eighteenth-century poetry; there was a set of the classics in fine editions, Bodonis and Baskervilles and suchlike; there was much county history, and one or two valuable old herbals and itineraries. I was certain that two years before Giffen would have had no use for literature except some muddy Russian oddments, and I am positive that he would not have known the name of Surtees. Yet there stood the tall octavos recording the unedifying careers of Mr Jorrocks, Mr Facey Romford, and Mr Soapy Sponge.

I was a little bewildered as I stretched my legs in a very deep armchair. Suddenly I had a strong impression of looking on at a play. My hosts seemed to be automata, moving docilely at the orders of a masterful stage-manager, and yet with no sense of bondage. And as I looked on they faded off the scene, and there was only one personality – that house so serene and secure, smiling at our modern antics, but weaving all the while an iron spell round its lovers. For a second I felt an oppression as of something to be resisted. But no. There was no oppression. The house was too well-bred and disdainful to seek to captivate. Only those who fell in love with it could know its mastery, for all love exacts a price. It was far more than a thing of stone and lime; it was a creed, an art, a scheme of life – older than any Carteron, older than England. Somewhere far back in time – in Rome, in Attica, or in an Aegean island – there must have been such places; but then they called them temples, and gods dwelt in them.

I was roused by Giffen's voice discoursing of his books.

'I've been rubbing up my classics again,' he was saying. 'Queer thing, but ever since I left Cambridge I have been out of the mood for them. And I'm shockingly ill-read in English literature. I wish I had more time for reading, for it means a lot to me.'

'There is such an embarrassment of riches here,' said his wife. 'The days are far too short for all there is to do. Even when there is nobody staying in the house I find every hour occupied. It's delicious to be busy over things one really cares for.'

'All the same I wish I could do more reading,' said Giffen. 'I've never wanted to so much before.'

'But you come in tired from shooting and sleep sound till dinner,' said the lady, laying an affectionate hand on his shoulder.

They were happy people, and I like happiness. Self-absorbed perhaps, but I prefer selfishness in the ordinary way of things. We are most of us selfish dogs, and altruism makes us uncomfortable. But I had somewhere in my mind a shade of uneasiness, for I was the witness of a transformation too swift and violent to be wholly natural. Years, no doubt, turn our eyes inward and abate our heroics, but not a trifle of two or three. Some agency had been at work here, some agency other and more potent than the process of time. The thing fascinated and partly frightened me. For the Giffens – though I scarcely dared to admit it – had deteriorated. They were far pleasanter people. I liked them infinitely better. I hoped to see them often again. I detested the type they used to represent, and shunned it like the plague. They were wise now, and mellow, and most agreeable human beings. But some virtue had gone out of them. An uncomfortable virtue, no doubt, but a virtue, something generous and adventurous. Before their faces had had a sort of wistful kindness. Now they had geniality – which is not the same thing.

What was the agency of this miracle? It was all around me: the ivory panelling, the olive-wood staircase, the lovely pillared hall. I got up to go to bed with a kind of awe on me. As Mrs Giffen lit my candle, she saw my eyes wandering among the gracious shadows.

'Isn't it wonderful,' she said, 'to have found a house which fits us like a glove? No! Closer. Fits us as a bearskin fits the bear. It has taken our impress like wax.'

Somehow I didn't think that the impress had come from the Giffens' side.

A November afternoon found Leithen and myself jogging* homewards from a run with the Heythrop. It had been a wretched day. Twice we had found and lost, and then a deluge had set in which scattered the field. I had taken a hearty toss into a swamp, and got as wet as a man may be, but the steady downpour soon reduced everyone to a like condition. When we turned towards Borrowby the rain ceased, and an icy wind blew out of the east which partially dried our sopping clothes. All the grace had faded from the Cotswold valleys. The streams were brown torrents, the meadows lagoons, the ridges bleak and grey, and a sky of scurrying clouds cast leaden shadows. It was a matter of ten miles to Borrowby: we had long ago emptied our flasks, and I longed for something hot to take the chill out of my bones.

'Let's look in at Fullcircle,' said Leithen, as we emerged on the highroad from a muddy lane. 'We'll make the Giffens give us tea. You'll find changes there.'

I asked what changes, but he only smiled and told me to wait and see.

My mind was busy with surmises as we rode up the

avenue. I thought of drink or drugs, and promptly discarded the notion. Fullcircle was above all things decorous and wholesome. Leithen could not mean the change in the Giffens' ways which had so impressed me a year before, for he and I had long ago discussed that. I was still puzzling over his words when we found ourselves in the inner hall, with the Giffens making a hospitable fuss over us.

The place was more delectable than ever. Outside was a dark November day, yet the little house seemed to be transfused with sunshine. I do not know by what art the old builders had planned it, but the airy pilasters, the perfect lines of the ceiling, the soft colouring of the wood seemed to lay open the house to a clear sky. Logs burned brightly on the massive steel andirons, and the scent and the fine blue smoke of them strengthened the illusion of summer.

Mrs Giffen would have had us change into dry things, but Leithen pleaded a waiting dinner at Borrowby. The two of us stood by the fireplace, drinking tea, the warmth drawing out a cloud of vapour from our clothes to mingle with the wood-smoke. Giffen lounged in an armchair, and his wife sat by the tea-table. I was looking for the changes of which Leithen had spoken.

I did not find them in Giffen. He was much as I remembered him on the June night when I had slept here, a trifle fuller in the face perhaps, a little more placid about the mouth and eyes. He looked a man completely content with life. His smile came readily and his easy laugh. Was it my fancy, or had he acquired a look of the picture in the dining-room? I nearly made an errand to go and see it. It seemed to me that his mouth had now something of the portrait's delicate complacence. Lely would have found him a fit subject, though he might have boggled at his lean hands.

But his wife! Ah, there the changes were unmistakable. She was comely now rather than pretty, and the contours of her face had grown heavier. The eagerness had gone from her eyes and left only comfort and good-humour. There was a suspicion, ever so slight, of rouge and powder. She had a string of good pearls – the first time I had seen her wear jewels. The hand that poured out the tea was plump, shapely, and well cared for. I was looking at a most satisfactory mistress of a country house, who would see that nothing was lacking to the part.

She talked more and laughed oftener. Her voice had an airy lightness which would have made the silliest prattle charming.

'We are going to fill the house with young people and give a ball at Christmas,' she announced. 'This hall is simply clamouring to be danced in. You must come both of you. Promise me. And, Mr Leithen, it would be very nice if you brought a party from Borrowby. Young men, please. We are overstocked with girls in these parts . . . We must do something to make the country cheerful in winter-time.'

I observed that no season could make Fullcircle other than cheerful.

'How nice of you!' she cried. 'To praise a house is to praise the householders, for a dwelling is just what its inmates make it. Borrowby is you, Mr Leithen, and Fullcircle us.'

'Shall we exchange?' Leithen asked.

She made a mouth. 'Borrowby would crush me, but it suits a Gothic survival like you. Do you think you would be happy here?'

'Happy,' said Leithen thoughtfully. 'Happy? Yes, undoubtedly. But it might be bad for my soul . . .

There's just time for a pipe, Giffen, and then we must be off.'

I was filling my pipe as we crossed the outer hall, and was about to enter the smoking-room I so well remembered when Giffen laid a hand on my arm.

'We don't smoke there now,' he said hastily.

He opened the door and I looked in . . . The place had suffered its third metamorphosis. The marble shrine which I had noticed on my first visit had been brought back, and the blue mosaic pavement and the ivory walls were bare. At the eastern end stood a little altar, with above it a copy of a Correggio Madonna.

A faint smell of incense hung in the air and the fragrance of hothouse flowers. It was a chapel, but, I swear, a more pagan place than when it had been work-room or smoking-room.

Giffen gently shut the door. 'Perhaps you didn't know, but some months ago my wife became a Catholic. It is a good thing for women, I think. It gives them a regular ritual for their lives. So we restored the chapel. It had always been there in the days of the Carterons and the Applebys.'

'And you?' I asked.

He shrugged his shoulders. 'I don't bother much about these things. But I propose to follow suit. It will please Ursula and do no harm to anybody.'

We halted on the brow of the hill and looked back on the garden valley. Leithen's laugh, as he gazed, had more awe than mirth in it.

'That little wicked house! I'm going to hunt up every scrap I can find about old Tom Carteron. He must have been an uncommon clever fellow. He's still alive down there and making people do as he did . . . In that kind of place you may expel the priest and sweep it and garnish it. But he always returns.'

The wrack was lifting before the wind and a shaft of late watery sun fell on the grey walls. It seemed to me that the little house wore an air of gentle triumph.

The Moor-Song

This is an early story which has a strong sense of Buchan's boyhood in Upper Tweeddale. It is characterized by the wry humour and affectionate tones of a Presbyterian manse.

The turns and twists of the story allow a fresh setting for what is, at its heart, a serious and beautifully phrased statement of the power of Romance. Part of it is that Ballad 'which makes him who hears it sick all the days of his life for something which he cannot name'. This Northern strain, to which Buchan was sensitive throughout his life is, particularly in its Caledonian richness of history and topography, a Scottish gift to the whole literature of feeling.

'The Moor-Song' first appeared in Macmillan's Magazine *for July 1897, when Buchan was twenty-one, and in* The Living Age *in Boston, Massachusetts a week or so later. Published in his first anthology,* Grey Weather, *in 1899, it has not been reprinted since.*

The Moor-Song

(The tale of the respectable whaup and the great godly man)

This is a story that I heard from the King of the Numidians, who with his tattered retinue encamps behind the peat-ricks. If you ask me where and when it happened I fear that I am scarce ready with an answer. But I will vouch my honour for its truth; and if any one seek further proof, let him go east the town and west the town and over the fields of Nomansland to the Long Muir, and if he find not the King there among the peat-ricks, and get not a courteous answer to his question, then times have changed in that part of the country, and he must continue the quest to His Majesty's castle in Spain.

Once upon a time, says the tale, there was a Great Godly Man, a shepherd to trade, who lived in a cottage among heather. If you looked east in the morning, you saw miles of moor running wide to the flames of sunrise, and if you turned your eyes west in the evening, you saw a great confusion of dim peaks with the dying eye of the sun set in a crevice. If you looked north, too, in the afternoon, when the life of the day is near its end and the world grows wise, you might have seen a country of low hills and haughlands with many waters running sweet among meadows. But if you looked south in the dusty forenoon or at hot midday, you saw the far-off glimmer of a white road, the roofs of the ugly little clachan* of Kilmaclavers, and the rigging of the fine new kirk of Threepdaidle.

It was a Sabbath afternoon in the hot weather, and the man had been to kirk all the morning. He had heard a grand sermon from the minister (or it may have been the priest, for I am not sure of the date and the King told the story quickly) – a fine discourse with fifteen heads and three parentheses. He held all the parentheses and fourteen of the heads in his memory, but he had forgotten the fifteenth; so for the purpose of recollecting it, and also for the sake of a walk, he went forth in the afternoon into the open heather. The air was mild and cheering, and with an even step he strolled over the turf and into the deeps of the moor.

The whaups were crying everywhere, making the air hum like the twanging of a bow. *Poo-eelie, Poo-eelie*, they cried, *Kirlew, Kirlew, Whaup, Wha- -up*. Sometimes they came low, all but brushing him, till they drove settled thoughts from his head. Often had he been on the moors, but never had he seen such a stramash among the feathered clan. The wailing iteration vexed him, and he *shoo'd* the birds away with his arms. But they seemed to mock him and whistle in his very face, and at the fluff of their wings his heart grew sore. He waved his great stick; he picked up bits of loose moor-rock and flung them wildly; but the godless crew paid never a grain of heed. The morning's sermon was still in his head, and the grave words of the minister still rattled in his ear, but he could get no comfort for this intolerable piping. At last his patience failed him and he swore unchristian words. 'Deil rax the birds' thrapples,' he cried.

At this all the noise was hushed and in a twinkling the moor was empty. Only one bird was left, standing on tall legs before him with its head bowed upon its breast, and its beak touching the heather.

Then the man repented his words and stared at the thing in the moss. 'What bird are ye?' he asked thrawnly.

'I am a Respectable Whaup,' said the bird, 'and I kenna why ye have broken in on our family gathering. Once in a hundred years we foregather for decent conversation, and here we are interrupted by a muckle, sweerin' man.'

Now the shepherd was a fellow of great sagacity, yet he never thought it a queer thing that he should be having talk in the mid-moss with a bird. Truth, he had no mind on the matter.

'What for were ye making siccan a din, then?' he asked. 'D'ye no ken ye were disturbing the afternoon of the holy Sabbath?'

The bird lifted its eyes and regarded him solemnly. 'The Sabbath is a day of rest and gladness,' it said, 'and is it no reasonable that we should enjoy the like?'

The shepherd shook his head, for the presumption staggered him. 'Ye little ken what ye speak of,' he said. 'The Sabbath is for them that have the chance of salvation, and it has been decreed that Salvation is for Adam's race and no for the beasts that perish.'

The whaup gave a whistle of scorn. 'I have heard all that long ago. In my great grandmother's time, which 'ill be a thousand years and mair syne, there came a people from the south with bright brass things on their heads and breasts and terrible swords at their thighs. And with them were some lang-gowned men who kenned the stars and would come out o' nights to talk to the deer and the corbies in their ain tongue. And one, I mind, foregathered with my great-grandmother and told her that the souls o' men flitted in the end to braw meadows where the gods bide or gaed down to the black pit which they ca' Hell. But the souls o' birds, he said, die wi' their bodies and that's the end o' them. Likewise in my mother's time, when there was a great abbey down yonder by the Threepdaidle Burn which they called the House of Kilmac-lavers, the auld monks would walk out in the evening to pick herbs for their distillings, and some were wise and kenned the ways of bird and beast. They would crack often o' nights with my ain family, and tell them that Christ had saved the souls o' men, but that birds and beasts were perishable as the dew o' heaven. And now ye have a black-gowned man in Threepdaidle who threeps on the same owercome. Ye may a' ken something o' your ain kitchen-midden, but certes! ye ken little o' the warld beyond it.'

Now this angered the man, and he rebuked the bird. 'These are great mysteries,' he said, 'which are no to be mentioned in the ears of an unsanctified creature. What can a thing like you wi' a lang neb and twae legs like stilts ken about the next warld?'

'Weel, weel,' said the whaup, 'we'll let the matter be. Everything to its ain trade, and I will not dispute with ye on metapheesics. But if ye ken something about the next warld, ye ken terrible little about this.'

Now this angered the man still more, for he was a shepherd reputed to have great skill in sheep and esteemed the nicest judge of hogg and wether in all the countryside. 'What ken ye about that?' he asked. 'Ye may gang east to Yetholm and west to Kells, and no find a better herd.'

'If sheep were a',' said the bird, 'ye micht be right; but what o' the wide warld and the folk in it? Ye are Simon Etterick o' the Lowe Moss. Do ye ken aucht o' your forebears?'

'My father was a God-fearing man at the Kennel-head, and my grandfather and great-grandfather afore him. One o' our name, folk say, was shot at a dyke-back by the Black Westeraw.'

'If that's a',' said the bird, 'ye ken little. Have ye never heard o' the little man, the fourth back from yoursel', who killed the Miller o' Bewcastle at the Lammas Fair? That was in my ain time, and from my mother I have heard o' the Covenanter, who got a bullet in his wame hunkering behind the divot-dyke and praying to his Maker. There were others o' your name rode in the Hermitage forays and burned Naworth and Warkworth and Castle Gay. I have heard o' an Etterick, Sim o' the Redcleuch, who cut the throat o' Jock Johnson in his ain house by the Annan side. And my grandmother had tales o' auld Ettericks who rade wi' Douglas and the Bruce and the ancient Kings o' Scots; and she used to tell o' others in her mother's time, terrible shock-headed men, hunting the deer and rinnin' on the high moors, and bidin' in the broken stane biggings on the hilltaps.'

The shepherd stared, and he, too, saw the picture. He smelled the air of battle and lust and foray, and forgot the Sabbath.

'And you yoursel',' said the bird, 'are sair fallen off from the auld stock. Now ye sit and spell in books, and talk about what ye little understand, when your fathers were roaming the warld. But little cause have I to speak, for I too am a downcome. My bill is two inches shorter than my mother's, and my grandmother was taller on her feet. The warld is getting weaklier things to dwell in it, ever since I mind mysel'.'

'Ye have the gift o' speech, bird,' said the man, 'and I would hear mair.' You will perceive that he had no mind of the Sabbath day or the fifteenth head of the forenoon's discourse.

'What things have I to tell ye when ye dinna ken the very horn-book o' knowledge? Besides, I am no clatter-vengeance to tell stories in the middle o' the muir, where there are ears open high and low. There's others than me wi' mair experience and a better skill at the telling. Our clan was well acquaint wi' the reivers* and lifters o' the muirs, and could crack fine o' wars and the taking of cattle. But the blue hawk that lives in the corrie o' the Dreichil can speak o' kelpies and the dwarfs that bide in the hill. The heron, the lang solemn fellow, kens o' the greenwood fairies and the wood elfins, and the wild geese that squatter on the tap o' the Muneraw will croak to ye of the merrymaidens and the girls o' the pool. The wren – he that hops in the grass below the birks – has the story of the *Lost Ladies of the Land*, which is ower auld and sad for any but the wisest to hear; and there is a wee bird bides in the heather – hill-lintie men call him – who sings the *Lay of the West Wind*, and the *Glee of the Rowan Berries*. But what am I talking of? What are these things to you, if ye have not first heard the Moor-Song, which is the beginning and end o' all things?'

'I have heard no songs,' said the man, 'save the sacred psalms o' God's Kirk.'

'Bonny sangs,' said the bird. 'Once I flew by the hinder end o' the Kirk and I keekit in. A wheen auld wives wi' mutches and a wheen solemn men wi' hoasts! Be sure the Moor-Song is no like you.'

'Can ye sing it, bird?' said the man, 'for I am keen to hear it.'

'Me sing,' cried the bird, 'me that has a voice like a craw! Na, na, I canna sing it, but maybe I can tak ye where ye may hear it. When I was young an auld bog-blitter did the same to me, and sae began my education. But are ye willing and brawly willing? – for if ye get but a sough of it ye will never mair have an ear for other music.'

'I am willing and brawly willing,' said the man.

'Then meet me at the Gled's Cleuch Head at the sun's setting,' said the bird, and it flew away.

Now it seemed to the man that in a twinkling it was sunset, and he found himself at the Gled's Cleuch Head with the bird flapping in the heather before him. The place was a long rift in the hill, made green with juniper and hazel, where it was said True Thomas came to drink the water.

'Turn ye to the west,' said the whaup, 'and let the sun fall on your face, then turn ye five times round about and say after me the Rune of the Heather and the Dew.' And before he knew, the man did as he was told, and found himself speaking strange words, while his head hummed and danced as if in a fever.

'Now lay ye down and put your ear to the earth,' said the bird, and the man did so. Instantly a cloud came over his brain, and he did not feel the ground on which he lay or the keen hill-air which blew about him. He felt himself falling deep into an abysm of space, then suddenly caught up and set among the stars of heaven. Then slowly from the stillness there welled forth music, drop by drop like the clear falling rain, and the man shuddered, for he knew that he heard the beginning of the Moor-Song.

High rose the air, and trembled among the tallest pines and the summits of great hills. And in it were the sting of rain and the blatter of hail, the soft crush of snow and the rattle of thunder among crags. Then it quieted to the low sultry croon which told of blazing midday when the streams are parched and the bent crackles like dry tinder. Anon it was evening, and the melody dwelled among the high soft notes which mean the coming of dark and the great light of sunset. Then the whole changed to a great pæan which rang like an organ through the earth. There were trumpet notes in it and flute notes and the plaint of pipes. 'Come forth,' it cried; 'the sky is wide and it is a far cry to the world's end. The fire crackles fine o' nights below the firs, and the smell of roasting meat and wood smoke is dear to the heart of man. Fine, too, is the sting of salt and the risp of the north-wind in the sheets. Come forth, one and all, to the great lands oversea, and the strange tongues and the fremit peoples. Learn before you die to follow the Piper's Son, and though your old bones bleach among grey rocks, what matter, if you have had your bellyful of life and come to the land of Heart's Desire?' And the tune fell low and witching, bringing tears to the eyes and joy to the heart; and the man knew (though no one told him) that this was the first part of the Moor-Song, the *Song of the Open Road*, the *Lilt of the Adventurer*, which shall be now and ever and to the end of days.

Then the melody changed to a fiercer and sadder note. He saw his forefathers, gaunt men and terrible, run stark among woody hills. He heard the talk of the bronze-clad invader, and the jar and clangour as flint met steel. Then rose the last coronach of his own people, hiding in wild glens, starving in corries, or going hopelessly to the death. He heard the cry of Border foray, the shouts of the poor Scots as they harried Cumberland, and he himself rode in the midst of them. Then the tune fell more mournful and slow, and Flodden lay before him. He saw the flower of Scots gentry around their king, gashed to the breast bone, still fronting the lines of the south, though the paleness of death sat on each forehead. 'The flowers of the Forest are gone,' cried the lilt, and through the long years he heard the cry of the lost, the desperate, fighting for kings over the water and princes in the heather. 'Who cares?' cried the air. 'Man must die, and how can he die better than in the stress of fight with his heart high and alien blood on his sword? Heigh-ho! One against twenty, a child against a host, this is the romance of life.' And the man's heart swelled, for he knew (though no one told him) that this was the *Song of Lost Battles*, which only the great can sing before they die.

But the tune was changing, and at the change the man shivered, for the air ran up to the high notes and then down to the deeps with an eldrich cry, like a hawk's scream at night, or a witch's song in the gloaming. It told of those who seek and never find, the quest that knows no fulfilment. 'There is a road,' it cries, 'which leads to the Moon and the Great Waters. No changehouse cheers it, and it has no end, but it is a fine road, a braw road – who will follow it?' And the man knew (though no one told him) that this was the *Ballad of Grey Weather*, which makes him who hears it sick all the days of his life for something which he cannot name. It is the song which the birds sing on the moor in the autumn nights, and the old crow on the treetops hears and flaps his wing. It is the lilt which old men and women hear in the darkening of their days, and sigh for the unforgettable; and love-sick girls get catches of it and play pranks with their lovers. It is a song so old that Adam heard it in the Garden before Eve came to comfort him, so young that from it still flows the whole joy and sorrow of earth.

Then it ceased, and all of a sudden the man was rubbing his eyes on the hillside, and watching the falling dusk. 'I have heard the Moor-Song,' he said to himself, and he walked home in a daze. The whaups were crying, but none came near him, though he looked hard for the bird that had spoken with him. It may be that it was there and he did not know it, or it may be that the whole thing was only a dream, but of this I cannot say.

The next morning the man rose and went to the manse.

'I am glad to see you, Simon,' said the minister, 'for it will soon be the Communion Season, and it is your duty to go round with the tokens.'

'True,' said the man, 'but it was another thing I came to talk about,' and he told him the whole tale.

'There are but two ways of it, Simon,' said the minister. 'Either ye are the victim of witchcraft, or ye are a self-deluded man. If the former (whilk I am loth to believe), then it behoves yet to watch and pray lest ye enter into temptation. If the latter then ye maun put a strict watch over a vagrom fancy, and ye'll be quit o' siccan whig-maleeries.'

Now Simon was not listening, but staring out of the window. 'There was another thing I had it in my mind to say,' said he. 'I have come to lift my lines, for I am thinking of leaving the place.'

'And where would ye go?' asked the minister, aghast.

'I was thinking of going to Carlisle and trying my luck as a dealer, or maybe pushing on with droves to the South.'

'But that's a cauld country where there are no faithfu' ministrations,' said the minister.

'Maybe so, but I am not caring very muckle about ministrations,' said the man, and the other looked after him in horror.

When he left the manse he went to a Wise Woman, who lived on the left side of the Kirkyard above Threepdaidle burn-foot. She was very old, and sat by the ingle day and night, waiting upon death. To her he told the same tale.

She listened gravely, nodding with her head. 'Ach,' she said, 'I have heard a like story before. And where will you be going?'

'I am going south to Carlisle to try the dealing and droving,' said the man, 'for I have some skill of sheep.'

'And will ye bide there?' she asked.

'Maybe aye, and maybe no,' he said. 'I had half a mind to push on to the big toun or even to the abroad. A man must try his fortune.'

'That's the way of men,' said the old wife. 'I, too, have heard the Moor-Song, and many women, who now sit decently spinning in Kilmaclavers, have heard it. But a woman may hear it and lay it up in her soul and bide at hame, while a man, if he get but a glisk of it in his fool's heart, must needs up and awa' to the warld's end on some daft-like ploy. But gang your ways and fare ye weel. My cousin Francie heard it, and he went north wi' a white cockade in his bonnet and a sword at his side, singing "Charlie's come hame". And Tam Crichtoun o' the Bourhopehead got a sough o' it one simmer's morning, and the last we heard o' Tam he was killed among the Frenchmen fechting like a fair deil. Once I heard a tinkler play a sprig of it on the pipes, and a' the lads were wud to follow him. Gang your ways, for I am near the end o' mine.' And the old wife shook with her coughing.

So the man put up his belongings in a pack on his back and went whistling down the Great South Road.

Whether or not this tale have a moral it is not for me to say. The King (who told it me) said that it had, and quoted a scrap of Latin, for he had been at Oxford in his youth before he fell heir to his kingdom. One may hear tunes from the Moor-Song, said he, in the thick of a storm on the scarp of a rough hill, in the low June weather, or in the sunset silence of a winter's night. But let none, he added, pray to have the full music, for it will make him who hears it a footsore traveller in the ways o' the world and a masterless man till death.

The Loathly Opposite

During the First World War Buchan was recalled from France to be Director of a new Department of Information, which later became a Ministry. With great energy he worked to create an organization which set new high standards for the dissemination of information. He initiated, and developed, new methods of communication, like the films of the Somme and Arras battles, and like the paintings of Paul Nash and C. R. W. Nevinson and others. His work brought him into close contact with Intelligence, especially Royal Navy intelligence.

All through the war, and for long after, Buchan was ill, sometimes seriously ill, with duodenal trouble. He always rested too little. He did not visit a German Kurhaus* himself, but he was well informed about them.

As he did so often, Buchan here creates fiction at his favourite spot, the point on the grid-reference where romance and reality just touch. He clearly enjoys approaching this point by way of the interpretation of a mysterious text.

The story first appeared in The Runagates Club *of 1928.*

The Loathly Opposite

OLIVER PUGH'S STORY

How loathly opposite I stood
To his unnatural purpose

KING LEAR

Burminster had been to a Guildhall dinner the night before, which had been attended by many – to him – unfamiliar celebrities. He had seen for the first time in the flesh people whom he had long known by reputation, and he declared that in every case the picture he had formed of them had been cruelly shattered. An eminent poet, he said, had looked like a starting-price bookmaker, and a financier of world-wide fame had been exactly like the music-master at his preparatory school. Wherefore Burminster made the profound deduction that things were never what they seemed.

'That's only because you have a feeble imagination,' said Sandy Arbuthnot. 'If you had really understood Timson's poetry you would have realized that it went with close-cropped red hair and a fat body, and you should have known that Macintyre (this was the financier) had the music-and-metaphysics type of mind. That's why he puzzles the City so. If you understand a man's work well enough you can guess pretty accurately what he'll look like. I don't mean the colour of his eyes and his hair, but the general atmosphere of him.'

It was Sandy's agreeable habit to fling an occasional

paradox at the table with the view of starting an argument. This time he stirred up Pugh, who had come to the War Office from the Indian Staff Corps. Pugh had been a great figure in Secret Service work in the East, but he did not look the part, for he had the air of a polo-playing cavalry subaltern. The skin was stretched as tight over his cheekbones as over the knuckles of a clenched fist, and was so dark that it had the appearance of beaten bronze. He had black hair, rather beady black eyes, and the hooky nose which in the Celt often goes with that colouring. He was himself a very good refutation of Sandy's theory.

'I don't agree,' Pugh said. 'At least not as a general principle. One piece of humanity whose work I studied with the microscope for two aching years upset all my notions when I came to meet it.'

Then he told us this story.

'When I was brought to England in November '17 and given a "hush" department on three floors of an eighteenth-century house in a back street, I had a good deal to learn about my business. That I learned it in reasonable time was due to the extraordinary fine staff that I found provided for me. Not one of them was a regular soldier. They were all educated men – they had to be in that job – but they came out of every sort of environment. One of the best was a Shetland laird, another was an Admiralty Court KC, and I had besides a metallurgical chemist, a golf champion, a leader-writer, a popular dramatist, several actuaries, and an East-end curate. None of them thought of anything but his job, and at the end of the war, when some ass proposed to make them OBEs, there was a very fair imitation of a riot. A more loyal crowd never existed, and they accepted me as their chief as unquestioningly as if I had been with them since 1914.

'To the war in the ordinary sense they scarcely gave a thought. You found the same thing in a lot of other behind-the-lines departments, and I daresay it was a good thing – it kept their nerves quiet and their minds concentrated. After all our business was only to decode and decypher German messages; we had nothing to do with the use which was made of them. It was a curious little nest, and when the Armistice came my people were flabbergasted – they hadn't realized that their job was bound up with the war.

'The one who most interested me was my second-in-command, Philip Channell. He was a man of forty-three, about five-foot-four in height, weighing, I fancy, under nine stone, and almost as blind as an owl. He was good enough at papers with his double glasses, but he could hardly recognize you three yards off. He had been a professor at some Midland college – mathematics or physics, I think – and as soon as the war began he had tried to enlist. Of course they wouldn't have him – he was about E5 in any physical classification, besides being well over age – but he would take no refusal, and presently he worried his way into the Government service. Fortunately he found a job which he could do superlatively well, for I do not believe there was a man alive with more natural genius for cryptography.

'I don't know if any of you have ever given your mind to that heart-breaking subject. Anyhow you know that secret writing falls under two heads – codes and cyphers, and that codes are combinations of words and cyphers of numerals. I remember how one used to be told that no code or cypher which was practically useful was really undiscoverable, and in a sense that is true, especially of codes. A system of communication which is in constant use must obviously not be too intricate, and a working code, if you get long enough for the job, can generally be read. That is why a code is periodically changed by the users. There are rules in worrying out the permutations and combinations of letters in most codes, for human ingenuity seems to run in certain channels, and a man who has been a long time at the business gets surprisingly clever at it. You begin by finding out a little bit, and then empirically building up the rules of de-coding, till in a week or two you get the whole thing. Then, when you are happily engaged in reading enemy messages, the code is changed suddenly, and you have to start again from the beginning . . . You can make a code, of course, that it is simply impossible to read except by accident – the key to which is a page of some book, for example – but fortunately that kind is not of much general use.

'Well, we got on pretty well with the codes, and read the intercepted enemy messages, cables and wireless, with considerable ease and precision. It was mostly diplomatic stuff, and not very important. The more valuable stuff was in cypher, and that was another pair of shoes. With a code you can build up the interpretation by degrees, but with a cypher you either know it or you don't – there are no half-way houses. A cypher, since it deals with numbers, is a horrible field for mathematical ingenuity. Once you have written out the letters of a message in numerals there are many means by which you can lock it and double-lock it. The two main devices, as you know, are transposition and substitution, and there is no limit to the ways one or other or both can be used. There is nothing to prevent a cypher having a double meaning, produced by two different methods, and, as a practical question, you have to decide which meaning is intended. By way of an extra complication, too, the message, when de-cyphered, may turn out to be itself in a difficult code. I can tell you our job wasn't exactly a rest cure.'

Burminster, looking puzzled, inquired as to the locking of cyphers.

'It would take too long to explain. Roughly, you write out a message horizontally in numerals; then you pour it into vertical columns, the number and order of which are determined by a keyword; then you write out the contents of the columns horizontally, following the lines across. To unlock it you have to have the key word, so as to put it back into the vertical columns, and then into the original horizontal form.'

Burminster cried out like one in pain. 'It can't be done. Don't tell me that any human brain could solve such an acrostic.'

'It was frequently done,' said Pugh.

'By you?'

'Lord bless you, not by me. I can't do a simple crossword puzzle. By my people.'

'Give me the trenches,' said Burminster in a hollow voice. 'Give me the trenches any day. Do you seriously mean to tell me that you could sit down before a muddle of numbers and travel back the way they had been muddled to an original that made sense?'

'I couldn't, but Channell could – in most cases. You see, we didn't begin entirely in the dark. We already knew the kind of intricacies that the enemy favoured, and the way we worked was by trying a variety of clues till we hit on the right one.'

'Well, I'm blessed! Go on about your man Channell.'

'This isn't Channell's story,' said Pugh. 'He only comes into it accidentally . . . There was one cypher which always defeated us, a cypher used between the German General Staff and their forces in the East. It was a locked cypher, and Channell had given more time to it than to any dozen of the others, for it put him on his mettle. But he confessed himself absolutely beaten. He wouldn't admit that it was insoluble, but he declared that he would need a bit of real luck to solve it. I asked him what kind of luck, and he said a mistake and a repetition. That, he said, might give him a chance of establishing equations.

'We called this particular cypher "PY", and we hated it poisonously. We felt like pygmies battering at the base of a high stone tower. Dislike of the thing soon became dislike of the man who had conceived it. Channell and I used to – I won't say amuse, for it was too dashed serious – but torment ourselves by trying to picture the fellow who owned the brain that was responsible for PY. We had a pretty complete dossier of the German Intelligence Staff, but of course we couldn't know who was responsible for this particular cypher. We knew no more than his code name, Reinmar, with which he signed the simpler messages to the East, and Channell, who was a romantic little chap for all his science, had got it into his head that it was a woman. He used to describe her to me as if he had seen her – a she-devil, young, beautiful, with a much-painted white face, and eyes like a cobra's. I fancy he read a rather low class of novel in his off-time.

'My picture was different. At first I thought of the histrionic type of scientist, the "ruthless brain" type, with a high forehead and a jaw puckered like a chimpanzee. But that didn't seem to work, and I settled on a picture of a first-class *Generalstaboffizier*, as handsome as Falkenhayn*, trained to the last decimal, absolutely passionless, with a mind that worked with the relentless precision of a fine machine. We all of us at the time suffered from the bogy of this kind of German, and, when things were going badly, as in March '18, I couldn't sleep for hating him. The infernal fellow was so water-tight and armour-plated, a Goliath who scorned the pebbles from our feeble slings.

'Well, to make a long story short, there came a moment in September '18 when PY was about the most important thing in the world. It mattered enormously what Germany was doing in Syria, and we knew that it was all in PY. Every morning a pile of the intercepted German wireless messages lay on Channell's table, which were as meaningless to him as a child's scrawl. I was prodded by my chiefs and in turn I prodded Channell. We had a week to find the key to the cypher, after which things must go on without us, and if we had failed to make anything of it in eighteen months of quiet work, it didn't seem likely that we would succeed in seven feverish days. Channell nearly went off his head with overwork and anxiety. I used to visit his dingy little room and find him fairly grizzled and shrunken with fatigue.

'This isn't a story about him, though there is a good story which I may tell you another time. As a matter of fact we won on the post. PY made a mistake. One morning we got a long message dated *en clair**, then a very short message, and then a third message almost the same as the first. The second must mean "Your message of today's date unintelligible, please repeat," the regular formula. This gave us a translation of a bit of the cypher. Even that would not have brought it out, and for twelve hours Channell was on the verge of lunacy, till it occurred to him that Reinmar might have signed the long message with his name, as we used to do sometimes in cases of extreme urgency. He was right, and, within three hours of the last moment Operations could give us, we had the whole thing pat. As I have said, that is a story worth telling, but it is not this one.

'We both finished the war too tired to think of much except that the darned thing was over. But Reinmar had been so long our unseen but constantly pictured opponent that we kept up a certain interest in him. We would like to have seen how he took the licking, for he must have known that we had licked him. Mostly when you lick a man at a game you rather like him, but I didn't like Reinmar. In fact I made him a sort of compost of everything I had ever disliked in a German. Channell stuck to his she-devil theory, but I was pretty certain that he was a youngish man with an intellectual arrogance which his country's débâcle would in no way lessen. He would never acknowledge defeat. It was highly improbable that I should ever find out who he was, but I felt that if I did, and met him face to face, my dislike would be abundantly justified.

'As you know, for a year or two after the Armistice I was a pretty sick man. Most of us were. We hadn't the fillip of getting back to civilized comforts, like the men in the trenches. We had always been comfortable enough in body, but our minds were fagged out, and there is no easy cure for that. My digestion went nobly to pieces, and I endured a miserable space of lying in bed and living on milk and olive-oil. After that I went back to work, but the darned thing always returned, and every leech had a different regime to advise. I tried them all – dry meals, a snack every two hours, lemon juice, sour milk, starvation, knocking off tobacco – but nothing got me more than half-way out of the trough. I was a burden to myself and a nuisance to others, dragging my wing through life, with a constant pain in my tummy.

'More than one doctor advised an operation, but I was chary about that, for I had seen several of my friends operated on for the same mischief and left as sick as before. Then a man told me about a German fellow called Christoph, who was said to be very good at handling my trouble. The best hand at diagnosis in the world, my informant said – no fads – treated every case on its merits – a really original mind. Dr Christoph had a modest Kurhaus at a place called Rosensee in the Sächischen Sweitz. By this time I was getting pretty desperate, so I packed a bag and set off for Rosensee.

'It was a quiet little town at the mouth of a narrow valley, tucked in under wooded hills, a clean fresh place with open channels of running water in the streets. There was a big church with an onion spire, a Catholic seminary, and a small tanning industry. The Kurhaus was half-way up a hill, and I felt better as soon as I saw my bedroom, with its bare scrubbed floors and its wide verandah looking up into a forest glade. I felt still better when I saw Dr Christoph. He was a small man with a grizzled beard, a high forehead, and a limp, rather like what I imagine the Apostle Paul must have been. He looked wise, as wise as an old owl. His English was atrocious, but even when he found that I talked German fairly well he didn't expand in speech. He would deliver no opinion of any kind until he had had me at least a week under observation, but somehow I felt comforted, for I concluded that a first-class brain had got to work on me.

'The other patients were mostly Germans with a sprinkling of Spaniards, but to my delight I found Channell. He also had been having a thin time since we parted. Nerves were his trouble – general nervous debility and perpetual insomnia, and his college had given him six months' leave of absence to try to get well. The poor chap was as lean as a sparrow, and he had the large dull eyes and the dry lips of the sleepless. He had arrived a week before me, and like me was under observation. But his vetting was different from mine, for he was a mental case, and Dr Christoph used to devote hours to trying to unriddle his nervous tangles. "He is a good man for a German," said Channell, "but he is on the wrong tack. There's nothing wrong with my mind. I wish he'd stick to violet rays and massage, instead of asking me silly questions about my great-grandmother."

'Channell and I used to go for invalidish walks in the woods, and we naturally talked about the years we had worked together. He was living mainly in the past, for the war had been the great thing in his life, and his professorial duties seemed trivial by comparison. As we tramped among the withered bracken and heather his mind was always harking back to the dingy little room where he had smoked cheap cigarettes and worked fourteen hours out of the twenty-four. In particular he was as eagerly curious about our old antagonist, Reinmar, as he had been in 1918. He was more positive than ever that she was a woman, and I believe that one of the reasons that had induced him to a try a cure in Germany was a vague hope that he might get on her track. I had almost forgotten about the thing, and I was amused by Channell in the part of the untiring sleuth-hound.

'"You won't find her in the Kurhaus," I said. "Perhaps she is in some old Schloss in the neighbourhood, waiting for you like the Sleeping Beauty."

'"I'm serious," he said plaintively. "It is purely a matter of intellectual curiosity, but I confess I would give a great deal to see her face to face. After I leave here, I thought of going to Berlin to make some inquiries. But I'm handicapped for I know nobody and I have no credentials. Why don't you, who have a large acquaintance and far more authority, take the thing up?"

'I told him that my interest in the matter had flagged

and that I wasn't keen on digging into the past, but I promised to give him a line to our Military Attaché if he thought of going to Berlin. I rather discouraged him from letting his mind dwell too much on events in the War. I said that he ought to try to bolt the door on all that had contributed to his present breakdown.

'"That is not Dr Christoph's opinion," he said emphatically. "He encourages me to talk about it. You see, with me it is a purely intellectual interest. I have no emotion in the matter. I feel quite friendly towards Reinmar, whoever she may be. It is, if you like, a piece of romance. I haven't had so many romantic events in my life that I want to forget this."

'"Have you told Dr Christoph about Reinmar?" I asked.

'"Yes," he said, "and he was mildly interested. You know the way he looks at you with his solemn grey eyes. I doubt if he quite understood what I meant, for a little provincial doctor, even though he is a genius in his own line, is not likely to know much about the ways of the Great General Staff . . . I had to tell him, for I have to tell him all my dreams, and lately I have taken to dreaming about Reinmar."

'"What's she like?" I asked.

'"Oh, a most remarkable figure. Very beautiful, but uncanny. She has long fair hair down to her knees."

'Of course I laughed. "You're mixing her up with the Valkyries," I said. "Lord, it would be an awkward business if you met that she-dragon in the flesh."

'But he was quite solemn about it, and declared that his waking picture of her was not in the least like his dreams. He rather agreed with my nonsense about the old Schloss. He thought that she was probably some penniless grandee, living solitary in a moated grange, with nothing now to exercise her marvellous brain on, and eating her heart out with regret and shame. He drew so attractive a character of her that I began to think that Channell was in love with a being of his own creation, till he ended with, "But all the same she's utterly damnable. She must be, you know."

'After a fortnight I began to feel a different man. Dr Christoph thought that he had got on the track of the mischief, and certainly, with his deep massage and a few simple drugs, I had more internal comfort than I had known for three years. He was so pleased with my progress that he refused to treat me as an invalid. He encouraged me to take long walks into the hills, and presently he arranged for me to go out roebuck-shooting with some of the local junkers.

'I used to start before daybreak on the chilly November mornings and drive to the top of one of the ridges, where I would meet a collection of sportsmen and beaters, shepherded by a fellow in a green uniform. We lined out along the ridge, and the beaters, assisted by a marvellous collection of dogs, including the sporting dachshund, drove the roe towards us. It wasn't very cleverly managed, for the deer generally broke back, and it was chilly waiting in the first hours with a powdering of snow on the ground and the fir boughs heavy with frost crystals. But later, when the sun grew stronger, it was a very pleasant mode of spending a day. There was not much of a bag, but whenever a roe or a capercailzie fell all the guns would assemble and drink little glasses of *Kirschwasser*. I had been lent a rifle, one of those appalling contraptions which are double-barrelled shot-guns and rifles in one, and to transpose from one form to the other requires a mathematical calculation. The rifle had a hair trigger too, and when I first used it I was nearly the death of a respectable Saxon peasant.

'We all ate our midday meal together and in the evening, before going home, we had coffee and cakes in one or other of the farms. The party was an odd mixture, big farmers and small squires, an hotel-keeper or two, a local doctor, and a couple of lawyers from the town. At first they were a little shy of me, but presently they thawed, and after the first day we were good friends. They spoke quite frankly about the war, in which every one of them had had a share, and with a great deal of dignity and good sense.

'I learned to walk in Sikkim*, and the little Saxon hills seemed to me inconsiderable. But they were too much for most of the guns, and instead of going straight up or down a slope they always chose a circuit, which gave them an easy gradient. One evening, when we were separating as usual, the beaters taking a short cut and the guns a circuit, I felt that I wanted exercise, so I raced the beaters downhill, beat them soundly, and had the better part of an hour to wait for my companions, before we adjourned to the farm for refreshment. The beaters must have talked about my pace, for as we walked away one of the guns, a lawyer called Meissen, asked me why I was visiting Rosensee at a time of year when few foreigners came. I said I was staying with Dr Christoph.

'"Is he then a private friend of yours?" he asked.

'I told him No, that I had come to his Kurhaus for treatment, being sick. His eyes expressed polite scepticism. He was not prepared to regard as an invalid a man who went down a hill like an avalanche.

'But, as we walked in the frosty dusk, he was led to speak of Dr Christoph, of whom he had no personal knowledge, and I learned how little honour a prophet may have in his own country. Rosensee scarcely knew him except as a doctor who had an inexplicable attraction for foreign patients. Meissen was curious about his methods and the exact diseases in which he specialized. "Perhaps he may yet save me a journey to Homburg*?" he laughed. "It is well to have a skilled physician at one's doorstep. The doctor is something of a hermit, and except for his patients does not appear to welcome his kind. Yet he is a good man, beyond doubt, and there are those who say that in the war he was a hero."

'This surprised me, for I could not imagine Dr Christoph in any fighting capacity, apart from the fact that he must have been too old. I thought that Meissen might refer to work in the base hospitals. But he was positive; Dr Christoph had been in the trenches; the limping leg was a war wound.

'I had had very little talk with the doctor, owing to my case being free from nervous complications. He would say a word to me morning and evening about my diet, and pass the time of day when we met, but it was not till the very eve of my departure that we had anything like a real conversation. He sent a message that he wanted to see me for not less than one hour, and he arrived with a batch of notes from which he delivered a kind of lecture on my case. Then I realized what an immense amount of care and solid thought he had expended on me. He had decided that his diagnosis was right – my rapid improvement suggested that – but it was necessary for some time to observe a simple regime, and to keep an eye on certain symptoms. So he took a sheet of notepaper from the table and in his small precise hand wrote down for me a few plain commandments.

'There was something about him, the honest eyes, the mouth which looked as if it had been often compressed in suffering, the air of grave goodwill, which I found curiously attractive. I wished that I had been a mental case like Channell, and had had more of his society. I detained him in talk, and he seemed not unwilling. By and by we drifted to the war and it turned out that Meissen was right.

'Dr Christoph had gone as medical officer in November '14 to the Ypres Salient with a Saxon regiment, and had spent the winter there. In '15 he had been in Champagne, and in the early months of '16 at Verdun, till he was invalided with rheumatic fever. That is to say, he had had about seventeen months of consecutive fighting in the worst areas with scarcely a holiday. A pretty good record for a frail little middle-aged man!

'His family was then at Stuttgart, his wife and one little boy. He took a long time to recover from the fever, and after that was put on home duty. "Till the war was almost over," he said, "almost over, but not quite. There was just time for me to go back to the front and get my foolish leg hurt." I must tell you that whenever he mentioned his war experience it was with a comical deprecating smile, as if he agreed with anyone who might think that gravity like this should have remained in bed.

'I assumed that this home duty was medical, until he said something about getting rusty in his professional work. Then it appeared that it had been some job connected with Intelligence. "I am reputed to have a little talent for mathematics," he said. "No. I am no mathematical scholar, but, if you understand me, I have a certain mathematical aptitude. My mind has always moved happily among numbers. Therefore I was set to construct and to interpret cyphers, a strange interlude in the noise of war. I sat in a little room and excluded the world, and for a little I was happy."

'He went on to speak of the enclave of peace in which he had found himself, and as I listened to his gentle monotonous voice, I had a sudden inspiration.

'I took a sheet of notepaper from the stand, scribbled the word *Reinmar* on it, and shoved it towards him. I had a notion, you see, that I might surprise him into helping Channell's researches.

'But it was I who got the big surprise. He stopped thunderstruck, as soon as his eye caught the word, blushed scarlet over every inch of face and bald forehead, seemed to have difficulty in swallowing, and then gasped. "How did you know?"

'I hadn't known, and now that I did, the knowledge left me speechless. This was the loathly opposite for which Channell and I had nursed our hatred. When I came out of my stupefaction I found that he had recovered his balance and was speaking slowly and distinctly, as if he were making a formal confession.

'"You were among my opponents . . . that interests me deeply . . . I often wondered . . . You beat me in the end. You are aware of that?"

'I nodded. "Only because you made a slip," I said.

'"Yes, I made a slip. I was to blame – very gravely to blame, for I let my private grief cloud my mind."

'He seemed to hesitate, as if he were loath to stir something very tragic in his memory.

'"I think I will tell you," he said at last. "I have often wished – it is a childish wish – to justify my failure to those who profited by it. My chiefs understood, of course, but my opponents could not. In that month when I failed I was in deep sorrow. I had a little son – his name was Reinmar – you remember that I took that name for my code signature?"

'His eyes were looking beyond me into some vision of the past.

'"He was, as you say, my mascot. He was all my family, and I adored him. But in those days food was not plentiful. We were no worse off than many million Germans, but the child was frail. In the last summer of the war he developed phthisis due to malnutrition, and in September he died. Then I failed my country, for with him some virtue seemed to depart from my mind. You see, my work was, so to speak, his also, as my name was his, and when he left me he took my power with him . . . So I stumbled. The rest is known to you."

'He sat staring beyond me, so small and lonely, that I could have howled. I remember putting my hand on his shoulder, and stammering some platitude about being sorry. We sat quite still for a minute or two, and then I remembered Channell. Channell must have poured his views of Reinmar into Dr Christoph's ear. I asked him if Channell knew.

'A flicker of a smile crossed his face.

'"Indeed no. And I will exact from you a promise never to breathe to him what I have told you. He is my patient, and I must first consider his case. At present he thinks that Reinmar is a wicked and beautiful lady whom he may some day meet. That is romance, and it is good for him to think so . . . If he were told the truth, he would be pitiful, and in Herr Channell's condition it is important that he should not be vexed with such emotions as pity."'

Streams of Water in the South

'Streams of Water in the South' is another very early story, from Grey Weather of 1899; it has not been reprinted since. It was almost certainly written when Buchan was in his teens and shows him alert to the realities of the Tweeddale shepherd's life which he knew so well. The landscape and the flood make a setting for the same kinds of truth about creativity as Wordsworth expounds in his poem 'Resolution and Independence'. So too does the figure of the old man who 'spoke in a broad, slow Scots, with so quaint a lilt in his speech that one seemed to be in an elder time among people of a quieter life and a quainter kindliness'. His great age, his solitariness and his authority enable Buchan to gather around his character some fine, unobtrusive writing about the eternal nature of moorland streams – the real subject of the tale, and a metaphor for the creative process itself.

Streams of Water in the South

Like streams of water in the South*
Our bondage, Lord, recall.

I

This is all a tale of an older world and a forgotten countryside. At this moment of time change has come; a screaming line of steel runs through the heather of no-man's-land, and the holiday-maker claims the valleys for his own. But this busyness is but of yesterday, and not ten years ago the fields lay quiet to the gaze of placid beasts and the wandering stars. This story I have culled from the grave of an old fashion, and set it down for the love of a great soul and the poetry of life.

It was at the ford of the Clachlands Water in a tempestuous August, that I, an idle boy, first learned the hardships of the Lammas droving. The shepherd of the Redswirehead, my very good friend, and his three shaggy dogs, were working for their lives in an angry water. The path behind was thronged with scores of sheep bound for the Gledsmuir market, and beyond it was possible to discern through the mist the few dripping dozen which had made the passage. Between raged yards of brown foam coming down from murky hills, and the air echoed with the yelp of dogs and the perplexed cursing of men.

Before I knew I was helping in the task, with water lipping round my waist and my arms filled with a terrified sheep. It was no light task, for though the water was no more than three feet deep, it was swift and strong, and a kicking hogg is a sore burden. But this was the only road; the stream might rise higher at any moment; and somehow or other those bleating flocks had to be transferred to their fellows beyond. There were six men at the labour, six men and myself, and all were cross and wearied and heavy with water.

I made my passages side by side with my friend the shepherd, and thereby felt much elated. This was a man who had dwelt all his days in the wilds and was familiar with torrents as with his own doorstep. Now and then a swimming dog would bark feebly as he was washed against us, and flatter his fool's heart that he was aiding the work. And so we wrought on, till by midday I was dead-beat, and could scarce stagger through the surf, while all the men had the same gasping faces. I saw the shepherd look with longing eye up the long green valley, and mutter disconsolately in his beard.

'Is the water rising?' I asked.

'It's no rising,' said he, 'but I likena the look o' that big, black clud upon Cairncraw. I doubt there's been a shoor up the muirs, and a shoor there means twae mair feet o' water in the Clachlands. God help Sandy Jamieson's lambs, if there is.'

'How many are left?' I asked.

'Three, fower – no abune a score and a half,' said he, running his eye over the lessened flocks. 'I maun try to tak twae at a time.'

So for ten minutes he struggled with a double burden, and panted painfully at each return. Then with a sudden swift look upstream he broke off and stood up. 'Get ower the water, every yin o' ye, and leave the sheep,' he said, and to my wonder every man of the five obeyed his word, for he was known for a wise counsellor in distress.

And then I saw the reason of his command, for with a sudden swift leap forward the Clachlands rose, and flooded up to where I had stood an instant before high and dry.

'It's come,' said the shepherd, in a tone of fate, 'and there's fifteen no ower yet, and Lord knows how they'll dae't. They'll hae to gang roond by Gledsmuir Brig, and that's twenty mile o' a differ. 'Deed, it's no like that Sandy Jamieson will get a guid price the morn for sic sair forfochen beasts.'

Then with firmly gripped staff he marched stoutly into the tide till it ran hissing below his armpits. 'I could dae't alane,' he cried, 'but no wi' a burden. For, losh, if ye slippit, ye'd be in the Manor Pool afore ye could draw breath.'

And so we waited with the great white droves and five angry men beyond, and the path blocked by a surging flood. For half an hour we waited, holding anxious consultation across the stream, when to us thus busied there entered a newcomer, a helper from the ends of the earth.

He was a man of something over middle size, but with a stoop forward that shortened him to something beneath it. His dress was ragged homespun, the cast-off clothes of some sportsman, and in his arms he bore a bundle of sticks and heather-roots which marked his calling. I knew him for a tramp who long had wandered in the place, but I could not account for the whole-voiced shout of greeting which met him as he stalked down the path. He lifted his eyes and looked solemnly and long at the scene. Then something of delight came into his eye, his face relaxed, and flinging down his burden, he stripped his coat and came towards us.

'Come on, Yeddie, ye're sair needed,' said the

shepherd, and I watched with amazement this grizzled, crooked man seize a sheep by the fleece and drag it into the water. Then he was in the midst, stepping warily, now up, now down the channel, but always nearing the farther bank. At last with a final struggle he landed his charge, and turned to journey back. Fifteen times did he cross that water, and at the end his mean figure had wholly changed. For now he was straighter and stronger, his eye flashed, and his voice, as he cried out to the drovers, had in it a tone of command. I marvelled at the transformation; and when at length he had donned once more his ragged coat and shouldered his bundle, I asked the shepherd his name.

'They ca' him Adam Logan,' said my friend, his face still bright with excitement, 'but maist folk ca' him "Streams o' Water".'

'Ay,' said I, 'and why "Streams of Water"?'

'Juist for the reason ye see,' said he.

Now I knew the shepherd's way, and I held my peace, for it was clear that his mind was revolving other matters, concerned most probably with the high subject of the morrow's prices. But in a little, as we crossed the moor toward his dwelling, his thoughts relaxed and he remembered my question. So he answered me thus – 'Oh, ay; as ye were sayin', he's a queer man, Yeddie – aye been; guid kens whaur he cam frae first, for he's been trampin' the countryside since ever I mind, and that's no yesterday. He maun be sixty year, and yet he's as fresh as ever. If onything, he's a thocht dafter in his ongaein's, mair silent-like. But ye'll hae heard tell o' him afore?'

I owned ignorance.

'Tut,' he said, 'ye ken nocht. But Yeddie had aye a queer crakin' for waters. He never gangs on the road. Wi' him it's juist up yae glen and doon anither, and aye keepin' by the burn-side. He kens every water i' the warld, every bit sheuch and burnie frae Gallowa' to Berwick. And then he kens the way o' spates the best I ever saw, and I've heard tell o' him fordin' waters when nae ither thing could leeve i' them. He can weyse and wark his road sae cunnin'ly on the stanes that the roughest flood, if it's no juist fair ower his heid, canna upset him. Mony a sheep has he saved to me, and it's mony a guid drove wad never hae won to Gledsmuir market but for Yeddie.'

I listened with a boy's interest in any romantic narration. Somehow, the strange figure wrestling in the brown stream took fast hold on my mind, and I asked the shepherd for farther tales.

'There's little mair to tell,' he said, 'for a gangrel life is nane the liveliest. But d'ye ken the lang-nebbit hill which cocks its tap abune the Clachlands heid? Weel, he's got a wee bit o' grund on the tap frae the Yerl, and there he's howkit* a grave for himsel'. He's sworn me and twae-three ithers to bury him there, wherever he may dee. It's a queer fancy in the auld dotterel.'

So the shepherd talked, and as at evening we stood by his door we saw a figure moving into the gathering shadows. I knew it at once, and did not need my friend's, 'There gangs "Streams o' Water"' to recognize it. Something wild and pathetic in the old man's face haunted me like a dream, and as the dusk swallowed him up, he seemed like some old Druid recalled of the gods to his ancient habitation of the moors.

II

Two years passed, and April came with her suns and rains, and again the waters brimmed full in the valleys. Under the clear, shining sky the lambing went on, and the faint bleat of sheep brooded on the hills. In a land of young heather and green upland meads, of faint odours of moor-burn, and hill-tops falling in lone ridges to the sky-line, the veriest St Anthony would not abide indoors; so I flung all else to the winds and went a-fishing.

At the first pool on the Callowa, where the great flood sweeps nobly round a ragged shoulder of hill, and spreads into broad deeps beneath a tangle of birches, I began my toils. The turf was still wet with dew and the young leaves gleamed in the glow of morning. Far up the stream rose the terrible hills which hem the mosses and tarns of that tableland, whence flow the greater waters of the country-side. An ineffable freshness, as of the morning alike of the day and the seasons, filled the clear hill-air, and the remote peaks gave the needed touch of intangible romance.

But as I fished, I came on a man sitting in a green dell, busy at the making of brooms. I knew his face and dress, for who could forget such eclectic raggedness? – and I remembered that day two years before when he first hobbled into my ken. Now, as I saw him there, I was captivated by the nameless mystery of his appearance. There was something startling to one, accustomed to the lack-lustre gaze of town-bred folk, in the sight of an eye as keen and wild as a hawk's from sheer solitude and lonely travelling. He was so bent and scarred with weather that he seemed as much a part of that woodland place as the birks themselves, and the noise of his labours did not startle the birds which hopped on the branches.

Little by little I won his acquaintance – by a chance reminiscence, a single tale, the mention of a friend. Then he made me free of his knowledge, and my fishing fared well that day. He dragged me up little streams to sequestered pools, where I had astonishing success; and then back to some great swirl in the Callowa where he had seen monstrous takes. And all the while he delighted me with his talk, of men and things, of weather and place, pitched high in his thin, old voice, and garnished with many tones of lingering sentiment. He spoke in a broad, slow Scots, with so quaint a lilt in his speech that one seemed to be in an elder time among people of a quieter life and a quainter kindliness.

Then by chance I asked him of a burn of which I had heard, and how it might be reached. I shall never forget the tone of his answer as his face grew eager and he poured forth his knowledge.

'Ye'll gang up the Knowe Burn, which comes down into the Cauldshaw. It's a wee tricklin' thing, trowin' in and out o' pools i' the rock, and comin' doun out o' the side o' Caerfraun. Yince a merrymaiden bided there, I've heard folks say, and used to win the sheep frae the Cauldshaw herd, and bile them i' the muckle pool below the fa'. They say that there's a road to the Ill Place there, and when the Deil likit he sent up the lowe and garred the water faem and fizzle like an auld kettle. But if ye've gaun to the Coln Burn ye maun haud atower the rig o' the hill frae the Knowe heid, and ye'll come to it wimplin' among green brae faces. It's a bonny bit, rale lonesome, but awfu' bonny, and there's mony braw trout in its siller flows.'

Then I remembered all I had heard of the old man's

craze, and I humoured him.

'It's a fine countryside for burns,' I said.

'Ye may say that,' said he, gladly, 'a weel-watered land. But a' this braw south country is the same. I've traivelled frae the Yeavering Hill in the Cheviots to the Caldons in Galloway, and it's a' the same. When I was young, I've seen me gang north to the Hielands and doun to the English lawlands, but now that I'm gettin' auld, I maun bide i' the yae place. There's no a burn in the South I dinna ken, and I never cam to the water I couldna ford.'

'No?' said I. 'I've seen you at the ford o' Clachlands in' the Lammas floods.'

'Often I've been there,' he went on, speaking like one calling up vague memories. 'Yince, when Tam Rorison was drooned, honest man. Yince again, when the brigs were ta'en awa', and the Back House o' Clachlands had nae bread for a week. But o' Clachlands is a bit easy water. But I've seen the muckle Aller come roarin' sae high that it washed awa' a sheep-fold that stood weel up on the hill. And I've seen this verra burn, this bonny clear Callowa, lyin' like a loch for miles i' the haugh. But I never heeds a spate, for if a man just kens the way o't it's a canny, hairmless thing. I couldna wish to dee better than just be happit i' the waters o' my ain countryside, when my legs fail and I'm ower auld for the trampin'.'

Something in that queer figure in the setting of the hills struck a note of curious pathos. And towards evening as we returned down the glen the note grew keener. A spring sunset of gold and crimson flamed in our backs and turned the clear pools to fire. Far off down the vale the plains and the sea gleamed half in shadow. Somehow in the fragrance and colour and the delectable crooning of the stream, the fantastic and the dim seemed tangible and present, and high sentiment revelled for once in my prosaic heart.

And still more in the breast of my companion. He stopped and sniffed the evening air, as he looked far over hill and dale and then back to the great hills above us. 'Yon's Crappel, and Caerdon and the Laigh Law,' he said, lingering with relish over each name, 'and the Gled comes doun atween them. I haena been there for a twalmonth, and I maun hae anither glisk o't, for it's a braw place.' And then some bitter thought seemed to seize him, and his mouth twitched. 'I'm an auld man,' he cried, 'and I canna see ye a' again. There's burns and mair burns in the high hills that I'll never win to.' Then he remembered my presence, and stopped. 'Ye maun excuse me,' he said huskily, 'but the sicht o' a' thae lang blue hills makes me daft, now that I've faun i' the vale o' years. Yince I was young and could get where I wantit, but now I am auld and maun bide i' the same bit. And I'm aye thinkin' o' the waters I've been to, and the green heichs and howes and the bricht pools that I canna win to again. I maun e'en be content wi' the Callowa, which is as bonny as the best.'

And then I left him, wandering down by the stream-side and telling his crazy meditations to himself.

III

A space of years elapsed ere I met him, for fate had carried me far from the upland valleys. But once again I was afoot on the white moor-roads; and, as I swung along one autumn afternoon up the path which leads from the Glen of Callowa to the Gled, I saw a figure before me which I knew for my friend. When I overtook him, his appearance puzzled and vexed me. Age seemed to have come on him at a bound, and in the tottering figure and the stoop of weakness I had difficulty in recognizing the hardy frame of the man as I had known him. Something, too, had come over his face. His brow was clouded, and the tan of weather stood out hard and cruel on a blanched cheek. His eye seemed both wilder and sicklier, and for the first time I saw him with none of the appurtenances of his trade.

He greeted me feebly and dully, and showed little wish to speak. He walked with slow, uncertain step, and his breath laboured with a new panting. Every now and then he would look at me sidewise, and in his feverish glance I could detect none of the free kindliness of old. The man was ill in body and mind.

I asked him how he had done since I saw him last.

'It's an ill world now,' he said in a slow, querulous voice. 'There's nae need for honest men, and nae leevin'. Folk dinna care for me ava now. They dinna buy my besoms, they winna let me bide a' nicht in their byres, and they're no like the kind canty folk in the auld times. And a' the countryside is changin'. Doun by Goldieslaw they're makkin' a dam for takin' water to the toun, and they're thinkin' o' daein' the like wi' the Callowa. Guid help us, can they no let the works o' God alane? Is there no room for them in the dirty lawlands that they maun file the hills wi' their biggins?'

I conceived dimly that the cause of his wrath was a scheme for waterworks at the border of the uplands, but I had less concern for this than his strangely feeble health.

'You are looking ill,' I said. 'What has come over you?'

'Oh, I canna last for aye,' he said mournfully. 'My auld body's about dune. I've warkit ower sair when I had it, and it's gaun to fail on my hands. Sleepin' out o' wat nichts and gangin' lang wantin' meat are no the best ways for a long life;' and he smiled the ghost of a smile.

And then he fell to wild telling of the ruin of the place and the hardness of the people, and I saw that want and bare living had gone far to loosen his wits. I knew the countryside with the knowledge of many years, and I recognized that change was only in his mind. And a great pity seized me for this lonely figure toiling on in the bitterness of regret. I tried to comfort him, but my words were useless, for he took no heed of me; with bent head and faltering step he mumbled his sorrows to himself.

Then of a sudden we came to the crest of the ridge where the road dips from the hill-top to the sheltered valley. Sheer from the heather ran the white streak till it lost itself among the reddening rowans and the yellow birks* of the wood. All the land was rich in autumn colour, and the shining waters dipped and fell through a pageant of russet and gold. And all around hills huddled in silent spaces, long brown moors crowned with cairns, or steep fortresses of rock and shingle rising to foreheads of steel-like grey. The autumn blue faded in the far skyline to white, and lent distance to the farther peaks. The hush of the wilderness, which is far different from the hush of death, brooded over the scene, and like faint music came the sound of a distance scythe-swing, and the tinkling whisper which is the flow of a hundred streams.

I am an old connoisseur in the beauties of the uplands, but I held my breath at the sight. And when I glanced at my companion, he, too, had raised his head, and stood with wide nostrils and gleaming eye revelling in this glimpse of Arcady. Then he found his voice, and the weakness and craziness seemed for one moment to leave him.

'It's my ain land,' he cried, 'and I'll never leave it. D' ye see yon broun hill wi' the lang cairn?' and he gripped my arm fiercely and directed my gaze. 'Yon's my bit. I howkit it richt on the verra tap, and ilka year I gang there to mak it neat and orderly. I've trystit wi' fower men in different pairishes, that whenever they hear o' my death, they'll cairry me up yonder and bury me there. And then I'll never leave it, but lie still and quiet to the warld's end. I'll aye hae the sound o' water in my ear, for there's five burns tak' their rise on that hillside, and on a' airts the glens gang doun to the Gled and the Aller. I'll hae a brawer buryin' than ony, for a hill-top's better than a dowie kirkyaird.'

Then his spirit failed him, his voice sank, and he was almost the feeble gangrel once more. But not yet, for again his eye swept the ring of hills, and he muttered to himself names which I knew for streams, lingeringly, lovingly, as of old affections. 'Aller and Gled and Callowa,' he crooned, 'braw names, and Clachlands and Cauldshaw and the Lanely Water. And I maunna forget the Stark and the Lin and the bonny streams o' the Creran. And what mair? I canna mind a' the burns, the Howe and the Hollies and the Fawn and the links o' the Manor. What says the Psalmist about them?

> Like streams o' water in the South
> Our bondage, Lord, recall.

Ay, but that's the name for them. "Streams o' water in the South".'

And as we went down the slopes to the darkening vale I heard him crooning to himself in a high, quavering voice the single distich; then in a little his weariness took him again, and he plodded on with no thought save for his sorrows.

IV

The conclusion of this tale belongs not to me but to the shepherd of the Redswirehead, and I heard it from him in his dwelling, as I stayed the night, belated on the darkening moors. He told me it after supper in a flood of misty Doric, and his voice grew rough at times, and he poked viciously at the dying peat.

'In the last back-end I was at Gledfoot wi' sheep, and a weary job I had and little credit. Ye ken the place, a lang dreich shore wi' the wind swirlin' and bitin' to the bane, and the broun Gled water choked wi' Solloway sand. There was nae room in ony inn in the town, so I made good to gang to a bit public on the Harbour Walk, where sailor-folk and fishermen feucht and drank, and nae dacent men frae the hills thocht o' gangin'. I was in a gey ill way, for I had sell't my beasts dooms cheap, and I thocht o' the lang miles hame in the wintry weather. So after a bite o' meat I gangs out to get the air and clear my heid, which was a' rammled wi' the auction-ring.

'And whae did I find, sittin' on a bench at the door, but the auld man Yeddie. He was waur changed than ever. His lang hair was hingin' ower his broo, and his face was thin and white as a ghaist's. His claes fell loose about him, and he sat wi' his hand on his auld stick and his chin on his hand, hearin' nocht and glowerin' afore him. He never saw nor kenned me till I shook him by the shoulders, and cried him by his name.

'"Whae are ye?" says he, in a thin voice that gaed to my hert.

'"Ye ken me fine, ye auld fule," says I. "I'm Jock

Rorison o' the Redswirehead, whaur ye've stoppit often."

'"Redswirehead," he says, like a man in a dream, "Redswirehead! That's at the tap o' the Clachlands Burn as ye gang ower to the Dreichil."

'"And what are ye daein' here? It's no your countryside ava, and ye're no fit noo for lang trampin'."

'"No," says he, in the same weak voice and wi' nae fushion in him, "but they winna hae me up yonder noo. I'm ower auld and useless. Yince a'body was gled to see me, and wad keep me as lang's I wantit, and had aye a guid word at meeting and pairting. Noo it's a' changed, and my wark's dune."

'I saw fine that the man was daft, but what answer could I gie to his havers? Folk in the Callowa Glens are as kind as afore, but ill weather and auld age had put queer notions intil his heid. Forbye, he was seeck, seeck unto death, and I saw mair in his ee than I likit to think.

'"Come in by and get some meat, man," I said. "Ye're famishin' wi' cauld and hunger."

'"I canna eat," he says, and his voice never changed. "It's lang since I had a bite, for I'm no hungry. But I'm awfu' thirsty. I cam here yestereen, and I can get nae water to drink like the water in the hills. I maun be settin' out back the morn, if the Lord spares me."

'I mindit fine that the body wad tak nae drink like an honest man, but maun aye draibble wi' burn water, and noo he had got the thing on the brain. I never spak a word, for the maitter was bye ony mortal's aid.

'For lang he sat quiet. Then he lifts his heid and looks awa ower the grey sea. A licht for a moment cam intil his een.

'"Whatna big water's that?" he said, wi' his puir mind aye rinnin' on waters.

'"That's the Solloway," says I.

'"The Solloway," says he; "it's a big water, and it wad be an ill job to ford it."

'"Nae men ever fordit it," I said.

'"But I never yet cam to the water I couldna ford," says he. "But what's the queer smell i' the air? Something snell and cauld and unfreendly, no like the reek o' bogs and hills."

'"That's the salt, for we're at the sea here, the mighty ocean."

'He keepit repeatin' the word ower in his mouth. "The salt, the salt, I've heard tell o' it afore, but I dinna like it. It's terrible cauld and unhamely."

'By this time an onding o' rain was comin' up frae the water, and I bade the man come indoors to the fire. He followed me, as biddable as a sheep, draggin' his legs like yin far gone in seeckness. I set him by the fire, and put whisky at his elbow, but he wadna touch it.

'"I've nae need o' it," said he. "I'm fine and warm;" and he sits staring at the fire, aye comin' ower again and again. "The Solloway, the Solloway. It's a guid name and a muckle water." But sune I gaed to my bed, being heavy wi' sleep, for I had travelled for twae days.'

'The next morn I was up at six and out to see the weather. It was a' changed. The muckle tides lay lang and still as our ain Loch o' the Lee, and far ayont I saw the big blue hills o' England shine bricht and clear. I thankit Providence for the day, for it was better to tak the lang miles back in sic a sun than in a blast of rain.

'But as I lookit I saw some folk comin' up frae the beach cairryin' something atween them. My hert gied a loup, and "some puir, drooned sailor-body," says I to mysel', "whae has perished in yesterday's storm." But as they came nearer I got a glisk which made me run like daft, and lang ere I was up on them I saw it was Yeddie.

'He lay drippin' and white, wi' his puir auld hair lyin' back frae his broo and his duds clingin' to the legs. But out o' the face there seemed to have gone a' the seeckness and weariness. His een were stelled, as if he had been lookin' forrit to something, and his lips were set like a man on a lang errand. And mair, his stick was grippit sae firm in his hand that nae man could loose it, so they e'en let it be.

'Then they tellt me the tale o' 't, how at the earliest licht they had seen him wanderin' alang the sands, juist as they were putting out their boats to sea. They wondered and watched him, till of a sudden he turned to the water and wadit in, keepin' straucht on till he was oot o' sicht. They rowed a' their pith to the place, but they were ower late. Yince they saw his heid appear abune water, still wi' his face to the ither side; and then they got his body, for the tide was rinnin' low in the mornin'. I tell't them a' I kenned o' him and they were sair affected. "Puir cratur," said yin, "he's shurely better now."

'So we brocht him up to the house and laid him there till the folk i' the town had heard o' the death. Syne I got a wooden coffin made and put him in it, juist as he was, wi' his staff in his hand and his auld duds about him. I mindit o' my sworn word, for I was yin o' the four that had promised, and I ettled to dae his bidding. It was three-and-twenty mile to the hills, and thirty to the lanely tap whaur he had howkit his grave. But I never heedit it. I'm a strong man, weel-used to the walkin', and my hert was sair for the puir auld man I had kenned sae well. Now that he had gotten deliverance from his affliction, it was mine to leave him in the place he want it. Forbye he wasna muckle heavier than a bairn.

'It was a long road, a sair road, but I did it, and by seven o'clock I was at the edge o' the muirlands. There was a braw mune, and a' the glens and taps stood out as clear as midday. Bit by bit, for I was gey tired, I warstled ower the rigs and up the cleuchs to the Gled-head, syne up the stany Gled-cleuch to the lang grey hill which they ca' the Hurlybackit. By ten I had come to the cairn, and black i' the yellow licht I saw the grave. So there I buried him, and though I'm no a releegious man, I couldna help sayin' ower him the guid words o' the Psalmist,

> Like streams of water in the South
> Our bondage, Lord, recall.'

This was the shepherd's tale, and I heard it out in silence.

So if you go from the Gled to the Aller, and keep far over the north side of the Muckle Muneraw, you will come in time to a stony ridge which ends in a cairn. There you will see the whole hill-country of the south, a hundred lochs, a myriad streams, and a forest of hill-tops. There on the very crest lies the old man, in the heart of his own land, at the fountain-head of his many waters. If you listen you will hear a hushed noise as of the swaying in trees or a ripple on the sea. It is the sound of the rising of burns, which, innumerable and unnumbered, flow thence to the silent glens forevermore.

Ship to Tarshish

In the Old Testament story Jonah lived near Joppa (the modern Tel Aviv). He was told to go to Nineveh, seven hundred miles north-east. Instead he set off west, in a ship bound for Tarshish, usually identified as Tartessus, in south-east Spain: that is, two and a half thousand miles in the opposite direction, through the Strait of Gibraltar, facing the Atlantic. Jonah was trying to run as far as he possibly could, almost to the edge of the known world, to get away from the command of God that in His name he should 'cry against' the very centre of the heathen Assyrian empire, Nineveh. Nor was it only the extreme distance that demonstrated Jonah's extreme feelings: the Jews were never seafarers, and a journey of that length for the only non-sailor aboard would have been agony, to say nothing of storms and 'great fish'.

Buchan gives the story, in The Runagates Club, to a modern ex-sailor to tell, for added emphasis on this Old Testament Jew's courage. As he says, when Jonah eventually did go to Nineveh, he might have found it less daunting than the whale's belly. Buchan's story gives an ironic twist to Jonah's lesson.

Ship to Tarshish

RALPH COLLATT'S STORY

> Now the word of the Lord came unto Jonah the son of
> Amittai, saying, Arise, go to Nineveh . . . But Jonah . . .
> found a ship going to Tarshish: so he paid the fare thereof,
> and went down into it, to go with them unto Tarshish from
> the presence of the Lord.
>
> JONAH I. i–iii

The talk one evening turned on the metaphysics of
courage. It is a subject which most men are a little shy of
discussing. They will heartily applaud a friend's pluck, but
it is curious how rarely they will label a man a coward.
Perhaps the reason is that we are all odd mixtures of
strength and weakness, brave in certain things, timid in
others; and since each is apt to remember his private funks
more vividly than the things about which he is bold, we
are chary about dogmatizing.

Lamancha propounded the thesis that everybody had a
yellow streak in them. We all, he said, at times shirk
unpleasant duties, and invent an honourable explanation,
which we know to be a lie.

Sandy Arbuthnot observed that the most temerarious
deeds were often done by people who had begun by
funking, and then, in the shame of the rebound, did a
good deal more than those who had no qualms. 'The man
who says I go not, and afterwards repents and goes,
generally travels the devil of a long way.'

'Like Jonah,' said Lamancha, 'who didn't like the job

allotted him, and took ship to Tarshish to get away from it, and then repented and went like a raging lion to Nineveh.'

Collatt, who had been a sailor and one of the Q-boat heroes in the war, demurred. 'I wonder if Nineveh was as unpleasant as the whale's belly,' he said. Then he told us a story in illustration, not as one would have expected, out of his wild sea memories, but from his experience in the City, where he was now a bill-broker.

I got to know Jim Hallward first when he had just come down from the University. He was a tall, slim, fair-haired lad, with a soft voice and the kind of manners which make the ordinary man feel a lout. Eton and Christ Church had polished him till he fairly glistened. His clothes were sober works of art, and he was the cleanest thing you ever saw – always seemed to have just shaved and bathed after a couple of hours' hard exercise. We all liked him, for he was a companionable soul and had no frills, but in the City he was about as useless as a lily in a quickset hedge. Somebody called him an 'apolaustic epicene'*, which sounded accurate, though I don't know what the words mean. He used to come down to business about eleven o'clock and leave at four – earlier in summer, when he played polo at Hurlingham.

This lotus-eating existence lasted for two years. His father was the head of Hallwards, the merchant-bankers who had been in existence since before the Napoleonic wars. It was an old-fashioned private firm with a tremendous reputation, but for some years it had been dropping a little out of the front rank. It had very few of the big issues, and, though reckoned as solid as the Bank of England, it had hardly kept pace with new developments. But just about the time Jim came down from

Oxford his father seemed to get a new lease of life. Hallwards suddenly became ultra-progressive, took in a new manager from one of the big joint-stock banks, and launched out into business which before it would not have touched with the end of a barge-pole. I fancy the old man wanted to pull up the firm before he died, so as to leave a good thing to his only child.

In this new activity Jim can't have been of much use. His other engagements did not leave him a great deal of time to master the complicated affairs of a house like Hallwards. He spoke of his City connection with a certain distaste. The set he had got into were mostly eldest sons with political ambitions, and if Jim had any serious inclination it was towards Parliament, which he proposed to enter in a year or two. For the rest he played polo, and hunted, and did a little steeplechasing, and danced assiduously. Dancing was about the only thing he did really well, for he was only a moderate horseman and his politics were not to be taken seriously. So he was the complete *flâneur*, agreeable, popular, beautifully mannered, highly ornamental, and the most useless creature on earth. You see, he had slacked at school, and had just scraped through college, and had never done a real piece of work in his life.

In the autumn of 192–, whispers began to circulate about Hallwards. It seemed that they were doing a very risky class of business, and people shrugged their shoulders. But no one was prepared for the almighty crash which came at the beginning of the New Year. The firm had been trying to get control of a colonial railway, and for this purpose was quietly buying up the ordinary stock. But an American group, with unlimited capital was out on the same tack, and the result was that the price was forced up, and Hallwards were foolish enough to go on buying.

They borrowed up to the limit of their capacity, and called a halt too late. If the thing had been known in time the City might have made an effort to keep the famous old firm on its legs, but it all came like a thunderclap. Hallwards went down, the American group got their railway stock at a knock-out price, and old Mr Hallward, who had been ailing for some months, had a stroke of paralysis and died.

I was desperately sorry for Jim. The foundations of his world were upset, and he hadn't a notion what to do about it. You see, he didn't know the rudiments of the business, and couldn't be made to understand it. He went about in a dream, with staring, unseeing eyes, like a puzzled child. At first he screwed himself up to a sort of effort. He had many friends who would help, he thought, and he made various suggestions, all of a bottomless futility. Very soon he found that his Mayfair popularity was no sort of asset to him. He must have realized that people were beginning to turn a colder eye on a pauper than on an eligible young man, and his overtures were probably met with curt refusals. Anyhow, in a week he had given up hope. He felt himself a criminal and behaved as such. He saw nobody but his solicitors, and when he met a friend in the street he turned and ran. A perfectly unreasonable sense of disgrace took possession of him, and there was a moment when I was afraid he might put an end to himself.

This went on for the better part of a month, while I and one or two others were trying to save something from the smash. We put up a fund and bought some of the wreckage, with the idea of getting together a little company to nurse it. It was important to do something, for though Jim was an only child and his mother was dead, there were various elderly female relatives who had their incomes from Hallwards. The firm had been much respected and old Hallward had been popular, and Jim had no enemies. There is a good deal of camaraderie in the City, and a lot of us were willing to combine and keep Jim going. We were all ready to help him, if he would only sit down and put his back into the job.

But that was just what Jim would not do. He had got a horror of the City, and felt a pariah whenever he met anybody who knew about the crash. He had eyes like a hunted hare's, and one couldn't get any sense out of him. I don't think he minded the change in his comforts – the end of polo and hunting and politics, and the prospect of cheap lodgings and long office hours. I believe he welcomed all that as a kind of atonement. It was the disgrace of the thing that came between him and his sleep. He knew only enough of the City to have picked up a wrong notion of its standards, and imagined that everybody was pointing a finger at him as a fool, and possibly a crook.

It was very little use reasoning with him. I pointed out that the right thing for him to do was to shoulder the burden and retrieve his father's credit. He laughed bitterly.

'Much good I'd be at that,' he said. 'You know I'm a baby in business, though you're too polite to tell me so.'

'You can have a try,' I said. 'We'll all lend you a hand.'

It was no use. References to his father and the firm's ancient prestige and his old great-aunts only made him shiver. You could see that his misery made him blind to argument. Then I began to lose my temper. I told him that it was his duty as a man to face the music. I asked him what else he proposed to do.

He said he meant to go to Canada and start life anew. He would probably change his name. I got out of patience with his silliness.

'You're offered a chance here to make good,' I told him. 'In Canada you'll have to find your chance, and how

in God's name are you going to do it? You haven't been
bred the right way to succeed in the Dominions. You'll
probably starve.'

'Quite likely,' was his dismal answer. 'I'll make my book
for that. I don't mind anything so long as I'm in a place
where nobody knows me.'

'Remember, you are running away,' I said, 'running
away from what I consider your plain duty. You can't
expect to win out if you begin by funking.'

'I know – I know,' he wailed. 'I am a coward.'

I said no more, for when a man is willing to admit that he
is a coward his nerves have got the better of his reason.

Well, the upshot was that Jim sailed for Canada with a
little short of two hundred pounds in his pocket – what was
left of his last allowance. He could have had plenty of
introductions, but he wouldn't take them. He seemed to be
determined to bury himself, and I daresay, too, he got a
morbid satisfaction out of discomfort. He had still the
absurd notion of disgrace, and felt that any handicap he laid
on himself was a kind of atonement.

He reached Montreal in the filthy weeks when the spring
thaw begins – the worst sample of weather to be found on
the globe. Jim had not procured any special outfit, and he
landed with a kit consisting of two smart tweed suits, a suit
of flannels, riding breeches and knickerbockers – the
remnants of his London wardrobe. It wasn't quite the rig
for a poor man to go looking for a job in. He had travelled
steerage, and, as might have been expected from one in his
condition, had not made friends, but he had struck up a
tepid acquaintanceship with an Irishman who was em-
ployed in a lumber business. The fellow was friendly, and
was struck by Jim's obvious air of education and good-
breeding, so, when he heard that he wanted work, he
suggested that a clerkship might be got in his firm.

Jim applied, and was taken on as the clerk in charge of timber-cutting rights in Eastern Quebec. The work was purely mechanical, and simply meant keeping a record of numbered lots, checking them off on the map, and filling in the details in the register as they came to hand. But it required accuracy and strict attention, and Jim had little of either. Besides, he wrote the vile fist* which is the special privilege of our public schools. He held down the job for a fortnight and then was fired.

He had found cheap lodgings in a boarding-house down east, and trudged the two miles in the slush to his office. His fellow-lodgers were willing enough to be friendly – clerks and shop-boys and typists and newspaper reporters most of them. Jim wasn't a snob, but he was rapidly becoming a hermit, for all his nerves were exposed and he shrank from his fellows. His shyness was considered English swank, and the others invented nicknames for him and sniggered when he appeared. Luckily he was too miserable to pay much attention. He had no interest in their games, their visits to the movies and to cheap dance-halls, and their precocious sweethearting. He could not get the hang of their knowing commercial jargon. They set him down as a snob, and he shrank from them as barbarians.

But there was one lodger, a sub-editor on a paper which I shall call the *Evening Hawk*, who saw a little farther than the rest. He realized that Jim was an educated man – a 'scholar' he called it, and he managed to get part of his confidence. So when Jim lost his lumber job he was offered a billet on the *Hawk*. There was no superfluity of men of his type in local journalism, and the editor thought it might give tone to his paper to have someone on the staff who could write decent English and keep them from making howlers about Europe. The *Hawk* was a lively, up-to-date production, very much Americanized in its traditions and its literary style, but it had just acquired some political influence and it hankered after more.

But Jim was no sort of success in journalism. He was tried out in a variety of jobs – as reporter, special correspondent, sub-editor – but he failed to give satisfaction in any. To begin with he had no news-sense. Not many things interested him in his present frame of mind, and he had no notion what would interest the *Hawk*'s readers. He couldn't compose snappy headlines, and it made him sick to try. His writing was no doubt a great deal more correct than that of his colleagues, but it was dull as ditch-water. To add to everything else he was desperately casual. It was not that he meant to be slack, but that he had no stimulus to make him concentrate his attention, and he was about the worst sub-editor, I fancy, in the history of the press.

Summer came, and sleet and icy winds gave place to dust and heat. Jim tramped the grilling streets, one vast ache of homesickness. He had to stick to his tweeds, for his flannel suit had got lost in his journeys between boarding-houses, and, as he mopped his brow in the airless newspaper rooms smelling of printers' ink and shaken by the great presses, he thought of green lawns at Hurlingham, and cool backwaters of the Isis, and clipped yew hedges in old gardens, and a pleasant club window overlooking St James's Street. He hungered for fresh air, but when on a Sunday morning he went for a long walk, he found no pleasure in the adjacent countryside. It all seemed dusty and tousled and unhomely. He wasn't complaining, for it seemed to him part of a rightful expiation, but he was very lonely and miserable.

I have said that he had landed with a couple of hundred pounds, and this he had managed to keep pretty well intact. One day at a quick-luncheon counter he got into talk with a man called McNee, a Manitoban who had fought in the war, and knew something about horses. McNee, like Jim, did not take happily to town life, and was very sick of his job with an automobile company, and looking about for a better. There was not much in common between the two men, except a dislike of Montreal, for I picture McNee as a rough diamond, an active enterprising fellow meant by Providence for a backwoodsman. He had heard of a big dam somewhere down in the Gaspé district, which was being constructed in connection with a pulp scheme. He knew one of the foremen, and believed that money might be made by anyone who could put up a little capital and run a store in the construction camp. He told Jim that it was a fine wild country with plenty of game in the woods, and that, besides making money easily, a storekeeper could have a white man's life. But every bit of a thousand dollars capital would be needed, and he could only lay his hands on a couple of hundred. To Jim in his stuffy lodging-house the scheme offered a blessed escape. He wanted to make money, he wanted fresh air and trees and running water, for your Englishman, though town-bred, always hankers after the country. So he gave up his job on the *Hawk*, just when it was about to give him up, and started out with McNee.

The place was his first disappointment. It was an ugly clearing in an interminable forest of dull spruces, which ran without a break to New Brunswick. However far you walked there was nothing to see except the low muffled hills and the monotonous green of the firs. The partners were given a big shack for their store, and made their sleeping quarters in one end of it. For stock they had laid in a quantity of tinned goods, tobacco, shirts and socks and boots, and a variety of musical instruments. But they found that most of their stuff was unmarketable, since the men were well fed and clothed by the company, and after a week their store had become a rough kind of café, selling hot-dogs, and icecream and soft drinks. McNee was immensely proud of it and ornamented the walls with 'ideal faces' from the American magazines. He was a born restaurant keeper, if he had got his chance, but unfortunately there was not much profit in coco-cola and ginger-ade.

In about a fortnight the place became half eating-house, half club, where the workmen gathered of an evening to play cards. McNee was in his element, but Jim was no more use than a sick pup. He didn't understand the lingo, and his shyness and absorption made him as unpopular as in the Montreal boarding-houses. He saw his little capital slipping away, and there was no compensation in the way of a pleasant life. He tried to imitate McNee's air of hearty bonhomie, and miserably failed. His partner was a good fellow, and stood up for him when an irate navvy consigned him to perdition as a 'God-darned London dude', and Jim's own good temper and sense of only getting what he deserved did something to protect him. But he soon realized that he was a ghastly failure, and this knowledge prevented him expostulating with the other for his obvious shortcomings. For McNee soon became too much of a social success. Gaspé was not 'dry', and there was more than soft drinks consumed in the store, especially by the joint proprietor and his friend the foreman. Also McNee was a bit of a gambler and was perpetually borrowing small sums from capital to meet his losses.

Now and then Jim took a holiday, and tramped all of a long summer day. The country around being only partially surveyed, there was no map to be had, and he repeatedly lost himself. Once he struck a lumber camp and was given pork and beans by cheerful French-Canadians whose *patois* he could not follow. Once he had almost a happy day, when he saw his first moose. But generally he came back from stifling encounters with cedar swamps and *bois brûlé*, weary but unrefreshed. He was not in the frame of mind to get much comfort out of the Canadian wilds, for he was always sore with longing for a different kind of landscape.

The river on which the camp lay was the famous Maouchi, and twelve miles down on the St Lawrence shore was a big fishing-lodge owned by a rich New Yorker. Jim used to see members of the party – young men in marvellous knickerbockers and young women in jumpers like Joseph's coat, and he hid himself at the sight of them. Occasionally a big roadster would pass the store, conveying fishermen to some of the upper lakes. Once, when he was feeling specially dispirited after a long hot day, a car stopped at the door, and two people descended. They came into the store, and the young man asked for lemonade, declaring that their tongues were hanging out of their mouths. Happily McNee was there to serve them, while Jim sheltered behind the curtain of the sleeping-room. He knew them both. One was a subaltern in the cavalry with whom he had played bridge in the club, the other was a girl whom he had danced with. Their workmanlike English clothes, their quiet clear English voices gave him a bad dose of homesickness. They were returning, he reflected, to hot baths and cool clean clothes and delicate food and civilized talk . . . For a moment he sickened at the sour stale effluvia of the eating-house, and the rank smell of the pork which McNee had been frying. Then he cursed himself for a fool and a child.

In the fall the work on the dam was shut down, and the store was closed. The partners couldn't remove their unsaleable goods, so the whole stock was sold at junk prices among the nearest villages. Jim found himself with about three hundred dollars in the world, and the long Canadian winter to get through. The fall on the other side of the Atlantic is the pick of the year, and the beauty of the flaming hillsides did a little to revive his spirits. McNee wanted to get back to Manitoba, where he had heard of a job, and Jim decided that he would try Toronto, which was supposed to be rather more healthy for Englishmen than the other cities. So the two travelled west together, and Jim insisted on paying McNee's fare to Winnipeg, thereby leaving himself a hundred and fifty dollars or so on which to face the world.

Toronto is the friendliest place on earth for the man who knows how to make himself at home there. There were plenty to help him if he had looked for them, for nowhere will you find more warm-hearted people to the square mile. But Jim's shyness and prickliness put him outside the pale. He made no effort to advertise the few assets he had, he was desperately uncommunicative, and his self-absorption was not unnaturally taken for 'side'. Also he made the mistake of letting himself get a little too far down in the social scale. His clothes had become very shabby, and his boots were bad; when the first snows came in November he bought himself a thick overcoat, and that left him no money to supplement the rest of his wardrobe, so that by Christmas he was a very good imitation of a tramp.

He tried journalism first, but as he gave no information about himself except that he had been for a few weeks on the Montreal *Hawk*, he had some difficulty in getting a job. At last he got work on a weekly rag simply because he had some notion of grammar. It lasted exactly a fortnight. Then he tried tutoring, and spent some of his last dollars on advertising; he had several nibbles, but always fell down at the interviews. One kind of parent jibbed at his superior manners, another at his inferior clothes. After that he jolted from one temporary job to another – a book-canvasser, an extra hand in a dry-goods-store in the Christmas week, where the counter hid the deficiencies of his raiment, a temporary clerk during a municipal election, a packer in a fancy-stationery business, and finally a porter in a third-class hotel. His employment was not continuous, and between jobs he must have nearly starved. He had begun in the ordinary cheap boarding-house, but, before he found quarters in the attic of the hotel he worked at, he had sunk to a pretty squalid kind of doss-house.

The physical discomfort was bad enough. He tramped the streets ill-clad and half-fed, and saw prosperous people in furs, and cheerful young parties, and fire-lit, book-lined rooms. But the spiritual trouble was worse. Sometimes, when things were very bad, he was fortunate enough to have his thoughts narrowed down to the obtaining of food and warmth. But at other times he would be tormented by a feeling that his misfortunes were deserved, and that Fate with a heavy hand was belabouring him because he was a coward. His trouble was no longer the idiotic sense of guilt about his father's bankruptcy; it was a much more rational penitence, for he was beginning to realize that I had been right, and that he had behaved badly in running away from a plain duty. At first he choked down the thought, but all that miserable winter it grew upon him. His disasters were a direct visitation of the Almighty on one who had shown the white feather. He came to have an almost mystical feeling about it. He felt that he was branded like Cain, so that everybody knew that he had funked, and yet he realized that a rotten morbid pride ironly prevented him from retracing his steps.

The second spring found him thin from bad feeding and with a nasty cough. He had the sense to see that a summer in that hotel would be the end of him, so, although he was in the depths of hopelessness, the instinct of self-preservation drove him to make a move. He wanted to get into the country, but it was impossible to get work on a farm from Toronto, and he had no money to pay for railway fares. In the end he was taken on as a navvy on a bit of railway construction work in the wilds of northern Ontario. He was given the price of his ticket and ten dollars advance on his wages to get an outfit, and one day late in April he found himself dumped at a railhead on a blue lake, with firs, firs, as far as the eye could reach. But it was spring-time, the mating wildfowl were calling, the land was greening, and Jim drew long breaths of sweet air and felt that he was not going to die just yet.

But the camp was a roughish place, and he had no McNee to protect him. There was every kind of rough-neck and deadbeat there, and Jim was a bad mixer. He was an obvious softy and new chum and a natural butt, and, since he was being tortured all the time by his conscience, his good nature and humblemindedness were not so proof as they had been in Gaspé. His poor physical condition made him a bad workman, and he came in for a good deal of abuse as a slacker from the huskies who wrought beside him. The section boss was an Irishman called Malone with a tongue like a whiplash, and he found plenty of opportunities for practising his gift on Jim. But he was a just man, and after a bit of rough-tonguing he saw that Jim was very white about the gills and told him to show his hands. Not being accustomed to the pick, these were one mass of sores. Malone cross-examined him, found that he had been at college, and took him off construction and put him in charge of stores.

There he had an easier life, but he was more than ever the butt of the mess shack and the sleeping quarters. His crime was not only speaking with an English accent and looking like Little Willie, but being supposed to be a favourite of the boss. By and by the ragging became unbearable, and after his mug of coffee had been three times struck out of his hand at one meal, Jim lost his temper and hit out. In the fight which followed he was ridiculously outclassed. He had been fairly good at games, but he had never boxed since his private school, and it is well for Jim's kind of man to think twice before he takes on a fellow who has all his life earned his living by his muscles. But he stood up pluckily, and took a good deal of punishment before he was knocked out, and he showed no ill-will afterwards. The incident considerably improved his position. Malone, who heard of it, asked him where in God's name he had been brought up that he couldn't use his hands better, but didn't appear ill-pleased. The fight had another consequence. It gave him just a suspicion of self-confidence, and helped him on his way to the decision to which he was slowly being compelled.

A week later he was sent a hundred miles into the forest to take supplies to an advance survey party. It was something of a compliment that Malone should have picked him for the job, but Jim did not realize that. His brain was beating like a pendulum on his private trouble – that he had run away, that all his misfortunes were the punishment for his cowardice, and that, though he confessed his fault, he could not make his shrinking flesh go back. He saw England as an Eden indeed, but with angels and flaming swords at every gate. He pictured the lifted eyebrows and the shrugged shoulders as he crept into a clerk's job, with not only his father's shame on his head, but the added disgrace of his own flight. It seemed impossible a year ago to stay on in London, but now it was a thousandfold more impossible to go home.

Yet the thought gave him no peace by day or night. He had six men in his outfit, two of them half-breeds, and the journey was partly by canoe – with heavy portages – and partly on foot with the stores in pack loads. It rained in torrents, the river was in flood, and the first day they made a bare twenty miles. The half-breeds were tough old customers, but the other four were not much to bank on, and on the third day, when they had to hump their packs and foot it on a bad trail through swampy woods in a cloud of flies, they decided that they had had enough. There was a new gold area just opened not so far away, and they announced that they intended to help themselves to what they wanted from the stores and then make a bee-line for the mines. They were an ugly type of tough, and had physically the upper hand of Jim and his half-breeds.

It was a nasty situation, and it shook Jim out of his private vexations. He spoke them fair, and proposed to make camp and rest for a day to talk it out. Privately he sent one of the half-breeds ahead to the survey-party for help, while he kept his ruffians in play. Happily he had some whisky with him and he had them drinking and playing cards, which took him well into the afternoon. Then they discovered the half-breed's absence, and wouldn't believe Jim's yarn that he had gone off to find fresh meat. His only chance was to bluff high, and, since he didn't much care what happened to him, he succeeded. He went to bed that night with a tough beside him who had announced his intention of putting a bullet through his head if there was any dirty work. Sometime after midnight his messenger arrived with help, and fortunately his bedside-companion's bullet went wide. The stores, a bit depleted, were safely delivered, and when Jim got back to his bass he received a solid cursing from his boss for his defective stewardship. But Malone concluded with one of his rare compliments. 'You'll train on, sonny,' he said. 'There's guts in you for all your goo-goo face.'

That episode put an end to Jim's indecision. His time in Canada had been one long chapter of black disasters, and he was confident that they were sent to him as a punishment. His last adventure had somehow screwed up his manhood. He hated Canada like poison, but the thought of going back to England made him green with apprehension. Yet he was clear that he must do it or never have a moment's peace. So he wrote to me and told me that for a year he had been considering things, and had come to the conclusion that he had behaved like a cad. He was coming back to get into any kind of harness I directed, and would I advance him thirty pounds for his journey?

Now the little company we had put together to nurse the wreckage of Hallwards had been doing rather well. One or two things had unexpectedly turned up trumps. There was enough money to keep the maiden aunts going, and it looked as if there would be a good deal presently for Jim. He had gone off leaving no address, so I had had no means of communicating with him. I cabled him a hundred pounds, and told him to come along.

One afternoon near the end of June he turned up in my office. He had crossed the Atlantic steerage, and his clothes were those of a docker who has been months out of work. The first thing he did was to plank eighty pounds on my desk. 'You sent me too much,' he said. 'I don't want to owe more than is necessary. You can stop the twenty quid out of my wages.'

At first sight I thought him very little changed in face. He was incredibly lean and tanned and his hair wanted cutting, but he had the same shy, hunted eyes as the boy who had bolted a year before. He did not seem to have won any self-confidence, except that the set of his mouth was a little firmer.

'I want to start work at once,' he said. 'I've come home to make atonement.'

It took me a long time to make him understand the position of affairs – that he could count even now on a respectable income, and that, if he put his back into it, Hallwards might once again become a power in the City. 'I was only waiting for you to come back,' I said, 'to revive the old name. Hallwards has a better sound than the Anglo-Orient Company.'

'But I can't touch a penny,' he said. 'What about the people who suffered through the bankruptcy?'

'There were very few,' I told him. 'None of the widow-and-orphan business. The banks were amply se-cured. The chief sufferers were your aunts and yourself, and that's going to be all right now.'

He listened with wide eyes, and slowly bewilderment gave place to relief, and relief to rapture. 'The first thing you've got to do,' I said, 'is to go to your tailor and get some clothes. You'd better put up at an hotel till you can find a flat. I'll see about your club membership. If you want to play polo I'll lend you a couple of ponies. Come and dine with me tonight and tell me your story.'

'My God!' he murmured. 'Do you realize that for a year I've been on my uppers? That's my story.'

The rest of that summer Jim walked about in a happy mystification. Once he was decently dressed, I could see that Canada had improved him. He was better-looking, tougher, manlier; his shyness was now wariness and he had got a new and sounder code of values. He worked like a beaver in the office, and, though he was curiously slow and obtuse about some things, I began to see that he had his father's brains, and something, too, that old Hallward had never had, a sensitive, subtle imagination. For the rest he enjoyed himself. He came in for the end of the polo season, and he was welcomed back to his old set as if nothing had happened.

Then I ceased to see much of him. I had been over-working badly and needed a long holiday, so I went off to a Scotch deer-forest in the middle of August and did not return till the beginning of October. Jim stuck tight to the office; he said that he had had all the holidays he wanted for a year or two.

On the second day after my return he came into my room and said that he wanted to speak to me privately. He wished, he said, that nothing should be done about the restoring the name of Hallwards. He would like the Anglo-Orient to go on just as it was before he returned, and he did not want the directorship which had been arranged.

'Why in the world?' I asked in amazement.

'Because I am going away. And I may be away for quite a time.'

When I found words, and that took some time, I asked if he had grown tired of England.

'Bless you, no! I love it better than any place on earth. The autumn scents are beginning, and London is snugging down for its blessed cosy winter, and the hunting will soon be starting, and last Sunday, I heard the old cock pheasants shouting – '

'Where are you going? Canada?'

He nodded.

'Have you fallen in love with it?'

'I hate it worse than hell,' he said solemnly, and proceeded to say things which in the interests of Imperial good feeling I refrain from repeating.

'Then you must be mad!'

'No,' he said, 'I'm quite sane. It's very simple, and I've thought it all out. You know I ran away from my duty eighteen months ago. Well, I was punished for it. I was a howling failure in Canada . . . I haven't told you half . . . I pretty well starved . . . I couldn't hold down any job . . . I was simply a waif and a laughing stock. And I loathed it – my God, how I loathed it! But I couldn't come back – the very thought of facing London gave me a sick pain. It took me a year to screw up my courage to do what I knew was my manifest duty. Well, I turned up, as you know.'

'Then that's all right, isn't it?' I observed obtusely. 'You find London better than you thought?'

'I find it Paradise,' and he smiled sadly. 'But it's a Paradise I haven't deserved. You see, I made a failure in Canada and I can't let it go at that. I hate the very name of the place and most of the people in it . . . Oh, I daresay there is nothing wrong with it, but one always hates a place where one has been a fool . . . I have to go back and make good. I shall take two hundred pounds, just what I had when I first started out.'

I only stared, and he went on: 'I funked once, and that may be forgiven. But a man who funks twice is a coward. I funk Canada like the devil, and that is why I am going back. There was a man there – only one man – who said I had guts. I'm going to prove to that whole damned Dominion that I have guts, but principally I've got to prove it to myself . . . After that I'll come back to you, and we'll talk business.'

I could say nothing: indeed I didn't want to say anything. Jim was showing a kind of courage several grades ahead of old Jonah's. He had returned to Nineveh and found that it had no terrors, and was now going back to Tarshish, whales and all.

The Earlier Affection

This is another Grey Weather *story, again not reprinted since 1899. It seems to have been written while Buchan was at Oxford: it shares some matter of style, though not of content, with his first novel,* Sir Quixote, *of 1895.*

The young English boy, 'let loose from college', self-conscious, even a little conceited at first in his encounters with the strange people of Scotland, makes a useful narrator for an episode in the confusing and tragic events following the Young Pretender's defeat. The boy's highland ancestry united him with his Cameron cousins, but the atavistic forces released in fighting make a stronger bond still between opposite kinds of men – some of whose present affections, for Whiggism, money and their curious kind of Christianity, are so forcibly supplanted. The title is a reference to the Apostle Paul's 'Set your affection on things above' (Colossians III.ii).

The Earlier Affection

My host accompanied me to the foot of the fine avenue which looks from Portnacroish to the steely sea-loch. The smoke of the clachan was clear in the air, and the morn was sweet with young leaves and fresh salt breezes. For all about us were woods, till the moor dipped to the water, and then came the great shining spaces straight to the edge of Morven and the stony Ardgower Hills.

'You will understand, Mr Townshend,' said my entertainer, 'that I do not fall in with your errand. It is meet that youth should be wild, but you had been better playing your pranks about Oxford than risking your neck on our Hieland hills, and this but two years gone come Whitsuntide since the late grievous troubles. It had been better to forget your mother and give your Cameron kin the go-by, than run your craig into the same tow as Ewan's by seeking him on Brae Mamore. Stewart though I be, and proud of my name, I would think twice before I set out on such a ploy. It's likely that Ewan will be blithe to see you and no less to get your guineas, but there are easier ways of helping a friend than just to go to his hidy-hole.'

But I would have none of Mr Stewart's arguments, for my heart was hot on this fool's journey. My cousin Ewan was in the heather, with his head well-priced by his enemies and his friends dead or broken. I was little more than a boy let loose from college, and it seemed paradise itself to thus adventure my person among the wilds.

'Then if you will no take an old man's telling, here's a word for you to keep mind of on the road. There are more that have a grudge against the Cameron than King George's soldiers. Be sure there will be pickings going up Lochaber-ways, and all the Glasgow pack-men and low-country trading-bodies that have ever had their knife in Lochiel will be down on the broken house like a pack of kites. It's not impossible that ye may meet a wheen on the road, for I heard news of some going north from the Campbell country, and it bodes ill for any honest gentle-man who may foregather with the black clan. Forbye, there'll be them that will come from Glenurchy-side and Breadalbin, so see you keep a quiet tongue and a watchful eye if ye happen on strangers.'

And with this last word I had shaken his hand, turned my horse to the north, and ridden out among the trees.

The sound of sea-water was ever in my ears, for the road twined in the links of coast and crooks of hill, now dipping to the tide's edge, and now rising to a great altitude amid the heather. The morn was so fresh and shining that I fell in love with myself and my errand, and when I turned a corner and saw a wall of blue hill rise gleaming to the heavens with snow-filled corries, I cried out for the fair land I had come to, and my fine adventure.

By the time I came to Duror it was midday, and I stopped for refreshment. There is an inn in Duror, where cheese and bread and usquebagh* were to be had – fare enough for a hungry traveller. But when I was on the road again, as I turned the crook of hill by the Heugh of Ardsheal, lo! I was in the thick of a party of men.

They were five in all, dressed soberly in black and brown and grey, and riding the soberest of beasts. Mr Stewart's word rose in my memory, and I shut my mouth and composed my face to secrecy. They would not trouble me long, this covey of merchant-folk, for they would get the ferry at Ballachulish, which was not my road to Brae Mamore.

So I gave them a civil greeting, and would have ridden by, had not Fate stepped in my way. My horse shied at a stick by the roadside, and ere I knew I was jostling and scattering them trying to curb the accursed tricks of my beast.

After this there was nothing for it but to apologize, and what with my hurry and chagrin I was profuse enough. They looked at me with startled eyes, and one had drawn a pistol from his holster, but when they found I was no reiver they took the thing in decent part.

'It's a sma' maitter,' said one with a thick burr in his voice. 'The hert o' a man and the hoofs o' a horse are controlled by nane but our Makker, a my father aye said. Ye're no to blame, young sir.'

I fell into line with the odd man – for they rode in pairs, and in common civility. I could not push on through them. As I rode behind I had leisure to look at my company. All were elderly men, their ages lying perhaps between five and thirty and twoscore, and all rode with the air of townsmen out on a holiday. They talked gravely among themselves, now looking at the sky (which was clouding over, as is the fashion in a Highland April), and now casting inquiring glances towards my place at the back. The man with whom I rode was a little fellow, younger than the rest and more ruddy and frank of face. He was willing to talk, which he did in a very vile Scots accent which I had hard work to follow. His name he said was Macneil, but he knew nothing of the Highlands, for his abode was Paisley. He questioned me of myself with some curiosity.

'Oh, my name is Townshend,' said I, speaking the truth at random, 'and I have come up from England to see if the report of your mountains be true. It is a better way of seeing the world, say I, than to philander through Italy and France. I am a quiet man of modest means with a taste for the picturesque.'

'So, so,' said the little man. 'But I could show you corn-rigs by the Cart side which are better and bonnier than a wheen muckle stony hills. But every man to his taste, and doubtless since ye're an Englander, ye'll no hae seen mony brae-faces?'

Then he fell to giving me biographies of each of the travellers, and as we were some way behind the others he could speak without fear. 'The lang man in the grey coat is the Deacon o' the Glesca Fleshers*, a man o' great substance and good repute. He's lang had trouble wi' thae Hieland bodies, for when he bocht nowt frae them they wad seek a loan of maybe mair than the price, and he wad get caution on some o' their lands and cot-houses.' Deed, we're a' in that line, as ye micht say'; and he raked the horizon with his hand.

'Then ye go north to recover monies?' said I, inadver-tently.

He looked cunningly into my face, and, for a second, suspicion was large in his eyes. 'Ye're a gleg yin, Mr Townds, and maybe our errand is just no that far frae what ye mean. But, speaking o' the Deacon, he has a grand-gaun business in the Trongate, and he has been elder this sax year in the Barony, and him no forty year auld. Laidly's his name, and nane mair respeckit among the merchants o' the city. Yon ither man wi' him is a Maister Graham, whae comes frae the Menteith way, a kind o' Hielander by bluid, but wi' nae Hieland tricks in his heid. He's a sober wud-merchant at the Broomielaw, and he has come up here on a job about some fir-wuds. Losh, there's a walth o' timmer in this bit,' and he scanned greedily the shady hills.

'The twae lang red-heided men are Campbells, brithers, whae deal in yairn and wabs o' a' kind in the Saltmarket. Gin ye were wantin' the guid hamespun or the fine tartan in a' the clan colours ye wad be wise to gang there. But I'm forgetting ye dinna belang to thae pairts ava'.'

By this time the heavens had darkened to a storm and the great rain-drops were already plashing on my face. We were now round the ribs of the hill they call Sgordhonuill and close to the edge of the Leven loch. It was a desolate, wild place, and yet on the very brink of the shore amid the birk-woods we came on the inn and the ferry.

I must needs go in with the others, and if the place was better than certain hostels I had lodged in on my road – notably in the accursed land of Lorne – it was far short of the South. And yet I dare not deny the comfort, for there was a peat-fire glowing on the hearth and the odour of cooking meat was rich for hungry nostrils. Forbye, the out-of-doors was now one pour of hail-water, which darkened the evening to a murky twilight.

The men sat round the glow after supper and there was no more talk of going further. The loch was a chaos of white billows, so the ferry was out of the question; and as for me, who should have been that night in Glen Leven-side, there was never a thought of stirring in my head, but I fell into a deep contentment with the warmth and a full meal, and never cast a look to the blurred window. I had not yet spoken to the others, but comfort loosened their tongues, and soon we were all on terms of gossip. They set themselves to find out every point in my career and my intentions, and I, mindful of Mr Stewart's warning, grew as austere in manner as the Deacon himself.

'And ye say ye traivel to see the world?' said one of the Campbells. 'Man, ye've little to dae. Ye maunna be thrang at hame. If I had a son who was a drone like you, he wad never finger siller o' mine.'

'But I will shortly have a trade,' said I, 'for I shall be cutting French throats in a year, Mr Campbell, if luck favours me.'

'Hear to him,' said the grave Campbell. 'He talks of war, bloody war, as a man wad talk of a penny-wedding. Know well, young man, that I value a sodger's trade lower than a flesher-lad's, and have no respect for a bright sword and a red coat. I am for peace, but when I speak, for battle they are strong,' said he, finishing with a line from one of his Psalms*.

I sat rebuked, wishing myself well rid of this company. But I was not to be let alone, for the Deacon would play the inquisitor on the matter of my family.

'What brought ye here of a' places? There are mony pairts in the Hielands better worth seeing. Ye'll hae some freends belike, here-aways?'

I told him, 'No,' that I had few friends above the Border; but the persistent man would not be pacified. He took upon himself, as the elder, to admonish me on the faults of youth.

'Ye are but a lad,' said he with unction, 'and I wad see no ill come to ye. But the Hielands are an unsafe bit, given up to malignants and papists and black cattle. Tak your ways back, and tell your freends to thank the Lord that they see ye again.' And then he broke into a most violent abuse of the whole place, notably the parts of Appin and Lochaber. It was, he said, the last refuge of all that was vicious and wasteful in the land.

'It is at least a place of some beauty,' I broke in with.

'Beauty,' he cried scornfully, 'd'ye see beauty in black

rocks and a grummly sea? Gie me the lown fields about Lanerick, and a' the kind canty south country, and I wad let your bens and corries alane.'

And then Graham launched forth in a denunciation of the people. It was strange to hear one who bore his race writ large in his name talk of the inhabitants of these parts as liars and thieves and good-for-nothings. 'What have your Hielands done,' he cried, 'for the well-being of this land? They stir up rebellions wi' papists and the French, and harry the lands o' the god-fearing. They look down on us merchants, and turn up their hungry noses at decent men, as if cheatry were mair gentrice than honest wark. God, I wad have the lot o' them shipped to the Indies and set to earn a decent living.'

I sat still during the torrent, raging at the dull company I had fallen in with, for I was hot with youth and had little admiration for the decencies. Then the Deacon, taking a Bible from his valise, declared his intention of conducting private worship ere we retired to rest. It was a ceremony I had never dreamed of before, and in truth I cannot fancy a stranger. First the company sang a psalm with vast unction and no melody. Then the Deacon read from some prophet or other, and finally we were all on our knees while a Campbell offered up a prayer.

After that there was no thought of sitting longer, for it seemed that it was the rule of these people to make their prayers the last article in the day. They lay and snored in their comfortless beds, while I, who preferred the safety of a chair to the unknown dangers of such bedding, dozed uneasily before the peats till the grey April morning.

Dawn came in with a tempest, and when the household was stirring and we had broken our fast, a storm from the north-west was all but tearing the roof from above our heads. Without, the loch was a chasm of mist and white foam, and waves broke hoarsely over the shore-road. The landlord, who was also the ferryman, ran about, crying the impossibility of travel. No boat could live a moment in that water, and unless our honours would go round the loch-head into Mamore there was nothing for it but to kick our heels in the public.

The merchants conferred darkly among themselves, and there was much shaking of heads. Then the Dean came up to me with a long face.

'There's nothing for't,' said he, 'but to risk the loch-head and try Wade's road to Fort William. I dinna mind if that was to be your way, Mr Townds, but it maun be ours, for our business winna wait; so if you're so inclined, we'll be glad o' your company.'

Heavens knows I had no further desire for theirs, but I dared not evade. Once in the heart of Brae Mamore I would find means to give them the slip and find the herd's shieling I had been apprised of, where I might get shelter and news of Ewan. I accepted with as cordial a tone as I could muster, and we set out into the blinding weather.

The road runs up the loch by the clachan of Ballachulish, fords the small stream of Coe which runs down from monstrous precipices, and then, winding round the base of the hill they call Pap of Glencoe, comes fairly into Glen Levin. A more desert place I have not seen. On all sides rose scarred and ragged hills; below, the loch gleamed dully like lead; and the howling storm shook the lone fir-trees and dazed our eyes with wrack. The merchants pulled their cloak-capes over their heads and set themselves manfully to the toil, but it was clear not to their stomach, for they said scarcely a word to themselves or me. Only Macneil kept a good temper, but his words were whistled away into the wind.

All the way along that dreary brae-face we were slipping and stumbling cruelly. The men had poor skill in guiding a horse, for though they were all well-grown fellows they had the look of those who are better used to bare-leg, rough-foot walking than to stirrup and saddle. Once I had to catch the Deacon's rein and pull him up on the path, or without doubt he would soon have been feeding the ravens at the foot of Corrynakeigh. He thanked me with a grumble, and I saw how tight-drawn were his lips and eyebrows. The mist seemed to get into my brain, and I wandered befogged and foolish in this unknown land. It was the most fantastic misery: underfoot wet rock and heather, on all sides grey dripping veils of rain, and no sound to cheer save a hawk's scream or the crying of an old blackcock from the height, while down in the glen-bottom there was the hoarse roaring of torrents.

And then all of a sudden from the darkness there sprang out a gleam of scarlet, and we had stumbled on a party of soldiers. Some twenty in all, they were marching slowly down the valley, and at the sight of us they grew at once alert. We were seized and questioned till they had assured themselves of our credentials. The merchants they let go at once, but I seemed to stick in their throat.

'What are you after, sir, wandering at such a season north of the Highland line?' the captain of them kept asking.

When I told him my tale of seeking the picturesque he would not believe it, till I lost all patience under the treatment.

'Confound it, sir,' I cried, 'is my speech like that of a renegade Scots Jacobite? I thought my English tongue sufficient surety. And if you ask for a better you have to find some decent military headquarters where they will tell you that Arthur Townshend is gazetted ensign in the King's own regiment and will proceed within six months to service abroad.'

When I had talked him over, the man made an apology of a sort, but he still looked dissatisfied. Then he turned roundly on us. 'Do you know young Fassiefern?' he asked.

My companions disclaimed any knowledge save by repute, and even I had the grace to lie stoutly.

'If I thought you were friends of Ewan Cameron,' said he, 'you should go no further. It's well known that he lies in hiding in these hills, and this day he is to be routed out and sent to the place he deserves. If you meet a dark man of the middle size with two-three ragged Highlanders at his back, you will know that you have foregathered with Ewan Cameron and that King George's men will not be far behind him.'

Then the Deacon unloosed the bands of his tongue and spoke a homily. 'What have I to dae,' he cried, 'with the graceless breed of the Camerons? If I saw this Ewan of Fassiefern on the bent then I wad be as hot to pursue him as any redcoat. Have I no suffered from him and his clan, and wad I no gladly see every yin o' them clapped in the Tolbooth?' And with the word he turned to a Campbell for approval and received a fierce nod of his red head.

'I must let you pass, sirs,' said the captain, 'but if you would keep out of harm's way you will go back to the Levin shore. Ewan's days of freedom are past, and he will be hemmed in by my men here and a like party from Fort William in front, and outflanked on both sides by other companies. I speak to you as honest gentlemen, and I bid you keep a good watch for the Cameron, if you would be in good grace with the King.' And without more ado he bade his men march.

Our company after this meeting was very glum for a mile or two. The Deacon's ire had been roused by the hint of suspicion, and he grumbled to himself till his anger found vent in a free cursing of the whole neighbourhood and its people. 'Deil take them,' he cried, 'and shame that I should say it, but it's a queer bit where an honest man canna gang his ways without a red-coated sodger casting een at him.' And Graham joined his plaint, till the whole gang lamented like a tinker's funeral.

It was now about midday, and the weather, if aught, had grown fiercer. The mist was clearing, but blasts of chill snow drove down on our ears, and the strait pass before us was grey with the fall. In front lay the sheer mountains, the tangle of loch and broken rocks where Ewan lay hid, and into the wilderness ran our bridle-path. Somewhere on the hillside were sentries, somewhere on the road before us was a troop of soldiers, and between them my poor cousin was fairly enclosed. I felt a sort of madness in my brain, as I thought of his fate. Here was I in the company of Whig traders, with no power to warn him, but going forward to see his capture.

A desperate thought struck me, and I slipped from my horse and made to rush into the bowels of the glen. Once there I might climb unseen up the pass, and get far enough in advance to warn him of his danger. My seeing him would be the wildest chance, yet I might take it. But as I left the path I caught a tree-root and felt my heels dangle in the void. That way lay sheer precipice. With a quaking heart I pulled myself up, and made my excuse of an accident as best I could to my staring companions.

Yet the whole pass was traversed without a sight of a human being. I watched every moment to see the troop of redcoats with Ewan in their grip. But no redcoats came; only fresh gusts of snow and the same dreary ribs of hill.

Soon we had left the pass and were out on a windy neck of mountain where hags and lochans gloomed among the heather.

And then suddenly as if from the earth there sprang up three men. Even in the mist I saw the red Cameron tartan, and my heart leapt to my mouth. Two were great stalwart men, their clothes drenched and ragged, and the rust on their weapons. But the third was clearly the gentleman – of the middle size, slim, dressed well though also in some raggedness. At the sight the six of us stopped short and gazed dumbly at the three on the path.

I rushed forward and gripped my cousin's hand. 'Ewan,' I cried, 'I am your cousin Townshend come north to put his back to yours. Thank God you are still unharmed'; and what with weariness and anxiety I had almost wept on his neck.

At my first step my cousin had raised his pistol, but when he saw my friendliness he put it back in his belt. When he heard of my cousinship his eyes shone with kindliness, and he bade me welcome to his own sorry country. 'My dear cousin,' he said, 'you have found me in a perilous case and ill-fitted to play the host. But I bid you welcome for a most honest gentleman and kinsman to these few acres of heather that are all now left to me.'

And then before the gaping faces of my comrades I stammered out my story. 'Oh, Ewan, there's death before and behind you and on all sides. There's a troop waiting down the road and there are dragoons coming at your back. You cannot escape, and these men with me are Whigs and Glasgow traders and no friends to the Cameron name.'

The three men straightened themselves like startled deer.

'How many passed you?' cried Ewan.

'May be a score,' said I.

He stopped for a while in deep thought.

'Then there's not above a dozen behind me. There are four of us here, true men, and five who are no. We must go back or forward, for a goat could not climb these craigs. Well-a-day, my cousin, if we had your five whiggishly-inclined gentlemen with us we might yet make a fight of it.' And he bit his lip and looked doubtfully at the company.

'We will fight nane,' said the Deacon. 'We are men o' peace, traivelling to further our lawful calling. Are we to dip our hands in bluid to please a Hieland Jaicobite?' The two Campbells groaned in acquiescence, but I thought I saw a glint of something not peaceful in Graham's eye.

'But ye are Scots folk,' said Ewan, with a soft, wheedling note in his voice. 'Ye will never see a countryman fall into the hands of redcoat English soldiers?'

'It's the law o' the land,' said a Campbell, 'and what for should we resist it to pleesure you? Besides, we are merchants and no fechtin' tinklers.'

I saw Ewan turn his head and look down the road. Far off in the stillness of the grey weather one could hear the sound of feet on the hill-gravel.

'Gentlemen,' he cried, turning to them with a last appeal, 'you see I have no way of escape. You are all proper men, and I beseech you in God's name to help a poor gentleman in his last extremity. If I could win past the gentry in front, there would be the seacoast straight before, where even now there lies a vessel to take me to a kinder country. I cannot think that loyalty to my clan and kin should be counted an offence in eyes of honest men. I do not know whether you are Highland or Lowland, but you are at least men, and may God do to you as you do to me this day. Who will stand with me?'

I sprang to his side, and the four of us stood looking down the road, where afar off came into sight the moving shapes of the foe.

Then he turned again to the others, crying out a word in Gaelic. I do not know what it was, but it must have gone to their hearts' core, for the little man Macneil with a sob came running toward us, and Graham took one step forward and then stopped.

I whispered their names in Ewan's ear and he smiled. Again he spoke in Gaelic, and this time Graham could forbear no more, but with an answering word in the same tongue he flung himself from his horse and came to our side. The two red-headed Campbells stared in some perplexity, their eyes bright with emotion and their hands twitching towards their belts.

Meantime the sound of men came nearer and the game grew desperate. Again Ewan cried in Gaelic, and this time it was low entreaty, which to my ignorant ears sounded with great pathos. The men looked at the Deacon and at us, and then with scarlet faces they too dropped to the ground and stepped to our backs.

Out of the mist came a line of dark weather-browned faces and the gleam of bright coats. 'Will you not come?' Ewan cried to the Deacon.

'I will see no blood shed,' said the man, with set lips.

And then there was the sharp word of command, and ere ever I knew, the rattle of shots; and the next moment we were rushing madly down on the enemy.

I have no clear mind of what happened. I know that the first bullet passed through my coat-collar and a second grazed my boot. I heard one of the Highlanders cry out and clap his hand to his ear, and then we were at death-grips. I used my sword as I could, but I had better have had a dirk, for we were wrestling for dear life, and there was no room for fine play. I saw dimly the steel of Ewan and the Highlanders gleam in the rain; I heard Graham roaring like a bull as he caught at the throat of an opponent. And then all was mist and madness and a great horror. I fell over a little brink of rock with a man a-top of me, and there we struggled till I choked the life out of him. After that I remember nothing till I saw the air clear and the road vacant before us.

Two bodies lay on the heath, besides the one I had accounted for in the hollow. The rest of the soldiers had fled down the pass, and Ewan had his way of escape plain to see. But never have I seen such a change in men. My cousin's coat was red and torn, his shoes all but cut from his feet. A little line of blood trickled over his flushed brow, but he never heeded it, for his eyes burned with the glory of battle. So, too, with his followers, save that one had a hole in his ear and the other a broken arm, which they minded as little as midge-bites. But how shall I tell of my companions? The two Campbells sat on the ground nursing wounds, with wild red hair dishevelled and hoarse blasphemy on their lips. Every now and then one would raise his head and cry some fierce word of triumph. Graham had a gash on his cheek, but he was bending sword-point on the ground and calling Ewan his blood-brother. The little man Macneil, who had fought like a Trojan, was whimpering with excitement, rubbing his eyes, and staring doubtfully at the heavens. But the Deacon, that man of peace – what shall I say of him? He stood some fifty yards down the pass, peering through the mist at the routed fugitives, his naked sword red in his hand, his whole apparel a ruin of blood and mire, his neatly dressed hair flying like a beldame's. There he stood hurling the maddest oaths. 'Hell!' he cried. 'Come back and I'll learn ye, my lads. Wait on, and I'll thraw every neck and give the gleds a feed this day.'

Ewan came up and embraced me. 'Your Whigamores are the very devil, cousin, and have been the saving of me. But now we are all in the same boat, so we had better improve our time. Come, lads!' he cried, 'is it for the seashore and a kinder land?'

And all except the Deacon cried out in Gaelic the word of consent, which, being interpreted, is 'Lead and we follow.'

The Wind in the Portico

'*The Wind in the Portico*' *appeared for the first time in* The Runagates Club. *It is prefaced by a characteristic remark by Richard Hannay, the South African mining engineer and soldier, whose lack of imagination is obvious. He is corrected by 'Peckwether the historian' and Nightingale, another academic, who are susceptible to forces that Hannay cannot dream of.*

Buchan was a classicist before he was anything else, and he remained one all his life. In 'The Wind in the Portico' he sets up a contrast between Theocritus, the first pastoral writer, and the events that are appearing in the English Shropshire countryside, clearly not a hundred miles from the old Roman Uriconium (the modern Wroxeter).

The Wind in the Portico

HENRY NIGHTINGALE'S STORY

A dry wind of the high places . . . not to fan nor to cleanse, even a full wind from those places shall come unto me.

JEREMIAH IV. xi–xii

Nightingale was a hard man to draw. His doings with the Bedawin had become a legend, but he would as soon have talked about them as claimed to have won the war. He was a slim dark fellow about thirty-five years of age, very short-sighted, and wearing such high-powered double glasses that it was impossible to tell the colour of his eyes. This weakness made him stoop a little and peer, so that he was the strangest figure to picture in a burnous* leading an army of desert tribesmen. I fancy his power came partly from his oddness, for his followers thought that the hand of Allah had been laid on him, and partly from his quick imagination and his flawless courage. After the war he had gone back to his Cambridge fellowship, declaring that, thank God, that chapter in his life was over.

As I say, he never mentioned the deeds which had made him famous. He knew his own business, and probably realized that to keep his mental balance he had to drop the curtain on what must have been the most nerve-racking four years ever spent by man. We respected his decision and kept off Arabia. It was a remark of Hannay's that drew from him the following story. Hannay was talking about his Cotswold house, which was on the Fosse Way, and saying that it always puzzled him how so elaborate a civilization as Roman Britain could have been destroyed so utterly and left no mark on the national history beyond a few roads and ruins and place-names. Peckwether, the historian, demurred, and had a good deal to say about how much the Roman tradition was woven into the Saxon culture. 'Rome only sleeps,' he said; 'she never dies.'

Nightingale nodded. 'Sometimes she dreams in her sleep and talks. Once she scared me out of my senses.'

After a good deal of pressing he produced this story. He was not much of a talker, so he wrote it out and read it to us.

There is a place in Shropshire which I do not propose to visit again. It lies between Ludlow and the hills, in a shallow valley full of woods. Its name in St Sant, a village with a big house and park adjoining, on a stream called the Vaun, about five miles from the little town of Faxeter. They have queer names in those parts, and other things queerer than the names.

I was motoring from Wales to Cambridge at the close of the long vacation. All this happened before the war, when I had just got my fellowship and was settling down to academic work. It was a fine night in early October, with a full moon, and I intended to push on to Ludlow for supper and bed. The time was about half-past eight, the road was empty and good going, and I was trundling pleasantly along when something went wrong with my headlights. It was a small thing, and I stopped to remedy it beyond a village and just at the lodge-gates of a house.

On the opposite side of the road a carrier's cart had drawn up, and two men, who looked like indoor servants, were lifting some packages from it on to a big barrow. The moon was up, so I didn't need the feeble light of the carrier's lamp to see what they were doing. I suppose I wanted to stretch my legs for a moment, for when I had finished my job I strolled over to them. They did not hear me coming, and the carrier on his perch seemed to be asleep.

The packages were the ordinary consignment from some big shop in town. But I noticed that the two men handled them very gingerly, and that, as each was laid in the barrow, they clipped off the shop label and affixed one of their own. The new labels were odd things, large and square, with some address written on them in very black capital letters. There was nothing in that, but the men's faces puzzled me. For they seemed to do their job in a fever, longing to get it over and yet in a sweat lest they should make some mistake. Their commonplace task seemed to be for them a matter of tremendous importance. I moved so as to get a view of their faces, and I saw that they were white and strained. The two were of the butler or valet class, both elderly, and I could have sworn that they were labouring under something like fear.

I shuffled my feet to let them know of my presence and remarked that it was a fine night. They started as if they had been robbing a corpse. One of them mumbled something in reply, but the other caught a package which was slipping and in a tone of violent alarm growled to his mate to be careful. I had a notion that they were handling explosives.

I had no time to waste, so I pushed on. That night, in my room at Ludlow, I had the curiosity to look up my map and identify the place where I had seen the men. The village was St Sant, and it appeared that the gate I had stopped at belonged to a considerable demesne called Vauncastle. That was my first visit.

At that time I was busy on a critical edition of Theocritus, for which I was making a new collation of the manuscripts. There was a variant of the Medicean Codex* in England, which nobody had seen since Gaisford*, and after a good deal of trouble I found that it was in the library of a man called Dubellay. I wrote to him at his London club, and got a reply to my surprise from Vauncastle Hall, Faxeter. It was an odd letter, for you could see that he longed to tell me to go to the devil, but couldn't quite reconcile it with his conscience. We exchanged several letters, and the upshot was that he gave me permission to examine his manuscript. He did not ask me to stay, but mentioned that there was a comfortable little inn in St Sant.

My second visit began on the 27th of December, after I had been home for Christmas. We had had a week of severe frost, and then it had thawed a little; but it remained bitterly cold, with leaden skies that threatened snow. I drove from Faxeter, and as we ascended the valley I remember thinking that it was a curiously sad country. The hills were too low to be impressive, and their outlines were mostly blurred with woods; but the tops showed clear, funny little knolls of grey bent that suggested a volcanic origin. It might have been one of those backgrounds you find in Italian primitives, with all the light and colour left out. When I got a glimpse of the Vaun in the bleached meadows it looked like the 'wan water' of the Border ballads. The woods, too, had not the friendly bareness of English copses in winter-time. They remained dark and cloudy, as if they were hiding secrets. Before I reached St Sant, I decided that the landscape was not only sad, but ominous.

I was fortunate in my inn. In the single street of one-storeyed cottages it rose like a lighthouse, with a cheery glow from behind the red curtains of the bar parlour. The inside proved as good as the outside. I found a bedroom with a bright fire, and I dined in a wainscoted room full of preposterous old pictures of lanky hounds and hollow-backed horses. I had been rather depressed on my journey, but my spirits were raised by this comfort, and when the house produced a most respectable bottle of port I had the landlord in to drink a glass. He was an ancient man who had been a gamekeeper, with a much younger wife, who was responsible for the management. I was curious to hear something about the owner of my manuscript, but I got little from the landlord. He had been with the old squire, and had never served the present one. I heard of Dubellays in plenty – the landlord's master, who had hunted his own hounds for forty years, the Major his brother, who had fallen at Abu Klea; Parson Jack, who had had the living till he died, and of all kinds of collaterals. The 'Deblays' had been a high-spirited, open-handed stock, and much liked in the place. But of the present master of the Hall he could or would tell me nothing. The Squire was a 'great scholar', but I gathered that he followed no sport and was not a convivial soul like his predecessors. He had spent a mint of money on the house, but not many people went there. He, the landlord, had never been inside the grounds in the new master's time, though in the old days there had been hunt break-fasts on the lawn for the whole countryside, and mighty tenantry dinners. I went to bed with a clear picture in my mind of the man I was to interview on the morrow. A scholarly and autocratic recluse, who collected treasures and beautified his dwelling and probably lived in his library. I rather looked forward to meeting him, for the bonhomous sporting squire was not much in my line.

After breakfast next morning I made my way to the Hall. It was the same leaden weather, and when I entered the gates the air seemed to grow bitterer and the skies darker. The place was muffled in great trees which even in their winter bareness made a pall about it. There was a long avenue of ancient sycamores, through which one caught only rare glimpses of the frozen park. I took my bearings, and realized that I was walking nearly due south, and was gradually descending. The house must be in a hollow. Presently the trees thinned, I passed through an iron gate, came out on a big untended lawn, untidily studded with laurels and rhododendrons, and there before me was the house front.

I had expected something beautiful – an old Tudor or Queen Anne façade or a dignified Georgian portico. I was disappointed, for the front was simply mean. It was low and irregular, more like the back parts of a house, and I guessed that at some time or another the building had been turned round, and the old kitchen door made the chief entrance. I was confirmed in my conclusion by observing that the roofs rose in tiers, like one of those recessed New York skyscrapers, so that the present back parts of the building were of an impressive height.

The oddity of the place interested me, and still more its dilapidation. What on earth could the owner have spent his money on? Everything – lawn, flower-beds, paths – was neglected. There was a new stone doorway, but the walls badly needed pointing, the window woodwork had not been painted for ages, and there were several broken panes. The bell did not ring, so I was reduced to hammering on the knocker, and it must have been ten minutes before the door opened. A pale butler, one of the men I had seen at the carrier's cart the October before, stood blinking in the entrance.

He led me in without question, when I gave my name, so I was evidently expected. The hall was my second surprise. What had become of my picture of the collector? The place was small and poky, and furnished as barely as the lobby of a farmhouse. The only thing I approved was its warmth. Unlike most English country houses there seemed to be excellent heating arrangements.

I was taken into a little dark room with one window that looked out on a shrubbery, while the man went to fetch his master. My chief feeling was of gratitude that I had not been asked to stay, for the inn was paradise compared with this sepulchre. I was examining the prints on the wall, when I heard my name spoken and turned round to greet Mr Dubellay.

He was my third surprise. I had made a portrait in my mind of a fastidious old scholar, with eye-glasses on a black cord, and a finical *weltkind*-ish manner. Instead I found a man still in his early middle age, a heavy fellow dressed in the roughest country tweeds. He was as untidy as his demesne, for he had not shaved that morning, his flannel collar was badly frayed, and his fingernails would have been the better for a scrubbing brush. His face was hard to describe. It was high-coloured, but the colour was not healthy; it was friendly, but it was also wary; above all, it was *unquiet*. He gave me the impression of a man whose nerves were all wrong, and who was perpetually on his guard.

He said a few civil words, and thrust a badly tied brown paper parcel at me.

'That's your manuscript,' he said jauntily.

I was staggered. I had expected to be permitted to collate the codex in his library, and in the last few minutes had realized that the prospect was distasteful. But here was this casual owner offering me the priceless thing to take away.

I stammered my thanks, and added that it was very good of him to trust a stranger with such a treasure.

'Only as far as the inn,' he said. 'I wouldn't like to send it by post. But there's no harm in your working at it at the inn. There should be confidence among scholars.' And he gave an odd cackle of a laugh.

'I greatly prefer your plan,' I said. 'But I thought you would insist on my working at it here.'

'No, indeed,' he said earnestly. 'I shouldn't think of such a thing . . . Wouldn't do at all . . . An insult to our freemasonry . . . That's how I should regard it.'

We had a few minutes' further talk. I learned that he had inherited under the entail from a cousin, and had been just over ten years at Vauncastle. Before that he had been a London solicitor. He asked me a question or two about Cambridge – wished he had been at the University – much hampered in his work by a defective education. I was a Greek scholar? – Latin, too, he presumed. Wonderful people the Romans . . . He spoke quite freely, but all the time his queer restless eyes were darting about, and I had a strong impression that he would have liked to say something to me very different from these commonplaces – that he was longing to broach some subject but was held back by shyness or fear. He had such an odd appraising way of looking at me.

I left without his having asked me to a meal, for which I was not sorry, for I did not like the atmosphere of the place. I took a short cut over the ragged lawn, and turned at the top of the slope to look back. The house was in reality a huge pile, and I saw that I had been right and that the main building was all at the back. Was it, I wondered, like the Alhambra, which behind a front like a factory concealed a treasure-house? I saw, too, that the woodland hollow was more spacious than I had fancied. The house, as at present arranged, faced due north, and behind the south front was an open space in which I guessed that a lake might lie. Far beyond I could see in the December dimness the lift of high dark hills.

That evening the snow came in earnest, and fell continuously for the better part of two days. I banked up the fire in my bedroom and spent a happy time with the codex. I had brought only my working boots with me and the inn boasted no library, so when I wanted to relax I went down to the taproom, or gossiped with the landlady in the bar parlour. The yokels who congregated in the former were pleasant fellows, but, like all the folk on the Marches, they did not talk readily to a stranger and I heard little from them of the Hall. The old squire had reared every year three thousand pheasants, but the present squire would not allow a gun to be fired on his land and there were only a few wild birds left. For the same reason the woods were thick with vermin. This they told me when I professed an interest in shooting. But of Mr Dubellay they would not speak, declaring that they never saw him. I daresay they gossiped wildly about him, and their public reticence struck me as having in it a touch of fear.

The landlady who came from a different part of the shire, was more communicative. She had not known the former Dubellays and so had no standard of comparison, but she was inclined to regard the present squire as not quite right in the head. 'They do say,' she would begin, but she, too, suffered from some inhibition, and what promised to be sensational would tail off into the commonplace. One thing apparently puzzled the neighbourhood above others, and that was his rearrangement of the house. 'They do say,' she said in an awed voice, 'that he have built a great church.' She had never visited it – no one in the parish had, for Squire Dubellay did not allow intruders – but from Lyne Hill you could see it through a gap in the woods. 'He's no good Christian,' she told me, 'and him and Vicar has quarrelled this many a day. But they do say as he worships summat there.' I learned that there were no women servants in the house, only the men he had brought from London. 'Poor benighted souls, they must live in a sad hobble,' and the buxom lady shrugged her shoulders and giggled.

On the last day of December I decided that I needed exercise and must go for a long stride. The snow had ceased that morning, and the dull skies had changed to a clear blue. It was still very cold, but the sun was shining, the snow was firm and crisp underfoot, and I proposed to survey the country. So after luncheon I put on thick boots and gaiters, and made for Lyne Hill. This meant a considerable circuit, for the place lay south of the Vauncastle park. From it I hoped to get a view of the other side of the house.

I was not disappointed. There was a rift in the thick woodlands, and below me, two miles off, I suddenly saw a strange building, like a classical temple. Only the entablature and the tops of the pillars showed above the trees, but they stood out vivid and dark against the background of snow. The spectacle in that lonely place was so startling that for a little I could only stare. I remember that I glanced behind me to the snowy line of the Welsh mountains, and felt that I might have been looking at a winter view of the Apennines two thousand years ago.

My curiosity was now alert, and I determined to get a nearer view of this marvel. I left the track and ploughed through the snowy fields down to the skirts of the woods. After that my trouble began. I found myself in a very good imitation of a primeval forest, where the undergrowth had been unchecked and the rides uncut for years. I sank into deep pits, I was savagely torn by briars and brambles, but

I struggled on, keeping a line as best I could. At last the trees stopped. Before me was a flat expanse which I knew must be a lake, and beyond rose the temple.

It ran the whole length of the house, and from where I stood it was hard to believe that there were buildings at its back where men dwelt. It was a fine piece of work – the first glance told me that – admirably proportioned, classical, yet not following exactly any of the classical models. One could imagine a great echoing interior dim with the smoke of sacrifice, and it was only by reflecting that I realized that the peristyle could not be continued down the two sides, that there was no interior, and that what I was looking at was only a portico.

The thing was at once impressive and preposterous. What madness had been in Dubellay when he embellished his house with such a grandiose garden front? The sun was setting and the shadow of the wooded hills darkened the interior, so I could not even make out the back wall of the porch. I wanted a nearer view, so I embarked on the frozen lake.

Then I had an odd experience. I was not tired, the snow lay level and firm, but I was conscious of extreme weariness. The biting air had become warm and oppressive. I had to drag boots that seemed to weigh tons across that lake. The place was utterly silent in the stricture of the frost, and from the pile in front no sign of life came.

I reached the other side at last and found myself in a frozen shallow of bulrushes and skeleton willow-herbs. They were taller than my head, and to see the house I had to look upward through their snowy traceries. It was perhaps eighty feet above me and a hundred yards distant, and, since I was below it, the delicate pillars seemed to spring to a great height. But it was still dusky, and the only detail I could see was on the ceiling, which seemed either to be carved or painted with deeply shaded monochrome figures.

Suddenly the dying sun came slanting through the gap in the hills, and for an instant the whole portico to its farthest recesses was washed in clear gold and scarlet. That was wonderful enough, but there was something more. The air was utterly still with not the faintest breath of wind – so still that when I had lit a cigarette half an hour before the flame of the match had burned steadily upward like a candle in a room. As I stood among the sedges not a single frost crystal stirred . . . But there was a wind blowing in the portico.

I could see it lifting feathers of snow from the base of the pillars and fluffing the cornices. The floor had already been swept clean, but tiny flakes drifted on to it from the exposed edges. The interior was filled with a furious movement, though a yard from it was frozen peace. I felt nothing of the action of the wind, but I knew that it was hot, hot as the breath of a furnace.

I had only one thought, dread of being overtaken by night near that place. I turned and ran. Ran with labouring steps across the lake, panting and stifling with a deadly hot oppression, ran blindly by a sort of instinct in the direction of the village. I did not stop till I had wrestled through the big wood, and come out on some rough pasture above the highway. Then I dropped on the ground, and felt again the comforting chill of the December air.

The adventure left me in an uncomfortable mood. I was ashamed of myself for playing the fool, and at the same time hopelessly puzzled, for the oftener I went over in my mind the incidents of that afternoon the more I was at a loss for an explanation. One feeling was uppermost, that I did not like this place and wanted to be out of it. I had already broken the back of my task, and by shutting myself up for two days I completed it; that is to say, I made my collation as far as I had advanced myself in my commentary on the text. I did not want to go back to the Hall, so I wrote a civil note to Dubellay, expressing my gratitude and saying that I was sending up the manuscript by the landlord's son, as I scrupled to trouble him with another visit.

I got a reply at once, saying that Mr Dubellay would like to give himself the pleasure of dining with me at the inn before I went, and would receive the manuscript in person.

It was the last night of my stay in St Sant, so I ordered the best dinner the place could provide, and a magnum of claret, of which I discovered a bin in the cellar. Dubellay appeared promptly at eight o'clock, arriving to my surprise in a car. He had tidied himself up and put on a dinner jacket, and he looked exactly like the city solicitors you see dining in the Junior Carlton.

He was in excellent spirits, and his eyes had lost their air of being on guard. He seemed to have reached some conclusion about me, or decided that I was harmless. More, he seemed to be burning to talk to me. After my adventure I was prepared to find fear in him, the fear I had seen in the faces of the men servants. But there was none; instead there was excitement, overpowering excitement.

He neglected the courses in his verbosity. His coming to dinner had considerably startled the inn, and instead of a maid the landlady herself waited on us. She seemed to want to get the meal over, and hustled the biscuits and the port on to the table as soon as she decently could. Then Dubellay became confidential.

He was an enthusiast, it appeared, an enthusiast with a

single hobby. All his life he had pottered among anti-
quities, and when he succeeded to Vauncastle he had the
leisure and money to indulge himself. The place, it
seemed, had been famous in Roman Britain – Vauni
Castra – and Faxeter was a corruption of the same. 'Who
was Vaunus?' I asked. He grinned, and told me to wait.

There had been an old temple up in the high woods.
There had always been a local legend about it, and the
place was supposed to be haunted. Well, he had had the
site excavated and he had found – Here he became the
cautious solicitor, and explained to me the law of treasure
trove. As long as the objects found were not intrinsically
valuable, not gold or jewels, the finder was entitled to
keep them. He had done so – had not published the results
of his excavations in the proceedings of any learned
society – did not want to be bothered by tourists. I was
different, for I was a scholar.

What had he found? It was really rather hard to follow
his babbling talk, but I gathered that he had found certain
carvings and sacrificial implements. And – he sunk his
voice – most important of all, an altar, an altar of Vaunus,
the tutelary deity of the vale.

When he mentioned this word his face took on a new
look – not of fear but of secrecy, a kind of secret
excitement. I have seen the same look on the face of a
street-preaching Salvationist.

Vaunus had been a British god of the hills, whom the
Romans in their liberal way appear to have identified with
Apollo. He gave me a long confused account of him,
from which it appeared that Mr Dubellay was not an exact
scholar. Some of his derivations of place-names were
absurd – like St Sant from Sancta Sanctorum – and in
quoting a line of Ausonius he made two false quantities.
He seemed to hope that I could tell him something more

about Vaunus, but I said that my subject was Greek, and that I was deeply ignorant about Roman Britain. I mentioned several books, and found that he had never heard of Haverfield*.

One word he used, 'hypocaust', which suddenly gave me a clue. He must have heated the temple, as he heated his house, by some very efficient system of hot air. I know little about science, but I imagined that the artificial heat of the portico, as contrasted with the cold outside, might create an air current. At any rate that explanation satisfied me, and my afternoon's adventure lost its uncanniness. The reaction made me feel friendly towards him, and I listened to his talk with sympathy, but I decided not to mention that I had visited his temple.

He told me about it himself in the most open way. 'I couldn't leave the altar on the hillside,' he said, 'I had to make a place for it, so I turned the old front of the house into a sort of temple. I got the best advice, but architects are ignorant people, and I often wished I had been a better scholar. Still the place satisfies me.'

'I hope it satisfies Vaunus,' I said jocularly.

'I think so,' he replied quite seriously, and then his thoughts seemed to go wandering, and for a minute or so he looked through me with a queer abstraction in his eyes.

'What do you do with it now you've got it?' I asked.

He didn't reply, but smiled to himself.

'I don't know if you remember a passage in Sidonius Apollinaris*,' I said, 'a formula for consecrating pagan altars to Christian uses. You begin by sacrificing a white cock or something suitable, and tell Apollo with all friendliness that the old dedication is off for the present. Then you have a Christian invocation – '

He nearly jumped out of his chair.

'That wouldn't do – wouldn't do at all! . . . Oh Lord, no! . . . Couldn't think of it for one moment!'

It was as if I had offended his ears by some horrid blasphemy, and the odd thing was that he never recovered his composure. He tried, for he had good manners, but his ease and friendliness had gone. We talked stiffly for another half-hour about trifles, and then he rose to leave. I returned him his manuscript neatly parcelled up, and expanded in thanks, but he scarcely seemed to heed me. He stuck the thing in his pocket, and departed with the same air of shocked absorption.

After he had gone I sat before the fire and reviewed the situation. I was satisfied with my hypocaust theory, and had no more perturbation in my memory about my afternoon's adventure. Yet a slight flavour of unpleasantness hung about it, and I felt that I did not quite like Dubellay. I set him down as a crank who had tangled himself up with a half-witted hobby, like an old maid with her cats, and I was not sorry to be leaving the place.

My third and last visit to St Sant was in the following June – the midsummer of 1914. I had all but finished my Theocritus, but I needed another day or two with the Vauncastle manuscript, and, as I wanted to clear the whole thing off before I went to Italy in July, I wrote to Dubellay and asked if I might have another sight of it. The thing was a bore, but it had to be faced, and I fancied that the valley would be a pleasant place in that hot summer.

I got a reply at once, inviting, almost begging me to come, and insisting that I should stay at the Hall. I couldn't very well refuse, though I would have preferred the inn. He wired about my train, and wired again saying he would meet me. This time I seemed to be a particularly welcome guest.

I reached Faxeter in the evening, and was met by a car from a Faxeter garage. The driver was a talkative young man, and, as the car was a closed one, I sat beside him for the sake of fresh air. The term had tired me, and I was glad to get out of stuffy Cambridge, but I cannot say that I found it much cooler as we ascended the Vaun valley. The woods were in their summer magnificence but a little dulled and tarnished by the heat, the river was shrunk to a trickle, and the curious hill-tops were so scorched by the sun that they seemed almost yellow above the green of the trees. Once again I had the feeling of a landscape fantastically un-English.

'Squire Dubellay's been in a great way about your coming, sir,' the driver informed me. 'Sent down three times to the boss to make sure it was all right. He's got a car of his own, too, a nice little Daimler, but he don't seem to use it much. Haven't seen him about in it for a month of Sundays.'

As we turned in at the Hall gates he looked curiously about him. 'Never been here before, though I've been in most gentlemen's parks for fifty miles round. Rum old-fashioned spot, isn't it, sir?'

If it had seemed a shuttered sanctuary in midwinter, in that June twilight it was more than ever a place enclosed and guarded. There was almost an autumn smell of decay, a dry decay like touchwood. We seemed to be descending through layers of ever-thickening woods. When at last we turned through the iron gate I saw that the lawns had reached a further stage of neglect, for they were as shaggy as a hayfield.

The white-faced butler let me in, and there, waiting at his back, was Dubellay. But he was not the man whom I had seen in December. He was dressed in an old baggy suit of flannels and his unwholesome red face was painfully drawn and sunken. There were dark pouches under his eyes, and these eyes were no longer excited, but dull and pained. Yes, and there was more than pain in them – there was fear. I wondered if his hobby were becoming too much for him.

He greeted me like a long-lost brother. Considering that I scarcely knew him, I was a little embarrassed by his warmth. 'Bless you for coming, my dear fellow,' he cried. 'You want a wash and then we'll have dinner. Don't bother to change, unless you want to. I never do.' He led me to my bedroom, which was clean enough but small and shabby like a servant's room. I guessed that he had gutted the house to build his absurd temple.

We dined in a fair-sized room which was a kind of library. It was lined with old books, but they did not look as if they had been there long; rather it seemed like a lumber room in which a fine collection had been stored. Once no doubt they had lived in a dignified Georgian chamber. There was nothing else, none of the antiques which I had expected.

'You have come just in time,' he told me. 'I fairly jumped when I got your letter, for I had been thinking of running up to Cambridge to insist on your coming down here. I hope you're in no hurry to leave.'

'As it happens,' I said, 'I *am* rather pressed for time, for I hope to go abroad next week. I ought to finish my work here in a couple of days. I can't tell you how much I'm in your debt for your kindness.'

'Two days,' he said. 'That will get us over midsummer. That should be enough.' I hadn't a notion what he meant.

I told him that I was looking forward to examining his collection. He opened his eyes. 'Your discoveries, I mean,' I said, 'the altar of Vaunus . . . '

As I spoke the words his face suddenly contorted in a spasm of what looked like terror. He choked and then recovered himself. 'Yes, yes,' he said rapidly. 'You shall see it – you shall see everything – but not now – not tonight. Tomorrow – in broad daylight – that's the time.'

After that the evening became a bad dream. Small talk deserted him, and he could only reply with an effort to my commonplaces. I caught him often looking at me furtively, as if he were sizing me up and wondering how far he could go with me. The thing fairly got on my nerves, and to crown all it was abominably stuffy. The windows of the room gave on a little paved court with a background of laurels, and I might have been in Seven Dials for all the air there was.

When coffee was served I could stand it no longer. 'What about smoking in the temple?' I said. 'It should be cool there with the air from the lake.'

I might have been proposing the assassination of his mother. He simply gibbered at me. 'No, no,' he stammered. 'My God, no!' It was half an hour before he could properly collect himself. A servant lit two oil lamps, and we sat on in the frowsty room.

'You said something when we last met,' he ventured at last, after many a sidelong glance at me. 'Something about a ritual for re-dedicating an altar.'

I remembered my remark about Sidonius Apollinaris.

'Could you show me the passage? There is a good classical library here, collected by my great-grandfather. Unfortunately my scholarship is not equal to using it properly.'

I got up and hunted along the shelves, and presently found a copy of Sidonius, the Plantin edition of 1609. I turned up the passage, and roughly translated it for him. He listened hungrily and made me repeat it twice.

'He says a cock,' he hesitated. 'Is that essential?'

'I don't think so. I fancy any of the recognized ritual stuff would do.'

'I am glad,' he said simply. 'I am afraid of blood.'

'Good God, man,' I cried out, 'are you taking my nonsense seriously? I was only chaffing. Let old Vaunus stick to his altar!'

He looked at me like a puzzled and rather offended dog.

'Sidonius was in earnest . . .'

'Well, I'm not,' I said rudely. 'We're in the twentieth century and not in the third. Isn't it about time we went to bed?'

He made no objection, and found me a candle in the hall. As I undressed I wondered into what kind of lunatic asylum I had strayed. I felt the strongest distaste for the place, and longed to go straight off to the inn; only I couldn't make use of a man's manuscripts and insult his hospitality. It was fairly clear to me that Dubellay was mad. He had ridden his hobby to the death of his wits and was now in its bondage. Good Lord! he had talked of his precious Vaunus as a votary talks of a god. I believed he had come to worship some figment of his half-educated fancy.

I think I must have slept for a couple of hours. Then I woke dripping with perspiration, for the place was simply an oven. My window was as wide open as it would go, and, though it was a warm night, when I stuck my head out the air was fresh. The heat came from indoors. The room was on the first floor near the entrance and I was looking on to the overgrown lawns. The night was very dark and utterly still, but I could have sworn that I heard wind. The trees were as motionless as marble, but somewhere close at hand I heard a strong gust blowing. Also, though there was no moon, there was somewhere near me a steady glow of light; I could see the reflection of it round the end of the house. That meant that it came from the temple. What kind of saturnalia was Dubellay conducting at such an hour?

When I drew in my head I felt that if I was to get any sleep something must be done. There could be no question about it; some fool had turned on the steam heat, for the room was a furnace. My temper was rising. There was no bell to be found, so I lit my candle and set out to find a servant.

I tried a cast downstairs and discovered the room where we had dined. Then I explored a passage at right angles, which brought me up against a great oak door. The light showed me that it was a new door, and that there was no apparent way of opening it. I guessed that it led into the temple, and, though it fitted close and there seemed to be no keyhole, I could hear through it a sound like a rushing wind . . . Next I opened a door on my right and found myself in a big store cupboard. It had a funny, exotic, spicy smell, and, arranged very neatly on the floor and shelves, was a number of small sacks and coffers. Each bore a label, a square of stout paper with very black lettering. I read '*Pro servitio Vauni*'.

I had seen them before, for my memory betrayed me if they were not the very labels that Dubellay's servants had been attaching to the packages from the carrier's cart that evening in the past autumn. The discovery made my suspicions an unpleasant certainty. Dubellay evidently meant the labels to read 'For the service of Vaunus'. He was no scholar, for it was an impossible use of the word 'servitium', but he was very patently a madman.

However, it was my immediate business to find some way to sleep, so I continued my quest for a servant. I followed another corridor, and discovered a second stair-case. At the top of it I saw an open door and looked in. It must have been Dubellay's, for his flannels were tumbled untidily on a chair, but Dubellay himself was not there and the bed had not been slept in.

I suppose my irritation was greater than my alarm – though I must say I was getting a little scared – for I still pursued the evasive servant. There was another stair which apparently led to attics, and in going up it I slipped and made a great clatter. When I looked up the butler in his nightgown was staring down at me, and if ever a mortal face held fear it was his. When he saw who it was he seemed to recover a little.

'Look here,' I said, 'for God's sake turn off that infernal hot air. I can't get a wink of sleep. What idiot set it going?'

He looked at me owlishly, but he managed to find his tongue.

'I beg your pardon, sir,' he said, 'but there is no heating apparatus in this house.'

There was nothing more to be said. I returned to my bedroom and it seemed to me that it had grown cooler. As I leaned out of the window, too, the mysterious wind seemed to have died away, and the glow no longer showed from beyond the corner of the house. I got into bed and slept heavily till I was roused by the appearance of my shaving water about half-past nine. There was no bath-room, so I bathed in a tin pannikin.

It was a hazy morning which promised a day of blister-ing heat. When I went down to breakfast I found Dubellay in the dining-room. In the daylight he looked a very sick man, but he seemed to have taken a pull on himself, for his manner was considerably less nervy than the night before. Indeed, he appeared almost normal, and I might have reconsidered my view but for the look in his eyes.

I told him that I proposed to sit tight all day over the manuscript, and get the thing finished. He nodded. 'That's all right. I've got a lot to do myself, and I won't disturb you.'

'But first,' I said, 'you promised to show me your discoveries.'

He looked at the window where the sun was shining on the laurels and on a segment of the paved court.

'The light is good,' he said – an odd remark. 'Let us go there now. There are times and seasons for the temple.'

He led me down the passage I had explored the previous night. The door opened not by a key but by some lever in the wall. I found myself looking suddenly at a bath of sunshine with the lake below as blue as a turquoise.

It is not easy to describe my impressions of that place. It was unbelievably light and airy, as brilliant as an Indian colonnade in midsummer. The proportions must have been good, for the columns soared and swam, and the roof (which looked like cedar) floated as delicately as a flower on its stalk. The stone was some local limestone, which on the floor took a polish like marble. All around was a vista of sparkling water and summer woods and far blue mountains. It should have been as wholesome as the top of a hill.

And yet I had scarcely entered before I knew that it was a prison. I am not an imaginative man, and I believe my nerves are fairly good, but I could scarcely put one foot before the other, so strong was my distaste. I felt shut off from the world, as if I were in a dungeon or on an ice-floe. And I felt, too, that though far enough from humanity, we were not alone.

On the inner wall there were three carvings. Two were imperfect friezes sculptured in low-relief, dealing apparently with the same subject. It was a ritual procession, priests bearing branches, the ordinary *dendrophori** business. The faces were only half-human, and that was from no lack of skill, for the artist had been a master. The striking thing was that the branches and the hair of the hierophants* were being tossed by a violent wind, and the expression of each was of a being in the last stage of endurance, shaken to the core by terror and pain.

Between the friezes was a great roundel of a Gorgon's head. It was not a female head, such as you commonly find, but a male head, with the viperous hair sprouting from chin and lip. It had once been coloured, and fragments of a green pigment remained in the locks. It was an awful thing, the ultimate horror of fear, the last dementia of cruelty made manifest in stone. I hurriedly averted my eyes and looked at the altar.

That stood at the west end on a pediment with three steps. It was a beautiful piece of work, scarcely harmed by the centuries, with two words inscribed on its face – APOLL. VAUN. It was made of some foreign marble, and the hollow top was dark with ancient sacrifices. Not so ancient either, for I could have sworn that I saw there the mark of a recent flame.

I do not suppose I was more than five minutes in the place. I wanted to get out, and Dubellay wanted to get me out. We did not speak a word till we were back in the library.

'For God's sake give it up!' I said. 'You're playing with fire, Mr Dubellay. You're driving yourself into Bedlam. Send these damned things to a museum and leave this place. Now, now, I tell you. You have no time to lose. Come down with me to the inn straight off and shut up this house.'

He looked at me with his lip quivering like a child about to cry.

'I will. I promise you I will . . . But not yet . . . After tonight . . . Tomorrow I'll do whatever you tell me . . . You won't leave me?'

'I won't leave you, but what earthly good am I to you if you won't take my advice?'

'Sidonius . . .' he began.

'Oh, damn Sidonius! I wish I had never mentioned him. The whole thing is arrant nonsense, but it's killing you. You've got it on the brain. Don't you know you're a sick man?'

'I'm not feeling very grand. It's so warm today. I think I'll lie down.'

It was no good arguing with him, for he had the appalling obstinacy of very weak things. I went off to my work in a shocking bad temper.

The day was what it had promised to be, blisteringly hot. Before midday the sun was hidden by a coppery haze, and there was not the faintest stirring of wind. Dubellay did not appear at luncheon – it was not a meal he ever ate, the butler told me. I slogged away all afternoon, and had pretty well finished my job by six o'clock. That would enable me to leave next morning, and I hoped to be able to persuade my host to come with me.

The conclusion of my task put me into a better humour, and I went for a walk before dinner. It was a very close evening, for the heat haze had not lifted; the woods were as silent as a grave, not a bird spoke, and when I came out of the cover to the burnt pastures the sheep seemed too languid to graze. During my walk I prospected the environs of the house, and saw that it would be very hard to get access to the temple except by a long circuit. On one side was a mass of outbuildings, and then a high wall, and on the other the very closest and highest quickset hedge I have ever seen, which ended in a wood with savage spikes on its containing wall. I returned to my room, had a cold bath in the exiguous tub, and changed.

Dubellay was not at dinner. The butler said that his master was feeling unwell and had gone to bed. The news pleased me, for bed was the best place for him. After that I settled myself down to a lonely evening in the library. I browsed among the shelves and found a number of rare editions which served to pass the time. I noticed that the copy of Sidonius was absent from its place.

I think it was about ten o'clock when I went to bed, for I was unaccountably tired. I remember wondering whether I oughtn't to go and visit Dubellay, but decided that it was better to leave him alone. I still reproach myself for that decision. I know now I ought to have taken him by force and haled him to the inn.

Suddenly I came out of heavy sleep with a start. A human cry seemed to be ringing in the corridors of my brain. I held my breath and listened. It came again, a horrid scream of panic and torture.

I was out of bed in a second, and only stopped to get my feet into slippers. The cry must have come from the temple. I tore downstairs expecting to hear the noise of an alarmed household. But where was no sound, and the awful cry was not repeated.

The door in the corridor was shut, as I expected. Behind it pandemonium seemed to be loose, for there was a howling like a tempest – and something more, a crackling like fire. I made for the front door, slipped off the chain, and found myself in the still, moonless night. Still, except for the rending gale that seemed to be raging in the house I had left.

From what I had seen on my evening's walk I knew that my one chance to get to the temple was by way of the quickset hedge. I thought I might manage to force a way between the end of it and the wall. I did it, at the cost of much of my raiment and my skin. Beyond was another rough lawn set with tangled shrubberies, and then a precipitous slope to the level of the lake. I scrambled along the sedgy margin, not daring to lift my eyes till I was on the temple steps.

The place was brighter than day with a roaring blast of fire. The very air seemed to be incandescent and to have become a flaming ether. And yet there were no flames – only a burning brightness. I could not enter, for the waft from it struck my face like a scorching hand and I felt my hair singe . . .

I am short-sighted, as you know, and I may have been mistaken, but this is what I think I saw. From the altar a great tongue of flame seemed to shoot upwards and lick the roof, and from its pediment ran flaming streams. In front of it lay a body – Dubellay's – a naked body, already charred and black. There was nothing else, except that the Gorgon's head in the wall seemed to glow like a sun in hell.

I suppose I must have tried to enter. All I know is that I found myself staggering back, rather badly burned. I covered my eyes, and as I looked through my fingers I seemed to see the flames flowing under the wall, where there may have been lockers, or possibly another entrance. Then the great oak door suddenly shrivelled like gauze, and with a roar the fiery river poured into the house.

I ducked myself in the lake to ease the pain, and then ran back as hard as I could by the way I had come. Dubellay, poor devil, was beyond my aid. After that I am not very clear what happened. I know that the house burned like a haystack. I found one of the men-servants on the lawn, and I think I helped to get the other down from his room by one of the rainpipes. By the time the neighbours arrived the house was ashes, and I was pretty well mother-naked. They took me to the inn and put me to bed, and I remained there till after the inquest. The coroner's jury were puzzled, but they found it simply death by misadventure; a lot of country houses were burned that summer. There was nothing found of Dubellay; nothing remained of the house except a few blackened pillars; the altar and the sculptures were so cracked and scarred that no museum wanted them. The place has not been rebuilt, and for all I know they are there today. I am not going back to look for them.

Nightingale finished his story and looked round his audience.

'Don't ask me for an explanation,' he said, 'for I haven't any. You may believe if you like that the god Vaunus inhabited the temple which Dubellay built for him, and, when his votary grew scared and tried Sidonius's receipt for shifting the dedication, became angry and slew him with his flaming wind. That wind seems to have been a perquisite of Vaunus. We know more about him now, for last year they dug up a temple of his in Wales.'

'Lightning,' someone suggested.

'It was a quiet night, with no thunderstorm,' said Nightingale.

'Isn't the countryside volcanic?' Peckwether asked. 'What about pockets of natural gas or something of the kind?'

'Possibly. You may please yourself in your explanation. I'm afraid I can't help you. All I know is that I don't propose to visit that valley again!'

'What became of your Theocritus?'

'Burned, like everything else. However, that didn't worry me much. Six weeks later came the war, and I had other things to think about.'

Fountainblue

In 1902, soon after Buchan was called to the Bar, and while he was one of Milner's Young Men in South Africa, his thirteenth book appeared, a volume containing two novellas and three stories, entitled The Watcher by the Threshold. *All the stories were connected by the idea of the strength of a hidden, primitive influence exerted by the topography of Lowland or Western Scotland. The second novella in the book is 'Fountainblue', written after leaving Oxford, while Buchan was working on the* Spectator *and reading for the Bar. It appeared first in* Blackwood's *in August 1901: Buchan was then twenty-five.*

The story is apparently simple, romantic, even obvious, but it is deceptive. It is in fact about a special sort of medieval romanticism in which the hero is ultimately more concerned to 'make' his soul than to achieve the pinnacle of worldly success and have the desirable girl. There is thus a direct link between this aspect of this early tale and the mature vision of Sir Edward Leithen in Buchan's last novel, Sick Heart River, *written forty years later.*

Fountainblue

I

Once upon a time, as the story-books say, a boy came over a ridge of hill, from which a shallow vale ran out into the sunset. It was a high, wind-blown country, where the pines had a crook in their backs and the rocks were scarred and bitten with winter storms. But below was the beginning of pastoral. Soft birch-woods, shady beeches, meadows where cattle had browsed for generations, fringed the little brown river as it twined to the sea. Farther, and the waves broke on white sands, the wonderful billows of the West which cannot bear to be silent. And between, in a garden wilderness, with the evening flaming in its windows, stood Fountainblue, my little four-square castle which guards the valley and the beaches.

The boy had torn his clothes, scratched his face, cut one finger deeply, and soaked himself with bog-water, but he whistled cheerfully and his eyes were happy. He had had an afternoon of adventure, startling emprises achieved in solitude, assuredly a day to remember and mark with a white stone. And the beginning had been most unpromising. After lunch he had been attired in his best raiment, and, in the misery of a broad white collar, despatched with his cousins to take tea with the small lady who domineered in Fountainblue. The prospect had pleased him greatly, the gardens fed his fancy, the hostess was an old confederate, and there were sure to be excellent things to eat. But his curious temper had arisen to torment him. On the way he quarrelled with his party, and in a moment found himself out of sympathy with the future. The enjoyment crept out of the prospect. He knew that he did not shine in society, he foresaw an afternoon when he would be left out in the cold and his hilarious cousins treated as the favoured guests. He reflected that tea was a short meal at the best, and that games on a lawn were a poor form of sport. Above all, he felt the torture of his collar and the straitness of his clothes. He pictured the dreary return in the twilight, when the afternoon, which had proved, after all, such a dismal failure, had come to a weary end. So, being a person of impulses, he mutinied at the gates of Fountainblue and made for the hills. He knew he should get into trouble, but trouble, he had long ago found out, was his destiny, and he scorned to avoid it. And now, having cast off the fear of God and man, he would for some short hours do exactly as he pleased.

Half-crying with regret for the delights he had forsworn, he ran over the moor to the craggy hills which had always been forbidden him. When he had climbed among the rocks awe fell upon the desolate little adventurer, and he bewailed his choice. But soon he found a blue hawk's nest, and the possession of a coveted egg inspired him to advance. By-and-by he had climbed so high that he could not return, but musts needs scale Stob Ghabhar itself. With a quaking heart he achieved it, and then, in the pride of his heroism, he must venture down the Grey Correi where the wild goats lived. He saw a bearded ruffian, and pursued him with stones, stalking him cunningly till he was out of breath. Then he found odd little spleenwort ferns, which he pocketed, and high up in the rocks a friendly raven croaked his encouragement. And then, when the shadows lengthened, he set off cheerily home-wards, hungry, triumphant, and very weary.

All the way home he flattered his soul. In one afternoon he had been hunter and trapper, and what to him were girls' games and pleasant things to eat? He pictured himself the hardy outlaw, feeding on oatmeal and goat's-flesh, the terror and pride of his neighbourhood. Could the little mistress of Fountainblue but see him now, how she would despise his prosaic cousins! And then, as he descended on the highway, he fell in with his forsaken party.

For a wonder they were in good spirits – so good that they forgot to remind him, in their usual way, of the domestic terrors awaiting him. A man had been there who had told them stories and shown them tricks, and there had been coconut cake, and Sylvia had a new pony on which they had ridden races. The children were breathless with excitement, very much in love with each other as common sharers in past joys. And as they talked all the colour went out of his afternoon. The blue hawk's egg was cracked, and it looked a stupid, dingy object as it lay in his cap. His rare ferns were crumpled and withered, and who was to believe his stories of Stob Ghabhar and the Grey Correi? He had been a fool to barter ponies and tea and a man who knew tricks for the barren glories of following his own fancy. But at any rate he would show no sign. If he was to be an outlaw, he would carry his outlawry well; so with a catch in his voice and tears in his eyes he jeered at his inattentive companions, upbraiding himself all the while for his folly.

II

The sun was dipping behind Stob Ghabhar when Maitland drove over the ridge of hill, whence the moor-road dips to Fountainblue. Twenty long miles from the last outpost of railway to the western sea-loch, and twenty of the barest, steepest miles in the bleak north. And all the way he had been puzzling himself with the half-painful, half-pleasing memories of a childhood which to the lonely man still overtopped the present. Every wayside bush was the home of recollection. In every burn he had paddled and fished: here he had found the jack-snipe's nest, there he had hidden when the shepherds sought him for burning the heather in May. He lost for a little the burden of his years and cares, and lived again in that old fresh world which had no boundaries, where sleep and food were all his thought at night, and adventure the sole outlook of the morning. The western sea lay like a thin line of gold beyond the moorland, and down in the valley in a bower of trees lights began to twinkle from the little castle. The remote mountains, hiding deep corries and woods in their bosom, were blurred by twilight to a single wall of hazy purple, which shut off this fairy glen impenetrably from the world. Fountainblue – the name rang witchingly in his ears. Fountainblue, the last home of the Good Folk, the last hold of the vanished kings, where the last wolf in Scotland was slain, and, as stories go, the last saint of the Great Ages taught the people – what had Fountainblue to do with his hard world of facts and figures? The thought woke him to a sense of the present, and for a little he relished the paradox. He had left it long ago, an adventurous child; now he was returning with success behind him and a portion of life's good things his own. He was rich, very rich and famous. Few men of forty had his power, and he had won it all in fair struggle with enemies and rivals and a niggardly world. He had been feared and hated, as he had been extravagantly admired; he had been rudely buffeted by fortune, and had met the blows with a fighter's joy. And out of it all something hard and austere had shaped itself, something very much a man, but a man with little heart and a lack of kindly human failings. He was master of himself in a curious degree, but the mastery absorbed his interests. Nor had he ever regretted it, when suddenly in this outlandish place the past swept over him, and he had a vision of a long avenue of vanished hopes. It pleased and disquieted him, and as the road dipped into the valley he remembered the prime cause of this mood of vagaries.

He had come up into the north with one purpose in view, he frankly told himself. The Etheridges were in Fountainblue, and ever since, eight months before, he had met Clara Etheridge, he had forgotten his ambitions. A casual neighbour at a dinner-party, a chance partner at a ball – and then he had to confess that this slim, dark, bright-eyed girl had broken in irrevocably upon his contentment. At first he hated it for a weakness, then he welcomed the weakness with feverish ecstasy. He did nothing by halves, so he sought her company eagerly, and, being a great man in his way, found things made easy for him. But the girl remained shy and distant, flattered doubtless by his attention, but watching him curiously as an intruder from an alien world. It was characterstic of the man that he never thought of a rival. His whole aim was to win her love; for rivalry with other men he had the contempt of a habitual conqueror. And so the uneasy wooing went on till the Etheridges left town, and he found himself a fortnight later with his work done and a visit before him to which he looked forward with all the vehemence of a nature whose strong point had always been its hope. As the road wound among the fir-trees, he tried to forecast the life at Fountainblue, and map out the future in his usual business-like way. But now the future refused to be thus shorn and parcelled: there was an unknown quantity in it which defied his efforts.

The house-party were sitting round the hall-fire when he entered. The high-roofed place, the flagged floor strewn with rugs, and the walls bright with the glow of fire on armour, gave him a boyish sense of comfort. Two men in knickerbockers were lounging on a settle, and at his entrance came forward to greet him. One was Sir Hugh Clanroyden, a follower of his own; the other he recognized as a lawyer named Durward. From the circle of women Miss Etheridge rose and welcomed him. Her mother was out, but would be back for dinner; meantime he should be shown his room. He noticed that her face was browner, her hair a little less neat, and there seemed something franker and kindlier in her smile. So in a very good humour he went to rid himself of the dust of the roads.

Durward watched him curiously, and then turned, laughing, to his companion, as the girl came back to her friends with a heightened colour in her cheeks.

'Romeo the second,' he said. 'We are going to be spectators of a comedy. And yet, heaven knows! Maitland is not cast for comedy.'

The other shook his head. 'It will never come off. I've known Clara Etheridge most of my life, and I would as soon think of marrying a dancing-girl to a bishop. She is a delightful person, and my very good friend, but how on earth is she ever to understand Maitland? And how on earth can he see anything in her? Besides, there's another man.'

Durward laughed. 'Despencer! I suppose he will be a serious rival with a woman; but imagine him Maitland's rival in anything else! He'd break him like a rotten stick in half an hour. I like little Despencer, and I don't care about Maitland; but all the same it is absurd to compare the two, except in love-making.'

'Lord, it will be comic,' and Clanroyden stretched his long legs and lay back on a cushion. The girls were still chattering beside the fire, and the twilight was fast darkening into evening.

'You dislike Maitland?' he asked, looking up. 'Now, I wonder why?'

Durward smiled comically at the ceiling. 'Oh, I know I oughtn't to. I know he's supposed to be a man's man, and that it's bad form for a man to say he dislikes him. But I'm honest enough to own to detesting him. I suppose he's great, but he's not great enough yet to compel one to fall down and worship him, and I hate greatness in the making. He goes through the world with his infernal arrogance and expects everybody to clear out of his way. I am told we live in an age of reason, but that fellow has burked* reason. He never gives a reason for a thing he does, and if you try to argue he crushes you. He has killed good talk for ever with his confounded rudeness. All the little sophistries and conventions which make life tolerable are so much rubbish to him, and he shows it. The plague of him is that he can never make-believe. He is as hard as iron, and as fierce as the devil, and about as unpleasant. You may respect the sledge-hammer type, but it's confoundedly dull. Why, the man has not the imagination of a rabbit, except in his description of people he dislikes. I liked him when he said that Layden reminded him of a dissipated dove, because I disliked Layden; but when Freddy Alton played the fool and people forgave him, because he was a good sort, Maitland sent him about his business, saying he had no further use for weaklings. He is so abominably cold-blooded and implacable that everyone must fear him, and yet most people can afford to despise him. All the kind simple things of life are shut out of his knowledge. He has no nature, only a heart of stone and an iron will and a terribly subtle brain. Of course he is a great man – in a way, but at the best he is only half a man. And to think that he should have fallen in love, and be in danger of losing to Despencer! It's enough to make one forgive him.'

Clanroyden laughed. 'I can't think of Despencer. It's too absurd. But, seriously, I wish I saw Maitland well rid of this mood, married or cured. That sort of man doesn't take things easily.'

'It reminds one of Theocritus and the Cyclops in love*. Who would have thought to see him up in this moorland place, running after a girl? He doesn't care for sport.'

'Do you know that he spent most of his childhood in this glen, and that he *is* keen about sport? He is too busy for many holidays, but he once went with Burton to the Caucasus, and Burton said the experience nearly killed him. He said that the fellow was tireless, and as mad and reckless as a boy with nothing to lose.'

'Well, that simply bears out what I say of him. He does not understand the meaning of sport. When he gets keen about anything he pursues it as carefully and relentlessly as if it were something on the Stock Exchange. Now little Despencer is a genuine sportsman in his canary-like way. He loves the art of the thing and the being out of doors.

Maitland, I don't suppose, ever thinks whether it is a ceiling or the sky above his august head. Despencer – '

But at the moment Clanroyden uncrossed his legs, bringing his right foot down heavily upon his companion's left. Durward looked up and saw a young man coming towards him, smiling.

The newcomer turned aside to say something to the girls round the fire, and then came and sat on an arm of the settle. He was a straight, elegant person, with a well-tanned, regular face, and very pleasant brown eyes.

'I've had such an afternoon,' he said. 'You never saw a place like Cairnlora. It's quite a little stone tower all alone in a firwood, and nothing else between the moor and the sea. It is furnished as barely as a prison, except for the chairs, which are priceless old Dutch things. Oh, and the silver at tea was the sort of thing that only Americans can buy nowadays. Mrs Etheridge is devoured with envy. But the wonder of the house is old Miss Elphinstone. She must be nearly seventy, and she looks forty-five, except for her hair. She speaks broad Scots, and she has the manners of a *marquise*. I would give a lot to have had Raeburn paint her. She reminded me of nothing so much as a hill-wind with her keen high-coloured old face. Yes, I have enjoyed the afternoon.'

'Jack has got a new enthusiasm,' said Durward. 'I wish I were like you to have a new one once a week. By the way, Maitland has arrived at last.'

'Really!' said Despencer. 'Oh, I forgot to tell you something which you would never have guessed. Miss Elphinstone is Maitland's aunt, and he was brought up a good deal at Cairnlora. He doesn't take his manners from her, but I suppose he gets his cleverness from that side of the family. She disapproves of him strongly, so of course I had to defend him. And what do you think she said? "He has betrayed his tradition. He has sold his birthright for a mess of pottage*, and I wish him joy of his bargain!" Nice one for your party, Hugh.'

Miss Etheridge had left the group at the fire and was standing at Despencer's side. She listened to him with a curious air of solicitude, like an affectionate sister. At the mention of Maitland's name Clanroyden had watched her narrowly, but her face did not change. And when Despencer asked, 'Where is the new arrival?' she talked of him with the utmost nonchalance.

Maitland came down to dinner, ravenously hungry and in high spirits. Nothing was changed in this house since he had stared at the pictures and imagined terrible things about the armour and broken teacups with childish impartiality. His own favourite seat was still there, where, hidden by a tapestry screen, he had quarrelled with Sylvia while their elders gossiped. This sudden flood of memories mellowed him towards the world. He was cordial to Despencer, forbore to think Durward a fool, and answered every one of Mr Etheridge's many questions. For the first time he felt the success of his life. The old house recalled his childhood, and the sight of Clanroyden, his devoted follower, reminded him of his power. Somehow the weariful crying for the moon, which had always tortured him, was exchanged for a glow of comfort, a shade of complacency in his haggard soul . . . And then the sight of Clara dispelled his satisfaction.

Here in this cheerful homely party of friends he found himself out of place. On state occasions he could acquit himself with credit, for the man had a mind. He could make the world listen to him when he chose, and the choice was habitual. But now his loneliness claimed its lawful consequences, and he longed for the little friendly graces which he had so often despised. Despencer talked of scenery and weather with a tenderness to which this man, who loved nature as he loved little else, was an utter stranger. This elegant and appropriate sentiment would have worried him past endurance, if Miss Clara had not shared it. It was she who told some folk-tale about the Grey Correi with the prettiest hesitancy which showed her feeling. And then the talk drifted to books and people, flitting airily about their petty world. Maitland felt himself choked by their accomplishments. Most of the subjects were ones no sane man would trouble to think of, and yet here were men talking keenly about trifles and disputing with nimble-witted cleverness on the niceties of the trivial. Feeling miserably that he was the only silent one, he plunged desperately into the stream, found himself pulled up by Despencer and deftly turned. The event gave him the feeling of having been foiled by a kitten.

Angry with the world, angrier with his own angularity, he waited for the end of the meal. Times had not changed in this house since he had been saved by Sylvia from social disgrace. But when the women left the room he found life easier. His host talked of sport, and he could tell him more about Stob Ghabhar than any keeper. Despencer, victorious at dinner, now listened like a docile pupil. Durward asked a political question, and the answer came sharp and definite. Despencer demurred gently, after his fashion. 'Well, but surely – ' and a grimly smiling 'What do you know about it?' closed the discussion. The old Maitland had returned for the moment.

The night was mild and impenetrably dark, and the fall of waters close at hand sounded like a remote echo. An open hall-door showed that some of the party had gone out to the garden, and the men followed at random. A glimmer of white frocks betrayed the women on the lawn, standing by the little river which slipped by cascade and glide from the glen to the low pasture-lands. In the featureless dark there was no clue to locality. The place might have been Berkshire or a suburban garden.

Suddenly the scream of some animal came from the near thicket. The women started and asked what it was.

'It was a hill-fox,' said Maitland to Clara. 'They used to keep me awake at nights on the hill. They come and bark close to your ear and give you nightmares.'

The lady shivered. 'Thank Heaven for the indoors,' she said. 'Now, if I had been the daughter of one of your old Donalds of the Isles, I should have known that cry only too well. Wild nature is an excellent background, but give me civilization in front.'

Maitland was looking into the wood. 'You will find it creeps far into civilization if you look for it. There is a very narrow line between the warm room and the savage out-of-doors.'

'There are miles of luxuries,' the girl cried, laughing. 'People who are born in the wrong country have to hunt over half the world before they find their savagery. It is all very tame, but I love the tameness. You may call yourself primitive, Mr Maitland, but you are the most complex and modern of us all. What would Donald of the Isles have said to politics and the Stock Exchange?'

They had strolled back to the house. 'Nevertheless I maintain my belief,' said the man. 'You call it miles of rampart; I call the division a line, a thread, a sheet of glass. But then, you see, you only know one side, and I only know the other.'

'What preposterous affectation!' the girl said, as with a pretty shiver she ran indoors. Maitland stood for a moment looking back at the darkness. Within the firelit hall, with its rugs and little tables and soft chairs, he had caught a glimpse of Despencer smoking a cigarette. As he looked towards the hills he heard the fox's bark a second time, and then somewhere from the black distance came a hawk's scream, hoarse, lonely, and pitiless. The thought struck him that the sad elemental world of wood and mountain was far more truly his own than this cosy and elegant civilization. And, oddly enough, the thought pained him.

III

The day following was wet and windy, when a fire was grateful, and the hills, shrouded in grey mist, had no attractions. The party read idly in armchairs during the morning, and in the afternoon Maitland and Clanroyden went down to the stream-mouth after sea-trout. So Despencer remained to talk to Clara, and, having played many games of picquet and grown heartily tired of each other, as tea-time approached they fell to desultory comments on their friends. Maitland was beginning to interest the girl in a new way. Formerly he had been a great person who was sensible enough to admire her, but something remote and unattractive, for whom friendship (much less love) was impossible. But now she had begun to feel his power, his manhood. The way in which other men spoke of him impressed her unconsciously, and she began to ask Despencer questions which were gall and wormwood to that young man. But he answered honestly, after his fashion.

'Isn't he very rich?' she asked. 'And I suppose he lives very plainly?'

'Rich as Crœsus, and he sticks in his ugly rooms in the

Albany because he never thinks enough about the thing to change. I've been in them once, and you never saw such a place. He's a maniac for fresh air, so they're large enough, but they're littered like a stable with odds and ends of belongings. He must have several thousand books, and yet he hasn't a decent binding among them. He hasn't a photograph of a single soul, and only one picture, which, I believe, was his father. But you never saw such a collection of whips and spurs and bits. It smells like a harness-room, and there you find Maitland, when by any chance he is at home, working half the night and up to the eyes in papers. I don't think the man has any expenses except food and rent, for he wears the same clothes for years. And he has given up horses.'

'Was he fond of horses?' Miss Clara asked.

'Oh, you had better ask him. I really can't tell you any more about him.'

'But how do his friends get on with him?'

'He has hardly any, but his acquaintances, who are all the world, say he is the one great man of the future. If you want to read what people think of him, you had better look at the "Monthly".'

Under cover of this one ungenerous word Despencer made his escape, for he hated the business, but made it the rule of his life 'never to crab a fellow'. Miss Clara promptly sought out the 'Monthly', and found twenty pages of super-fine analysis and bitter, grudging praise. She read it with interest, and then lay back in her chair and tried to fix her thoughts. It is only your unhealthy young woman who worships strength in the abstract, and the girl tried to determine whether she admired the man as a power or disliked him as a brute. She chose a compromise, and the feeling which survived was chiefly curiosity.

The result of the afternoon was that when the fishermen returned, and Maitland, in dry clothes, appeared for tea, she settled herself beside him and prepared to talk. Maitland, being healthily tired, was in an excellent temper, and he found himself enticed into what for him was a rare performance – talk about himself. They were sitting apart from the others, and, ere ever he knew, he was answering the girl's questions with an absent-minded frankness. In a little she had drawn from him the curious history of his life, which most men knew, but never from his own lips.

'I was at school for a year,' he said, 'and then my father died and our affairs went to pieces. I had to come back and go into an office, a sort of bank. I hated it, but it was good for me, for it taught me something, and my discontent made me ambitious. I had about eighty pounds a year, and I saved from that. I worked too at books incessantly, and by-and-by I got an Oxford scholarship, at an obscure college. I went up there, and found myself in a place where everyone seemed well-off, while I was a pauper. However, it didn't trouble me much, for I had no ambition to play the fool. I only cared about two things – horses and metaphysics. I hated all games, which I thought only fit for children. I daresay it was foolish, but then you see I had had a queer upbringing. I managed to save a little money, and one vacation when I was wandering about in Norfolk, sleeping under haystacks and working in harvest-fields when my supplies ran down, I came across a farmer. He was a good fellow and a sort of sportsman, and I took a fancy to him. He had a colt to sell which I fancied more, for I saw it had blood in it. So I bought it for what seemed a huge sum to me in those days, but I kept it at his farm and I superintended its education. I broke it myself and taught it to jump, and by-and-by in

my third year I brought it to Oxford and entered for the
Grind* on it. People laughed at me, but I knew my own
business. The little boys who rode in the thing knew
nothing about horses, and not one in ten could ride; so I
entered and won. It was all I wanted, for I could sell my
horse then, and the fellow who rode second bought it. It
was decent of him, for I asked a big figure, and I think he
had an idea of doing me a kindness. I made him my
private secretary the other day.'

'You mean Lord Drapier?' she asked.

'Yes – Drapier. That gave me money to finish off and
begin in town. Oh, and I had got a first in my schools. I
knew very little about anything except metaphysics, and I
never went to tutors. I suppose I knew a good deal more
than the examiners in my own subject, and anyhow they
felt obliged to give me my first after some grumbling.
Then I came up to town with just sixty pounds in my
pocket, but I had had the education of a gentleman.'

Maitland looked out of the window, and the sight of the
mist-clad hills recalled him to himself. He wondered why
he was telling the girl this story, and he stopped suddenly.

'And what did you do in town?' she asked, with
interest.

'I hung round and kept my eyes open. I nearly starved,
for I put half my capital on a horse which I thought was
safe, and lost it. By-and-by, quite by accident, I came
across a curious fellow, Ransome – you probably have
heard his name. I met him in some stables where he was
buying a mare, and he took a liking to me. He made me
his secretary, and then, because I liked hard work, he let
me see his business. It was enormous, for the man was a
genius after a fashion; and I slaved away in his office and
down at the docks for about three years. He paid me just
enough to keep body and soul together and cover them

with clothes; but I didn't grumble, for I had a sort of idea that I was on my probation. And then my apprenticeship came to an end.'

'Yes,' said the girl.

'Yes; for you see Ransome was an odd character. He had a sort of genius for finance, and within his limits he was even a great administrator. But in everything else he was as simple as a child. His soul was idyllic: he loved green fields and Herrick and sheep. So it had always been his fancy to back out some day and retire with his huge fortune to some country place and live as he pleased. It seemed that he had been training me from the first day I went into the business, and now he cut the rope and left the whole enormous concern in my hands. I needed every atom of my wits, and the first years were a hard struggle. I became of course very rich; but I had to do more, I had to keep the thing at its old level. I had no natural turn for the work, and I had to acquire capacity by sheer grind. However, I managed it, and then, when I felt my position sure, I indulged myself with a hobby and went into politics.'

'You call it a hobby?'

'Certainly. The ordinary political career is simply a form of trifling. There's no trade on earth where a man has to fear so few able competitors. Of course it's very public and honourable and that sort of thing, and I like it; but sometimes it wearies me to death.'

The girl was looking at him with curious interest. 'Do you always get what you want?' she asked.

'Never,' he said.

'Then is your success all disappointment?'

'Oh, I generally get a bit of my ambitions, which is all one can hope for in this world.'

'I suppose your ambitions are not idyllic, like Mr Ransome's?'

He laughed. 'No, I suppose not. I never could stand your Corot meadows and ivied cottages and village church bells. But I am at home in this glen, or used to be.'

'You said that last night, and I thought it was affectation,' said the girl; 'but perhaps you are right. I'm not at home in this scenery, at any rate in this weather. Ugh, look at that mist driving and that spur of Stob Ghabhar! I really must go and sit by the fire.'

IV

The next day dawned clear and chill, with a little frost to whiten the heather; but by midday the sun had turned August to June, and sea and land drowsed in a mellow heat. Maitland was roused from his meditations with a pipe on a garden-seat by the appearance of Miss Clara, her eyes bright with news. He had taken her in to dinner the night before, and for the first time in his life had found himself talking easily to a woman. Her interest of the afternoon had not departed; and Despencer in futile disgust shunned the drawing-room, his particular paradise, and played billiards with Clanroyden in the spirit of an unwilling martyr.

'We are going out in the yacht,' Miss Clara cried, as she emerged from the shadow of a fuchsia-hedge, 'to the Isles of the Waves, away beyond the Seal's Headland. Do you know the place, Mr Maitland?'

'Eilean na Cille? Yes. It used to be dangerous for currents, but a steam-yacht does not require to fear them.'

'Well, we'll be ready to start at twelve, and I must go in to give orders about lunch.'

A little later she came out with a bundle of letters in her

hands. 'Here are your letters, Mr Maitland; but you mustn't try to answer them, or you'll be late.' He put the lot in his jacket pocket and looked up at the laughing girl. 'My work is six hundred miles behind me,' he said, 'and today I have only the Eilean na Cille to think of.' And, as she passed by, another name took the place of the Eilean, and it seemed to him that at last he had found the link which was to bind together the two natures – his boyhood and his prime.

Out on the loch the sun was beating with that steady August blaze which is more torrid than midsummer. But as the yacht slipped between the horns of the land, it came into a broken green sea with rollers to the north where the tireless Atlantic fretted on the reefs. In a world of cool salt winds and the golden weather of afternoon, with the cries of tern and gull about the bows and the foam and ripple of green water in the wake, the party fell into a mood of supreme contentment. The restless Miss Clara was stricken into a figure of contemplation, which sat in the bows and watched the hazy blue horizon and the craggy mainland hills in silent delight. Maitland was revelling in the loss of his isolation. He had ceased to be alone, a leader, and for the moment felt himself one of the herd, a devotee of humble pleasures. His mind was blank, his eyes filled only with the sea, and the lady of his devotion, in that happy moment of romance, seemed to have come at last within the compass of his hopes.

The Islands of the Waves are low green ridges which rise little above the highest tide-mark. The grass is stiff with salt, the sparse heather and rushes are crooked with the winds, but there are innumerable little dells where a light wild scrub flourishes, and in one a spring of sweet water sends a tiny stream to the sea. The yacht's company came ashore in boats, and tea was made with a great bustle beside the well, while the men lay idly in the bent and smoked. All wind seemed to have died down, a soft, cool, airless peace like a June evening was abroad, and the heavy surging of the tides had sunk to a distant whisper. Maitland lifted his head, sniffed the air, and looked uneasily to the west, meeting the eye of one of the sailors engaged in the same scrutiny. He beckoned the man to him.

'What do you make of the weather?' he asked.

The sailor, an East-coast man from Arbroath, shook his head. 'It's ower lown a' of a sudden,' he said. 'It looks like mair wind nor we want, but I think it'll haud till the morn.'

Maitland nodded and lay down again. He smiled at the return of his old sea craft and weather-lore, on which he had prided himself in his boyhood; and when Miss Clara came up to him with tea she found him grinning vacantly at the sky.

'What a wonderful lull in the wind,' she said. 'When I was here last these were real isles of the waves, with spray flying over them and a great business to land. But now they might be the island in Fountainblue lake.'

'Did you ever hear of the Ocean Quiet?' he asked. 'I believe it to be a translation of a Gaelic word which is a synonym for death, but it is also a kind of natural phenomenon. Old people at Cairnlora used to talk of it. They said that sometimes fishermen far out at sea in blowing weather came into a place of extraordinary peace, where the whole world was utterly still and they could hear their own hearts beating.'

'What a pretty fancy!' said the girl.

'Yes; but it had its other side. The fishermen rarely came home alive, and if they did they were queer to the end of their days. Another name for the thing was the Breathing of God. It is an odd idea, the passing from the wholesome turmoil of nature to the uncanny place where God crushes you by His silence.'

'All the things to eat are down by the fire,' she said, laughing. 'Do you know, if you weren't what you are, people might think you a poet, Mr Maitland. I thought you cared for none of these things.'

'What things?' he asked. 'I don't care for poetry. I am merely repeating the nonsense I was brought up on. Shall I talk to you about politics?'

'Heaven forbid! And now I will tell you my own story about these isles. There is a hermit's cell on one of them and crosses, like Iona. The hermit lived alone all winter, and was fed by boats from the shore when the weather was calm. When one hermit died another took his place, and no one knew where he came from. Now one day a great lord in Scotland disappeared from his castle. He was the King's Warden of the Marches and the greatest soldier of his day, but he disappeared utterly out of men's sight, and people forgot about him. Long years after the Northmen in a great fleet came down upon these isles, and the little chiefs fled before them. But suddenly among them there appeared an old man, the hermit of the Wave Islands, who organized resistance and gathered a strong army. No one dared oppose him, and the quarrelsome petty chiefs forgot their quarrels under his banner, for he had the air of one born to command. At last he met the invaders in the valley of Fountainblue, and beat them so utterly that few escaped to their ships. He fell himself in the first charge, but not before his followers had heard his battle-cry of "Saint Bride", and known the Hermit of the Isles and the great King's Warden were the same.'

'That was a common enough thing in wild times. Men grew tired of murder and glory and waving banners, and wanted quiet to make their peace with their own souls. I should have thought the craving scarcely extinct yet.'

'Then here is your chance, Mr Maitland,' said the girl, laughing. 'A little trouble would make the hut habitable, and you could simply disappear, leaving no address to forward your letters to. Think of the sensation, "Disappearance of a Secretary of State", and the wild theories and the obituaries. Then some day when the land question became urgent on the mainland, you would turn up suddenly, settle it with extraordinary wisdom, and die after confiding your life-story to some country reporter. But I am afraid it would scarcely do, for you would be discovered by Scotland Yard, which would be ignominious.'

'It is a sound idea, but the old device is too crude. However, it could be managed differently. Some day, when civilization grows oppressive, Miss Clara, I will remember your advice.'

The afternoon shadows were beginning to lengthen and from the west a light sharp wind was crisping the sea. The yacht was getting up steam, and boats were coming ashore for the party. The deep blue waters were flushing rose-pink as the level westering sun smote them from the summit of a cloudbank. The stillness had gone, and the air was now full of sounds and colour. Miss Clara, with an eye on the trim yacht, declared her disapproval. 'It is an evening for the cutter,' she cried, and in spite of Mrs Etheridge's protests she gave orders for it to be made ready. Then the self-willed young woman looked around for company. 'Will you come, Mr Maitland?' she said. 'You can sail a boat, can't you? And Mr Despencer, I shall want you to talk to me when Mr Maitland is busy. We shall race the yacht, for we ought to be able to get through the Scart's Neck with this wind.'

'I am not sure if you are wise, Miss Clara,' and Maitland pulled down his brows as he looked to the west. 'It will be wind – in a very little, and you stand the chance of a wetting.'

'I don't mind. I want to get the full good of such an evening. You want to be near the water to understand one of our sunsets. I can be a barbarian too, you know.'

It was not for Maitland to grumble at this friendliness; so he followed her into the cutter with Despencer, who had no love for the orders but much for her who gave them. He took the helm and steered, with directions from the lady, from his memory of the intricate coast. Despencer with many rugs looked to Miss Clara's comfort, and, having assured his own, was instantly entranced with the glories of the evening.

The boat tripped along for a little in a dazzle of light into the silvery grey of the open water. Far in front lay the narrow gut called the Scart's Neck, which was the by-way to the loch of Fountainblue. Then Maitland at the helm felt the sheets suddenly begin to strain, and, looking behind, saw the the Isles of the Waves were almost lost in the gloom, and that the roseate heavens were quickly darkening behind. The wind which he had feared was upon them; a few seconds more and it was sending the cutter staggering among billows. He could hardly make himself heard in the din, as he roared directions to Despencer about disposing of his person in another part of the boat. The girl with flushed face was laughing in pure joy of the storm. She caught a glimpse of Maitland's serious eye and looked over the gunwale at the threatening west. Then she too became quiet, and meekly sat down on the thwart to which he motioned her.

The gale made the Scart's Neck impossible, and the murky sky seemed to promise greater fury ere the morning. Twilight was falling, and the other entrance to the quiet loch meant the rounding of a headland and a difficult course through a little archipelago. It was the only way, for return was out of the question, and it seemed vain to risk the narrow chances of the short-cut. Maitland looked down at his two companions, and reflected with pleasure that he was the controller of their fates. He had sailed much as a boy, and he found in this moment of necessity that his old lore returned to him. He felt no mistrust of his powers: whatever the gale he could land them at Fountainblue, though it might take hours and involve much discomfort. He remembered the coast like his own name; he relished the grim rage of the elements, and he kept the cutter's head out to sea with a delight in the primeval conflict.

The last flickering rays of light, coming from the screen of cloud, illuminated the girl's pale face, and the sight disquieted him. There was a hint of tragedy in this game. Despencer, nervously self-controlled, was reassuring Clara. Ploughing onward in the blackening night in a frail boat on a wind-threshed sea was no work for a girl. But it was Despencer who was comforting her! Well, it was his proper work. He was made for the business of talking soft things to women. Maitland, his face hard with spray, looked into the darkness with a kind of humour in his heart. And then, as the boat shore and dipped into the storm, its human occupants seemed to pass out of the picture, and it was only a shell tossed on great waters in the unfathomable night. The evening had come, moonless and starless, and Maitland steered as best he could by the deeper blackness which was the configuration of the shore. Something loomed up that he knew for the headland, and they were drifting in a quieter stretch of sea, with the breakers grumbling ahead from the little tangle of islands.

Suddenly he fell into one of the abstractions which had

always dogged him through his strenuous life. His mind was clear, he chose his course with a certain precision, but the winds and waves had become to him echoes of echoes. Wet with spray and shifting his body constantly with the movement of the boat, it yet was all a phantasmal existence, while his thoughts were following an airy morrice in a fairyland world. The motto of his house, the canting motto of old reivers, danced in his brain – *'Parmi ceu haut bois conduyrai m'amie'** – 'Through the high wood I will conduct my love' – and in a land of green forests, dragon-haunted, he was piloting Clara robed in a quaint medieval gown, himself in speckless plate-armour. His fancy fled through a score of scenes, sometimes on a dark heath, or by a lonely river, or among great mountains, but always the lady and her protector. Clara, looking up from Despencer's side, saw his lips moving, noted that his eyes were glad, and for a moment hoped better things of their chances.

Then suddenly she was dumb with alarm, for the cutter heeled over, and but that Maitland woke to clear consciousness and swung the sheet loose, all would have been past. The adventure nerved him and quickened his senses. The boat seemed to move more violently than the wind drove her, and in the utter blackness he felt for the first time the grip of the waters. The ugly cruel monster had wakened, and was about to wreak its anger on the toy. And then he remembered the currents which raced round Eilean Righ and the scattered isles. Dim shapes loomed up, shapes strange and unfriendly, and he felt miserably that he was as helpless now as Despencer. To the left night had wholly shut out the coast; his one chance was to run for one of the isles and risk a landing. It would be a dreary waiting for the dawn, but safety had come before any comfort. And yet, he remembered, the little islands were rock-bound and unfriendly, and he was hurrying forward in the grip of a black current with a gale behind and unknown reefs before.

And then he seemed to remember something of this current which swept along the isles. In a little – so he recalled a boyish voyage in clear weather – they would come to a place where the sea ran swift and dark beside a kind of natural wharf. Here he had landed once upon a time, but it was a difficult enterprise, needing a quick and a far leap at the proper moment, for the stream ran very fast. But if this leap were missed there was still a chance. The isle was the great Eilean Righ, and the current swung round its southern end, and then, joining with another stream, turned up its far side, and for a moment washed the shore. But if this second chance were missed, then nothing remained but to fall into the great sea-going stream and be carried out to death in the wide Atlantic. He strained his eyes to the right for Eilean Righ. Something seemed to approach, as they bent under an access of the gale. They bore down upon it, and he struggled to keep the boat's head away, for at this pace to grate upon rock would mean upsetting. The sail was down, fluttering amidships like a captive bird, and the gaunt mast bowed with the wind. A horrible fascination, the inertia of nightmare, seized him. The motion was so swift and beautiful; why not go on and onward, listlessly? And then, conquering the weakness, he leaned forward and called to Clara. She caught his arm like a child, and he pulled her up beside him. Then he beckoned Despencer, and, shrieking against the din, told him to follow him when he jumped. Despencer nodded, his teeth chattering with cold and the novel business. Suddenly out of the darkness, a yard on their right, loomed a great flat rock along which the current raced like a mill-lade. The boat made to strike, but Maitland forced her nose out to sea, and then as the stern swung round he seized his chance. Holding Clara with his left arm he stood up, balanced himself for a moment on the gunwale, and jumped. He landed sprawling on his side on some wet seaweed, over which the sea was lipping, but undeniably on land. As he pulled himself up he had a vision of the cutter, dancing like a cork, vanishing down the current into the darkness.

Holding the girl in his arms, he picked his way across the rock pools to the edge of the island heather. For a moment he thought Clara had fainted. She lay still the inert, her eyes shut, her hair falling foolishly over her brow. He sprinkled some water on her face, and she revived sufficiently to ask her whereabouts. He was crossing the island to find Despencer, but he did not tell her. 'You are safe,' he said, an he carried her over the rough ground as lightly as a child. An intense exhilaration had seized him. He ran over the flats and strode up the low hillocks with one thought possessing his brain. To save Despencer, that of course was the far-off aim on his mind's horizon, but all the foreground was filled with the lady. '*Parmi ceu haut bois*' – the old poetry of the world had penetrated to his heart. The black night and the wild wind and the sea were the ministrants of love. The hollow shams of life with their mincing conventions had departed, and in this savage out-world a man stood for a man. The girl's light tweed jacket was no match for this chill gale, so he stopped for a moment, took off his own shooting-coat and put it round her. And then, as he came over a little ridge, he was aware of a grumbling of waters and the sea.

The beach was hidden in a veil of surf which sprinkled the very edge of the bracken. Beyond, the dark waters were boiling like a caldron, for the tides in this little bay ran with the fury of a river in spate. A moon was beginning to struggle through the windy clouds, and surf, rock, and wave began to shape themselves out of the night. Clara stood on the sand, a slim, desolate figure, and clung to Maitland's arm. She was still dazed with the storm and the baffling suddenness of change. Maitland, straining his eyes out to sea, was in a waking dream. With the lady no toil was too great, no darkness terrible; for her he would scale the blue air and plough the hills and do all the lover's feats of romance. And then suddenly he shook her hand roughly from his arm and ran forward, for he saw something coming down the tide.

Before he left the boat he had lowered the sail, and the cutter swung to the current, an odd amorphous thing, now heeling over with a sudden gust and now pulled back to balance by the strong grip of the water. A figure seemed to sit in the stern, making feeble efforts to steer. Maitland knew the coast and the ways of the sea. He ran through the surf-ring into the oily black eddies, shouting to Despencer to come overboard. Soon he was not ten yards from the cutter's line, where the current made a turn towards the shore before it washed the iron rocks to the right. He found deep water, and in two strokes was in the grip of the tides and borne wildly towards the reef. He prepared himself for what was coming, raising his feet and turning his right shoulder to the front. And then with a shock he was pinned against the rock-wall, with the tides tugging at his legs, while his hands clung desperately to a shelf. Here he remained, yelling directions to the coming boat. Surf was in his eyes, so that at first he could not see, but at last in a dip of the waves he saw the cutter, a man's form in the stern, plunging not twenty yards away. Now was his chance or never, for while the tide would take a boat far from his present place of vantage, it would carry a lighter thing, such as a man's body, in a circle nearer to the shore. He yelled again, and the world seemed to him quiet for a moment, while his voice echoed eerily in the void. Despencer must have heard it, for the next moment he saw him slip pluckily overboard, making the cutter heel desperately with his weight. And then – it seemed an age – a man, choking and struggling weakly, came down the current, and, pushing his right arm out against the rush of water, he had caught the swimmer by the collar and drawn him in to the side of the rock.

Then came the harder struggle. Maitland's left hand was numbing, and though he had a foothold, it was too slight to lean on with full weight. A second lassitude oppressed him, a supreme desire to slip into those racing tides and rest. He was in no panic about death, but he had the practical man's love of an accomplished task, and it nerved him to the extreme toil. Slowly by inches he drew himself up the edge of the reef, cherishing jealously each grip and foothold, with Despencer, half-choked and all but fainting, hanging heavily on his right arm. Blind with spray, sick with sea-water, and aching with his labours, he gripped at last the tangles of sea-weed, which meant the flat surface, and with one final effort raised himself and Despencer to the top. There he lay for a few minutes with his head in a rock-pool till the first weariness had passed.

He staggered with his burden in his arms along the ragged reef to the strip of sand where Clara was weeping hysterically. The sight of her restored Maitland to vigour, the appeal of her lonely figure there in the wet brackens. She must think them all dead, he reflected, and herself desolate, for she could not have interpreted rightly his own wild rush into the waves. When she heard his voice she started as if at a ghost, and then seeing his burden, ran towards him. 'Oh, he is dead!' she cried. 'Tell me! tell

me!' and she clasped the inert figure so that her arm
crossed Maitland's. Despencer, stupefied and faint, was
roused to consciousness by a woman's kisses on his cheek,
and still more by his bearer abruptly laying him on the
heather. Clara hung over him like a mother, calling him
by soft names, pushing his hair from his brow, forgetful of
her own wet and sorry plight. And meanwhile Maitland
stood watching, while his palace of glass was being
shivered about his ears.

Aforetime his arrogance had kept him from any thought
of jealousy; now the time and place were too solemn for
trifling, and facts were laid bare before him. Sentiment
does not bloom readily in a hard nature, but if it once
comes to flower it does not die without tears and agonies.
The wearied man, who stood quietly beside the hysterical
pair, had a moment of peculiar anguish. Then he conquered sentiment, as he had conquered all other feelings
of whose vanity he was assured. He was now, as he was
used to be, a man among children; and as a man he had his
work. He bent over Clara. 'I know a hollow in the middle
of the island,' he said, 'where we can camp the night. I'll
carry Despencer, for his ankle is twisted. Do you think
you could try to walk?'

The girl followed obediently, her eyes only on her
lover. Her trust in the other was infinite, her indifference
to him impenetrable; while he, hopelessly conscious of his
fate, saw in the slim dishevelled figure at his side the lost
lady, the mistress for him of all romance and generous
ambitions. The new springs in his life were choked; he had
still his work, his power, and, thank God, his courage; but
the career which ran out to the horizon of his vision was
black and loveless. And he held in his arms the thing
which had frustrated him, the thing he had pulled out of
the deep in peril of his body; and at the thought life for a

moment seemed to be only a comic opera with tragedy to shift the scenes.

He found a cleft between two rocks with a soft floor of heather. There had been no rain, so the bracken was dry, and he gathered great armfuls and driftwood logs from the shore. Soon he had a respectable pile of timber, and then in the nick of the cleft he built a fire. His matches, being in his jacket pocket, had escaped the drenchings of salt water, and soon with a smoke and crackling and sweet scent of burning wood, a fire was going cheerily in the darkness. Then he made a couch of bracken, and laid there the still feeble Despencer. The man was more weak than ill; but for his ankle he was unhurt; and a little brandy would have brought him to himself. But this could not be provided, and Clara saw in his condition only the sign of mortal sickness. With haggard eyes she watched by him, easing his head, speaking soft kind words, forgetful of her own cold and soaking clothes. Maitland drew her gently to the fire, shook down the bracken to make a rest for her head, and left a pile of logs ready for use. 'I am going to the end of the island,' he said, 'to light a fire for a signal. It is the only part which they can see on the mainland, and if they see the blaze they will come off for us as soon as it is light.' The pale girl listened obediently. This man was the master, and in his charge was the safety of her lover and herself.

Maitland turned his back upon the warm nook, and stumbled along the ridge to the northern extremity of the isle. It was not a quarter of a mile away, but the land was so rough with gullies and crags that the journey took him nearly an hour. Just off the extreme point was a flat rock, sloping northwards to a considerable height, a place from which a beacon could penetrate far over the mainland. He gathered brackens for kindling, and driftwood which former tides had heaped on the beach; and then with an armful he splashed through the shallow surf to the rock. Scrambling to the top, he found a corner where a fire might be lit, a place conspicuous and yet sheltered. Here he laid his kindling, and then in many wet journeys he carried his stores of firewood from the mainland to the rock. The lighting was nervous work, for he had few matches; but at last the dampish wood had caught, and tongues of flame shot up out of the smoke. Meantime the wind had sunk lower, the breakers seemed to have been left behind, and the eternal surge of the tides became the dominant sound to the watcher by the beacon.

And then, it seemed to him, the great convulsions of the night died away, and a curious peace came down upon the waters. The fire leaped in the air, the one living thing in a hushed and expectant world. It was not the quiet of sleep but of a sudden cessation, like the lull after a great flood or a snowslip. The tides still eddied and swayed, but it was noiselessly; the world moved, yet without sound or friction. The bitter wind which chilled his face and stirred up the red embers was like a phantom blast, without the roughness of a common gale. For a moment he seemed to be set upon a high mountain with the world infinitely remote beneath his feet. To all men there come moments of loneliness of body, and to some few the mingled ecstasy and grief of loneliness of soul. The child-tale of the Ocean Quiet came back to him, the hour of the Breathing of God. Surely the great silence was now upon the world. But it was an evil presage, for all who sailed into it were homeless wanderers for ever after. Ah well! he had always been a wanderer, and the last gleam of home had been left behind, where by the firelight in the cold cranny a girl was crooning over her lover.

His past, his monotonous. brilliant past, slipped by with

the knotless speed of a vision. He saw a boy, haunted with dreams, chafing at present delights, clutching evermore at the faint things of fancy. He saw a man, playing with the counters which others played with, fighting at first for bare existence and then for power and the pride of life. Success came over his path like a false dawn, but he knew in his heart that he had never sought it. What was that remote ineffable thing he had followed? Here in the quiet of the shadowy waters he had the moment of self-revelation which comes to all, and hopes and dim desires seemed to stand out with the clearness of accomplished facts. There had always been something elect and secret at the back of his fiercest ambitions. The ordinary cares of men had been to him but little things to be played with; he had won by despising them; casting them from him, they had fallen into the hollow of his hand. And he had held them at little, finding his reward in his work, and in a certain alertness and freshness of spirit which he had always cherished. There is a story of island-born men who carry into inland places and the streets of cities the noise of sea-water in their ears, and hear continually the tern crying and the surf falling. So from his romantic boyhood this man had borne an arrogance towards the things of the world which had given him a contemptuous empire over a share of them. As he saw the panorama of his life no place or riches entered into it, but only himself, the haggard, striving soul, growing in power, losing, perhaps, in wisdom. And then, at the end of the way, Death, to shrivel the power to dust, and with the might of his sunbeam to waken to life the forgotten world of the spirit.

In the hush he seemed to feel the wheel and the drift of things, the cosmic order of nature. He forgot his weariness and his plashing clothes as he put more wood on the beacon and dreamed into the night. The pitiless sea, infinite, untamable, washing the Poles and hiding Earth's secrets in her breast, spoke to him with a far-remembered voice. The romance of the remote isles, the homes of his people, floating still in a twilight of old story, rose out of the darkness. His life, with its routine and success, seemed in a moment hollow, a child's game, unworthy of a man. The little social round, the manipulation of half-truths, the easy victories over fools – surely this was not the task for him. He was a dreamer, but a dreamer with an iron hand; he was scarcely in the prime of life; the world was wide and his chances limitless. One castle of cards had already been overthrown; the Ocean Quiet was undermining another. He was sick of domesticity of every sort – of town, of home, of civilization. The sad elemental world was his, the fury and the tenderness of nature, the peace of the wilds which old folk had called the Breathing of God. '*Parmi ceu haut bois conduyrai m'amie*' – this was still his motto, to carry untarnished to the end an austere and beautiful dream. His little ambitions had been but shreds and echoes and shadows of this supreme reality. And his love had been but another such simulacrum; for what he had sought was no foolish, laughing girl, but the Immortal Shepherdess, who, singing the old songs of youth, drives her flocks to the hill in the first dewy dawn of the world.

Suddenly he started and turned his head. Day was breaking in a red windy sky, and somewhere a boat's oars were plashing in the sea. And then he realized for the first time that he was cold and starving and soaked to the bone.

V

MR HENRY DURWARD TO LADY CLAUDIA ETHERIDGE

'. . . Things have happened, my dear Clo, since I last wrote; time has passed; tomorrow I leave this place and go to stalk with Drapier; and yet in the stress of departure I take time to answer the host of questions with which you assailed me. I am able to give you the best of news. You have won your bet. Your prophecy about the conduct of the "other Etheridge girl" has come out right. They are both here, as it happens, having come on from Fountain-blue, – both the hero and the heroine, I mean, of this most reasonable romance. You know Jack Despencer, one of the best people in the world, though a trifle given to chirping. But I don't think the grasshopper will become a burden to Miss Clara, for she likes that sort of thing. She must, for there is reason to believe that she refused for its sake the greatest match – I speak with all reverence – which this happy country could offer. I know you like Maitland as little as I do, but we agree in admiring the Colossus from a distance. Well, the Colossus has, so to speak, been laid low by a frivolous member of your sex. It is a most romantic tale. Probably you have heard the gist of it, but here is the full and circumstantial account.

'We found Maitland beside the fire he had been feeding all night, and I shall never forget his figure alone in the dawn on that rock, drenched and dishevelled, but with his haggard white face set like a Crusader's. He took us to a kind of dell in the centre of the island, where we found

Clara and Despencer shivering beside a dying fire. He had a twisted ankle and had got a bad scare, while she was perfectly composed, though she broke down when we got home. It must have been an awful business for both, but Maitland never seems to have turned a hair. I want to know two things. First, how in the presence of great danger he managed to get his dismissal from the lady? – for get it he assuredly did, and Despencer at once appeared in the part of the successful lover; second, what part he played in the night's events? Clara remembered little, Despencer only knew that he had been pulled out of the sea, but over all Maitland seems to have brooded like a fate. As usual he told us nothing. It was always his way to give the world results and leave it to find out his methods for itself . . .

'Despencer overwhelmed him with gratitude. His new happiness made him in love with life, and he included Maitland in the general affection. The night's events seemed to have left their mark on the great man also. He was very quiet, forgot to be rude to anybody, and was kind to both Clara and Despencer. It is his way of acknowledging defeat, the great gentleman's way, for, say what we like about him, he is a tremendous gentleman, one of the last of the breed . . .

'And then he went away – two days later. Just before he went Hugh Clanroyden and myself were talking in the library, which has a window opening on a flower-garden. Despencer was lying in an invalid's chair under a tree and Clara was reading to him. Maitland was saying goodbye, and he asked for Despencer. We told him that he was with Clara in the garden. He smiled one of those odd scarce smiles of his, and went out to them. When I saw his broad shoulders bending over the chair and the strong face looking down at the radiant Jack with his amiable good looks, confound it, Clo, I had to contrast the pair, and admit with Shakespeare the excellent foppery of the world*. Well-a-day! "Smooth Jacob stills robs homely Esau."* And perhaps it is a good thing, for we are most of us Jacobs, and Esau is an uncomfortable fellow in our midst.

'A week later came the surprising, the astounding news that he had taken the African Governorship. A career ruined, everyone said, the finest chance in the world flung away; and then people speculated, and the story came out in bits, and there was only one explanation. It is the right one, as I think you will agree, but it points to some hidden weakness in that iron soul that he could be moved to fling over the ambitions of years because of a girl's choice. He will go and bury himself in the wilds, and our party will have to find another leader. Of course he will do his work well, but it is just as if I were to give up my chances of the Woolsack for a county-court judgeship. He will probably be killed, for he has a million enemies; he is perfectly fearless, and he does not understand the arts of compromise. It was a privilege, I shall always feel, to have known him. He was a great man, and yet – intellect, power, character, were at the mercy of a girl's caprice. As I write, I hear Clara's happy laugh below in the garden, probably at some witticism of the fortunate Jack's. Upon which, with my usual pride in the obvious, I am driven to reflect that the weak things in life may confound the strong*, and that, after all, the world is to the young . . .'

VI

SIR HUGH CLANROYDEN TO MR HENRY DURWARD
SOME YEARS LATER

'. . . I am writing this on board ship, as you will see from the heading, and shall post it when I get to the Cape. You have heard of my appointment, and I need not tell you how deep were my searchings of heart before I found courage to accept. Partly I felt that I had got my chance; partly I thought – an inconsequent feeling – that Maitland, if he had lived, would have been glad to see me in the place. But I am going to wear the Giant's Robe, and Heaven knows I have not the shoulders to fill it. Yet I am happy in thinking that I am in a small sense faithful to his memory.

'No further news, I suppose, has come of the manner of his death? Perhaps we shall never know, for it was on one of those Northern expeditions with a few men by which he held the frontier. I wonder if anyone will ever write fully the history of all that he did? It must have been a titanic work, but his methods were always so quiet that people accepted his results like a gift from Providence. He was given, one gathers, a practically free hand, and he made the country – four years' work of a man of genius. They wished to bring his body home, but he made them bury him where he fell – a characteristic last testament. And so he has gone out of the world into the world's history.

'I am still broken by his death, but, now that he is away, I begin to see him more clearly. Most people, I think, misunderstood him. I was one of his nearest friends, and I only knew bits of the man. For one thing – and I hate to use the vulgar word – he was the only aristocrat I ever heard of. Our classes are three-fourths of them of yesterday's growth, without the tradition, character, manner, or any trait of an aristocracy. And the few, who are nominally of the blood, have gone to seed in mind, or are spoilt by coarse marriages, or, worst of all, have the little trifling superior airs of incompetence. But he, he had the most transcendent breeding in mind and spirit. He had no need for self-assertion, for his most casual acquaintances put him at once in a different class from all other men. He had never a trace of a vulgar ideal; men's opinions, worldly honour, the common pleasures of life, were merely degrees of the infinitely small. And yet he was no bloodless mystic. If race means anything he had it to perfection. Dreams and fancies to him were the realities, while facts were the shadows which he made dance as it pleased him.

'The truth is, that he was that rarest of mortals, the iron dreamer. He thought in æons and cosmic cycles, and because of it he could do what he pleased in life. We call a man practical if he is struggling in the crowd with no knowledge of his whereabouts, and yet in our folly we deny the name to the clear-sighted man who can rule the crowd from above. And here I join issue with you and everybody else. You thought it was Miss Clara's refusal which sent him abroad and interrupted his career. I read the thing otherwise. His love for the girl was a mere accident, a survival of the domestic in an austere spirit. Something I do not know what, showed him his true desires. She may have rejected him; he may never have spoken to her; in any case the renunciation had to come. You must remember that that visit to Fountainblue was the first that he had paid since his boyhood to his boyhood's home. Those revisitings have often a strange trick of self-revelation. I believe that in that night on the island he saw our indoor civilization and his own destiny in so sharp a contrast that he could not choose but make the severance. He found work where there could be small hope of honour or reward, but many a chance for a hero. And I am sure that he was happy, and that it was the longed-for illumination that dawned on him with the bullet which pierced his heart.

'But, you will say, the fact remains that he was once in love with Miss Clara, and that she would have none of him. I do not deny it. He was never a favourite with women; but, thank heaven, I have better things to do than study their peculiarities . . .'

Notes

Occasional minor variations, mostly of punctuation and spelling, between magazine publication and first hardback edition I have again ignored – 'Song of the Moor' instead of 'Moor-song' for the title of the fifth story, for example. Significant changes are recorded here.

On Cademuir Hill
18 *The Linton Ploughman*: a Peeblesshire dance.
19 *howe*: a hollow.
21 *hard-handed men* . . . Shakespeare, *A Midsummer Night's Dream*, V.i.72–3.
21 *stelled*: stellar or starred.
21 *lippened*: trusted. The verse means, 'Only when the room is spinning is it time to go; we've always trusted in Providence and we always will.'
22 *brae*: the slope of a hill.
23 *hills and mountains*: Psalm 114. v.4. 'The mountains skipped like rams, and the little hills like lambs.'
24 *whaups*: curlews.

A Lucid Interval
29 The first words of Robert Louis Stevenson's *The Master of Ballantrae* (1889) are, 'The full truth of this odd matter is what the world has long been looking for . . .'
30 *fakir*: from an Arab word; in the UK loosely used for a very poor religious man in India.
31 '*birsing yont*': 'birsing' is a Scots word for 'bruising', and 'yont' means 'beyond'. The sense of the phrase comes across in the record of the Morayshire farmer advising his son, who was going out in the world, 'Aye birse yont': the *Scottish National Dictionary* comments, 'No doubt he did push ahead.'
31 *Breadalbane* is a mountainous district in the north-west of central Scotland. John Campbell, first Earl of Breadal-

bane, is infamous for the atrocity known as the Massacre of Glencoe, when on 13 February 1692, soldiers billeted on the MacDonalds in Glencoe murdered their hosts, attempting to wipe out the entire clan. So 'like the Breadalbanes' here qualifies the previous phrase 'birsing yont' somewhat viciously.

31 *zemindars*: native Indians holding land for which they paid revenue directly to the British Government.

33 *Kissingen*: a Bavarian spa and health-resort.

33 *en garçon*: attended by a manservant.

34 *Doukhobor*: one of a small community of Russian peasants, now also found in small numbers in Canada. The word means 'Spirit-fighter': the communities live close to the New Testament doctrines of the Holy Spirit.

34 *Ethiopians . . . skin*: Jeremiah XIII. xxiii. 'Can the Ethiopian change his skin, or the leopard his spots?'

35 *troglodytic*: cave-dwelling.

38 *Newman's favourite quotation*: St Ambrose, *de Fide*, i.5. sec 42. John Henry, Cardinal Newman quotes it in *Apologia pro Vita Sua*, first published in 1864 (OUP 1964 p. 175).

38 *more Indico*: in the Indian manner.

40 *that accursed name*: the Empire.

41 *kailyard*: cabbage-patch.

41 *but-and-ben*: two-roomed cottage.

41 *yellow slaves*: the use of imported Chinese labourers on the Rand after the Boer War, and their bad living and working conditions, were an important issue in the General Election of 1905.

43 *Andamans*: the Andaman Islands, in the Indian Ocean.

43 *von Kladow*: probably a reference to the German Chancellor, von Bethmann Hollweg. The British relationship with Germany was one of extremely delicately balanced non-intervention: even the narrator does not quite grasp the full implications of what Mulross proposes to do.

44 *slow length*: Alexander Pope, *An Essay on Criticism*, 349–350:

A needless Alexandrine ends the song,
That, like a wounded snake, drags its slow length along.

44 *Westbury's language to the herald*: Richard Bethell, First Lord Westbury, was Lord Chancellor from 1861 till his

disgrace in 1865. He was notorious for his suavely-uttered sarcasms and was the subject of much gossip, and unnumbered stories, so that it is difficult at this distance to decide what he actually said. His biographer, T. A. Nash, in his two-volume work in 1888, gives the official version of Westbury's most famous remark:

> It was said that when one of the equity judges, in reference to some application to the Court, made answer that he would turn the matter over in his mind, Bethell, turning round to his junior with a smile, which seemed to bespeak intense amusement, said, loud enough to be heard by the bar, 'Take a note of that: his lordship says he will turn it over in what he is pleased to call his mind!'

Bethel was a Brasenose man, and he makes a brief appearance in Buchan's youthful, but official, history of that college. He is also the subject of five lively pages in Buchan's review-article, 'The Victorian Chancellors', which had appeared in *Blackwood's* eighteen months earlier, and been reprinted in his book *Some Eighteenth Century Byways* also in 1908. An unsigned article in *Macmillan's Magazine* in April 1883 gives a more rounded portrait, and hints at some large blemishes. Here are more anecdotes, a good deal livelier than those printed by Nash. In none of these places, however, is there any reference to language of a herald. The nearest to Buchan's narrator's context is the following, which appears in several versions. I give that by Nash:

> The late Sir William Erle [a respected judge] in reply to Lord Westbury, who asked him why he did not attend the Judicial Committee of the Privy Council, said that he was old and deaf and stupid. 'That is no sufficient excuse,' returned Lord Westbury, 'for Chelmsford and I are very old. Napier is very deaf, Colville is very stupid; but we four make an excellent tribunal'.

The book which Buchan reviews, by J. B. Atlay, includes many anecdotes but still none about a herald, though there is reference to 'language used . . . out of doors' which might give a hint about what is meant.

44   *satraps*: provincial governors; here, tyrannical persons.
45   *babus*: i.e. Indians. In some parts of India 'babu' is equivalent to 'Mr'.
51   *UP*: United Presbyterian, a denomination strong on total abstinence from alcohol.
52   *ryot*: Indian peasant.
54   *Tariff Reform*: the Liberals were, of course, Free Traders to a man. By the time of this story, most Opposition MPs were Tariff Reformers.
56   *stot*: heifer.
56   *amicus curiæ*: friend or ally of the senate.
57   *Bosnian Succession*: A Balkan crisis had begun in 1875 with a revolt in Bosnia (now in central Yugoslavia) against Turkish misrule. The Turks were presently defeated by Russia, and a peace of a kind was settled at the Congress of Berlin in 1878: but the stability of the whole of Europe had been shaken in that the Tsar could see himself as having been humiliated by the German Kaiser and the Austrian Emperor, backed by Britain. Then in October 1908, Austria – without even the knowledge of her close ally Germany – decided to annexe Bosnia, an act which could easily have stirred the wrath of the Russian Empire. A European war seemed not far away. In this volatile situation, the Kaiser suddenly declared that if the Tsar attacked Austria, Russia would have to face the might of the German Empire as well. In the uneasy peace which followed, Britain stood carefully aloof, particularly from the question of where Bosnia belonged, though she was desperately anxious. For Mulross to propose the deliberate aggravation of Germany under its unstable Kaiser would be appalling to the Prime Minister. Sadly, of course, Bosnia later overtook fiction, when on 28 June 1914 a young Bosnian fanatic assassinated the heir to the Austrian throne at Sarajevo, directly precipitating the First World War.
60   *Marienbad*: the Austrian spa.
61   *peace on the vexed tents of Israel*: not in fact a biblical quotation, though made up of Old Testament words.

The Lemnian
63   Gilbert Murray's Harvard lectures of 1907, attempting to

show what might have gone into the making of the *Iliad* were the basis of this book, possibly his best. By the time John and Susan Buchan were exploring the Aegean, Murray had been two years in Oxford as Regius Professor of Greek and a Fellow of New College. A lifelong friend since Buchan's rawer Glasgow days, Murray's combination of scholarship and imagination had much in common with Buchan's mind. A sentence in this *Greek Epic* book, about the fifth-century Athenians, shows something of the closeness: 'The jungle grew thick and close all around them, and the barrier between seemed very weak, very impalpable.' One section of Murray's book deals with the later succession of invasions from the north in the fourteenth and thirteenth centuries BC. A few pages of exposition of the complexity of the contemporary written references leads to Murray's sudden imaginative description of an outcast island tribe moving in fear of death across the sea from island to island, meeting and joining other outcasts, including more primitive men 'answering to babyish names like "Atta" and "Babba" and "Dadda" . . .' A page later comes a paragraph illuminating some peculiarities in the history – or mythology – of the island of Lemnos. These pages, and the imaginative stimulus of visiting the scenes, presumably lie behind this story.

64 *Carians*: the original inhabitants of a district of south-west Asia Minor, considered by the Greeks to be mean and stupid even as slaves.

65 ῧβρις: hubris; overweening arrogance, especially that pride that challenges the gods.

66 *Pelasgian*: the name of the earliest inhabitants of Greece. 'Pelasgia' was an ancient name of the islands of Delos and Lesbos.

68 *the Far-Darter*: Apollo is so called in the *Iliad*: Ἐκζβόλου, meaning far-shooting, with the idea of attaining his aim.

68 *A verse of Homer*: *Iliad*, ix. 497–501. It was spoken of course not by Phocion (a historical Athenian general) but by Phoenix, an old friend and one-time tutor of Achilles.

68 *a Lemnian song-maker*: not known.

69 *Thermopylæ*: the Hot Gates, in ancient times a narrow pass, between Mt Oeta and the Malic Gulf, famous for hot springs. It was the only pass by which an enemy could

penetrate from northern to southern Greece; thus it was always of the greatest importance. It was especially famous for the Spartan (Lacedæmonian) defence in 480 BC with only 300 men against the entire host of the Persians under Xerxes ('the Great King'). The Spartans under Leonidas only fell because the Persians discovered a path over the mountains and could attack the Greeks in the rear. Buchan is bringing together to one moment many centuries of history.

77   *Ares*: the Greek god of war; the equivalent of the Roman Mars.

82   *Klephts*: literally 'thieves' (cf. 'kleptomania') and a common word for brigand: but particularly used of bands of Greeks who maintained independence in the mountains after the Turkish conquest of Greece in the fifteenth century AD.

Fullcircle

In the magazine version, the first two paragraphs are omitted, and the narrator is called 'Jardine'.

86   *Martial*: first-century Roman poet and courtier, whose epigrams were especially popular in seventeenth-century England for their observation and wit.

86   *Bucolics*: pastoral poetry in the style of Theocritus or Virgil.

87   *Ars Vivendi*: on the art of living.

88   *crab*: pull to pieces, criticize.

90   *blue-books*: official reports of Parliament and the Privy Council.

90   *moots*: meetings.

90   *Lord Falkland*: Lucius Cary, second Viscount Falkland, was a distinguished Royalist who made his house at Great Tew, near Oxford, a centre for the most able and liberal-minded thinkers of his day. Leithen is quoting Clarendon's character of him in his *History of the Rebellion,* Book VII, written about 1647:

> His friends frequently resorted and dwelt with him, as in a Colledge scituated in a purer ayre, so that his house was a University bounde in a lesser volume, whither they came not so much for repose, as study: and to

examyne and refyne those grosser propositions, which laziness and consent made currant in vulgar conversation.

92 *Raleigh's phrase*: Buchan knew the work of Raleigh well: he had won the Stanhope Prize in 1897, while an undergraduate at Oxford, with a judicious essay on Raleigh, published as a book, and he later wrote of him for children. The phrase Leithen quotes could be a paraphrase of sentences in Raleigh's *History of the World*, Book 1, chapter 2, para 2: 'A divine understanding, and intellect or minde contemplative.'

100 *jogging*: Leithen and Peckwether are not of course on foot: they have been out with one of the most celebrated of the Cotswold hunts.

The Moor-Song

106 *clachan*: hamlet.
111 *reiver*: robber, pillager.

The Loathly Opposite

117 *Kurhaus*: private clinic.
123 *Falkenhayn*: German minister of war and chief of the general staff until 1916. A favourite of the Kaiser, he was of striking appearance.
124 *en clair*: not in cypher.
130 *Sikkim*: in the eastern Himalayas; a district containing Kanchen junga and other great peaks.
131 *Homburg*: fashionable German health resort in Hesse.

Streams of Water in the South

136 *streams of water in the south*: from a Scottish paraphrase of Psalm 126, the hymn beginning 'When Zion's bondage God turned back.' The third verse reads,

> As streams of water in the south
>   Our bondage, Lord, recall.
> Who sow in tears, a reaping time
>   Of love enjoy they shall.

140 *howkit*: digged, dug up.
146 *birks*: birch-trees.

Ship to Tarshish
155 *apolaustic epicene*: a bisexual (or possibly in this context asexual) person devoted to the search for enjoyment.
160 *fist*: handwriting.

The Earlier Affection
177 *usquebagh*: whisky; literally 'water of life'.
179 *Glesca Fleshers*: Glasgow butchers.
181 *one of his Psalms*: Psalm 120. v.7.

The Wind in the Portico
194 *burnous*: Arab hooded cloak.
197 *Medicean Codex*: a manuscript volume from the library at Florence founded by Lorenzo de' Medici.
197 *Gaisford*: an editor of Theocritus.
208 *Haverfield*: Francis John Haverfield (1860–1919), Oxford historian who founded the modern scientific study of Roman Britain.
208 *Sidonius Apollinaris*: much-honoured Roman poet of the fifth century AD who became a bishop in the last years of his life.
217 *dendrophori*: bearing trees.
217 *hierophants*: priests at ceremonies, especially of initiation.

Fountainblue
230 *burked*: murdered, especially by strangulation. The word comes directly from the Edinburgh criminal executed in 1829.
231 *Cyclops in love*: Theocritus, *Idylls*, XI.
233 *mess of pottage*: in *Genesis* XXV, the story is told of Esau who came so faint to his brother Jacob that he exchanged his birthright for 'bread and pottage of lentiles'.
239 *Grind*: a local steeplechase in Oxford slang of the time.
248 *'Parmi ceu haut bois . . .'*: 'the canting motto of old reivers', that is, the esoteric language of ancient plunderers, refers to the Norman invaders of these islands.
260 *the excellent foppery of the world*: Shakespeare, *King Lear*, 1.ii.120.
260 *'Smooth Jacob . . .'*: a proverbial remark based on the story in *Genesis* XXVII, in which Jacob robs his elder

brother of his blind father's blessing by wearing his
brother's clothes and putting goatskins on his hands to
imitate his brother's hairiness.

260   *confound the strong*: 1 Corinthians I. xxvii.